Full Figured 13:

Carl Weber Presents

Full Figured 13:

Carl Weber Presents

Mona Love

and Katt

www.urbanbooks.net

Urban Books, LLC
300 Farmingdale Road, NY-Route 109
Farmingdale, NY 11735

ISBN 13: 978-1-60162-110-8
ISBN 10: 1-60162-110-8

First Trade Paperback Printing March 2019
Printed in the United States of America

10 9 8 7 6 5 4 3 2 1

*This is a work of fiction. Any references or similarities
to actual events, real people, living or dead, or to real
locales are intended to give the novel a sense of reality.
Any similarity in other names, characters, places, and
incidents is entirely coincidental.*

Distributed by Kensington Publishing Corp.
Submit Orders to:
Customer Service
400 Hahn Road
Westminster, MD 21157-4627
Phone: 1-800-733-3000
Fax: 1-800-659-2436

A MILLION DOLLARS' WORTH OF FAT

by

Mona Love

Chapter 1

Lucky Day

I laughed at myself, but wasn't a damn thing funny. It was all I could do to keep myself from crying. Not only was I embarrassed as all hell, but I was seriously hurt. The way the ripples of pain rocked through my entire body, I felt like someone had beaten my ass with ten baseball bats. But nothing hurt worse than my left ankle. It was literally screaming, if that makes sense. I blinked a few times and tears eased out the sides of my eyes.

Do you know what it is like to be 320 pounds and bust your ass in a crowded mall after the cute, slim-heeled sandals you wore buckled under your weight? Of course you don't! But that's what happened. One minute I was getting my plus-sized-model walk on, heels just clacking, ample hips swaying sexily, and the next minute I was crashing to the floor like a brick building that had been hit with a wrecking ball.

Screech. Boom. Splat. That's what it sounded like.

So there I was, lying flat, staring up at the ogling eyes and contorted faces of all the mall hood rats and shoppers amused by the beached whale on the floor. You'd think all the fluffy cushion I had around my ass and midsection would've helped. Nope. I was hurting. I was hurting bad, physically and mentally.

I heard the groans mixed with snickering as soon as the sickening screech of my heel against the mall floor tiles let me know shit was about to get ugly. I imagined that my shoe had one last holler from the thin heels, saying, "Bitch, you knew damn well I wasn't strong enough to hold up all that ass!"

I was laughing to keep myself from crying. And then I heard it: a deep baritone that made me want to melt into the floor and disappear. "Miss, are you all right?" the voice asked.

I didn't even have to look to know that the owner of that voice was sexy as hell. And just like I suspected, within seconds there was a handsome face hovering over mine. *Dayum!* I stared up at the gorgeous man and the gawking crowd, feeling like a circus sideshow.

"Let me help you up," he said, as he spread his stance wide like he knew he'd have to dig down deep for strength to get my big ass up.

"I . . . I got it," I managed through fake chuckles. If I weren't embarrassed before, I was hot with shame now. My face felt like someone had lit it with a torch. But I was kind of used to stuff like this. I had been dealing with this all my life.

Just keep laughing, Keisha. You know the drill. Laugh at yourself first. Keep laughing. It'll make the pain and embarrassment less, I told myself. It was the same thing I'd been saying since I was the chubby girl in elementary school. I learned early on that if I laughed at myself, that would make everyone else's laughter null and void. Or so I always hoped.

"No, you could've seriously hurt yourself. Let me," the man with the beautiful voice said.

I couldn't, I wouldn't, I didn't look at him. But I took his hand and let him help me up. I got to my feet. One foot was still in the other high heel, and the other was throbbing from being twisted by the disloyal heel.

"Keep on walking. Y'all standing around watching and recording, but this woman is really hurt," my sexy-voiced Good Samaritan barked at the group of teens who remained for the show. They scattered, taking their mean comments and laughter with them.

"You really didn't have to," I said, my voice quivering with nerves. Now I had no choice but to look at the man who possessed that soul-stirring deep voice.

"I know I didn't have to, but common decency is something we need in this world," he replied.

I felt something flutter inside of me. It wasn't that usual flutter like tiny butterflies. This was more like huge winged bats banging around inside my stomach. There was definitely something different and special about this man.

Finally, I took a good look at him. Lawd! My heart sank immediately. This man was fine. He was Michael B. Jordan fine. He was Chadwick Boseman fine. He was Wakanda warrior fine. Right away I knew, like he'd said, that he was just being a Good Samaritan, because a fine-ass man like him would never want a thicker-than-a-snicker chick like me.

"Well, thank you," I said, unable to hold eye contact with him. "I appreciate the help."

"Andre," he said, extending his hand.

The heat that engulfed my face made me feel like I'd just stuck my entire head into a fire pit. I swallowed ten times before I was able to speak. "Kei . . . Keisha," I managed, accepting his hand for a shake.

"It's very nice to meet you, Keisha," he said with wink and a smile. Then out of nowhere, he bent down and unbuckled my other high heel shoe, slipped it off of my good foot, stood up, and handed it to me. "I think you should just go without these. I'll run to the Target and grab you some flip-flops. Be right back."

Before I could protest, this knight in shining armor was on the move. I flopped back on the mall bench, pinched myself, and looked around to make sure I wasn't dreaming. I felt like it was my lucky day. And trust me, I'd never felt lucky my entire life.

Dating and men . . . hmmm, where do I start? Let's just say I hadn't been lucky. Dating apps had resulted in dudes who acted like I had catfished them whenever we met up in person. There was this one guy who yelled out, "You big as fuck!" when I walked up to him in front of the restaurant. There had been many missed and failed dates: dating apps, speed dating, friend hookups, stranger approaches, and none had resulted in love. Forget about the "friend zone." I'd been told, "I like you as a friend," so many times that I stopped counting around the age of 16. That sentence really meant, "You're too fat for me, but I think you're crazy fun and nice and I don't want to let you down too hard." I'd also had the occasional, "I'm not ready for a relationship," only to see the dude in the next week or two canoodling with the next bitch. The next skinny bitch.

Okay, okay. Let me admit that I'm five feet nine inches tall, 320 pounds with size 44F breasts, and a waist that decides to show up when it wants to. But I am also a sexy caramel-skinned, almond-eyed beauty who has learned how to carry her weight in the highest BBW manner. I've been told I should do plus-sized modeling so many times I can't even count. Beautiful in the face does not equal beautiful to the world. Society is a cruel fucking place for thick girls. The beauty standard is and always will be some skinny bitch who, in my opinion, needs to eat a whole box of crackers and five sandwiches.

"Here you go, beautiful," Andre said, snapping me out of my own thoughts.

"Thank you so much." I was blushing, I could tell. There went that face flame again. My heart was hammering like I was running.

"Let me help you to your car," he said, flashing a megawatt smile that made me hot around the collar.

"Oh, um, okay," I stammered. I knew the confusion showed on my face because I was thinking, *what else can this day hold for me? Because this shit right here is straight out of a romantic comedy movie!*

"Yes, bitch, a total stranger lifted my big ass up off the mall floor, helped me out of my damn other shoe, and bought me a pair of flip-flops. He got the right size, mind you, and let me lean my big ass on his shoulder while he walked me to my damn car," I rambled into my cell phone, telling my best friend, Leitha, the story.

"Biiitcchh!" Leitha screamed into her phone so loudly that I pulled mine away from my ear for a minute. "Get theee whole fuck outta here!"

"I'm so serious right now, LeLe. I mean, it was like some fairytale shit, but the fat girl version. When I say this man was fine as shit, he was fine as shit. Why me? It's like he looked at me like I was a skinny bitch with a new wig and butt implants. You know that look dudes give them Instagram famous bitches? Yeah, mmm-hmmm, that look," I continued.

"Girl, what? Shit! This is your lucky day. Carry your ass to the store and play the lotto or some shit. My grandmama always said that if you get the stroke of luck, ride that bitch 'til the wheels fall off," Leitha said with feeling.

"I'm pretty sure that's not how the saying goes, LeLe," I said and busted out laughing.

"It don't even matter. Take your ass to the store and play the lotto and like ten scratch-offs. And, bitch, if you win, you better come get me so I can disappear with you," Leitha said jokingly, although I knew she was dead-ass serious.

"Girl, bye. I'll call you when I get home."

As soon as I hung up with Leitha I took her advice. I headed to the store to play the lotto. I mean shit, what did I have to lose? The whole time I couldn't stop thinking about Andre. His beautiful mocha skin. His strong hands. His white-ass teeth. But most of all, his muscular body. He looked like he worked out seven days a week. I hadn't seen a gym since that one time I tried to combine Weight Watchers with intense HIIT workouts and damn near had a heart attack and a breathing tube. I ran my ass out of that gym so fast, never to return. Every New Year I say I'm going back. Emphasis on "I say."

"You one dumb ass, Keisha. Why in the hell didn't you get his number?" I grumbled to myself. I could've shot my shot. What's the worst that could've happened? He could've said he was married and I'd be in the same boat I was in now: no number! But what if Leitha was right and it was my lucky day? I might've had that man's number and in six months been his lucky bride.

"Bitch, please," I scolded myself. "He helped you, but he don't want you."

"Ms. Keisha!" Habeeb, the store owner, sang as I walked into the bodega on the corner of my block. "You want ham and cheese hero, a lot of mayo, lettuce, tomato, oil, and vinegar?"

"Ugh, Habeeb. How come every time I come in here you think I'm about to buy food?"

He raised his eyebrows at me knowingly.

"Just because I'm three hundred pounds don't mean I eat all the time. I'm big-boned, and it runs in my family," I hissed and rolled my eyes.

Habeeb just smiled. He was thinking some slick shit, but he ain't want to say it.

"Let me get ten Mega Millions Quick Picks," I said, flustered as I slammed down my twenty-dollar bill.

Habeeb was about to type in the order.

"Wait, no. Let me get five Quick Picks and let me pick the rest," I corrected.

He slid me the card to pick the numbers.

I picked up one of the little pencils he had on the counter in an old-fashioned matchbox. I closed my eyes and pictured Andre again: his neatly cropped hair, his thinly trimmed goatee, and his eyes, those piercing, attentive eyes. Then, I used my cell phone keypad to spell out his name with numbers.

A: I colored in the number two on the card. N: I colored in the number six on the card. D: I colored in the number three on the card. R: I colored in the number seven on the card. E: I colored in the thirty-three since I had already used the three for the D. For the Mega Ball box, I colored in the eleven, since that was the date I met Andre.

I looked at the numbers one more time. I felt stupid, and I started to rip up the card. Playing letters associated with a total stranger's name? Who does that?

"You ready?" Habeeb asked, interrupting my thoughts.

"Yeah, just do it. Shit, what I got to lose?" I said, pushing the card across the counter. Within seconds I had my Mega Millions ticket. I shrugged and stuffed it into my pocketbook.

"Now, give me my damn hero, Habeeb," I said.

He busted out laughing.

His towel-head ass knew damn well I came in there for my usual hero. Shit, a girl got to eat.

Chapter 2

That Date Life

The usual rotation of dates in my life was exhausting. This time, I sat across from my "date," Darius, thinking, *Keisha Long, just what the fuck are you doing here?* And I use quotes on purpose. I could hardly call Darius a date. I didn't even know what the word date meant anymore. He was the fourth dude in a month, and if you looked up "total loser" in Webster's Dictionary, Darius's face would be the whole page.

"So I'm saying you cute for a big girl. Where you work at?" Darius asked after licking Buffalo wing sauce off of his thumb like he had way too much experience sucking something.

I closed my eyes for ten seconds and swallowed hard. It was all I could do to keep my composure. *Did this dude just ask me where I work at? Jesus, be an invisibility cloak.*

I stared at him for a few more long seconds. Yeah, I was stupid for even being at some damn Buffalo Wild Wings with this jank-ass loser. I had met Darius a few months before while I was clubbing and had gotten pissy drunk. Six drinks and he'd looked like a black Norse god at the time. I'd stumbled out of the club on his arm and into his car. Well, what I thought was his car. Anyway, Darius and I had had some sloppy one-night-stand sex. I didn't remember much about the details, but I did remember that his dick was just like that gotdamn egg-plant emoji and I wanted more. That night he'd promised to call me, and after five or six failed attempts at calling him, I had given up.

Lo and behold, three damn months later and there I was. Darius had called me with the "Hey, bighead" line and asked if I wanted to hang out. I didn't think anything of it, and if it meant one more personal eggplant Friday episode with him, I was down.

Through sober eyes, Darius was just average: fade haircut on some nappy-ass hair with some fake-ass waves, full beard, which is the way these dudes these days try to make themselves look sexier than they really are, and his clothes, um, he definitely wasn't dressed to the nines like he was the night I met him, which made me believe he had borrowed that Gucci belt and those Balenciaga sneakers he had on that night.

"I work. I think that's all that's important," I said dryly as I used my fork to push around the dry-ass bag salad this Buffalo Wild Wings had tried to pass off as gourmet cooking.

"Okay. Okay. I hear you. Independent woman, just what I'm looking for," Darius said.

"So you're looking for a woman?" I asked, baffled. First date in three months and he was looking for a woman? "Interesting. Very interesting."

"Well, you know, it's getting cold, and I was kind of thinking you'd be the perfect person for this cuffing season that's coming up," Darius replied with not one ounce of shame.

"Wow, okay. Let's just get right to the point why don't we?" I grumbled.

Just when I was about to call it quits, Darius hit me with, "I thought we was feeling each other that night. You know, *feeling* each other," he said, parting a sly smile.

Next thing I knew, I was on my knees with my big ass in the air with Darius's face wedged between my ass cheeks, eating my pussy from the back. When he was done doing that, he flipped me over onto my back as if I weighed a hundred pounds and not over 300. He laid that dick on me with so much skill I was yelling out, "Yes! It's cuffing season! You can cuff with me! Yes! Oh, yes!"

Took me almost two months to get him out of my house. He didn't have a job, a car, a house, decent clothes, and to top it off he had several (too many to count, so I'll say several) children and baby mamas. After I dodged that bullet, I had to ask myself, *why it is always the ones with the good dick who ain't got shit?* Thinking about his dick still made me shudder though.

"Yes, LeLe. I am going on a date. Yes, another date," I rolled my eyes, and my best friend sucked her teeth. This was my life: a proverbial Ferris wheel of dates. 'Round and 'round I went, each time hitting the bottom and letting the next no-good nigga off the ride and another half-no-good nigga on the ride. 'Round and 'round some more.

"I'm so over this shit, Keisha. Why don't you just give it a rest? You're beautiful. A man don't define you," Leitha said sincerely. "I think if you just wait and pray, God will send you the right man at the right time."

I sucked my teeth and kept on applying my makeup. That was easy for Leitha to say. She had a man. Everyone needed someone. In my eyes, human companionship was just as essential as oxygen. I wanted to tell myself I didn't need a man, but deep down it was ingrained in me that I did.

I sighed and threw my makeup brush on the vanity. I closed my eyes for a few long minutes and thought about what Leitha was saying. She was right. A man didn't define me, but something about getting men's approval seemed to haunt my life. I wanted to be accepted and loved and taken care of. Wasn't that what all women wanted? Maybe it was because my father had walked out on my mother and me when I was eight. I'd always blamed myself for being fat as his reason for leaving. After his abandonment, I'd eat and eat and grow bigger and bigger. That was my comfort. No matter how hard I tried, I loved food . . . oh, and men. So I ate to comfort myself after the rejection from men, but I kept pursuing men in my need for their approval and the sham of comfort it provided. Do you see how that could end up being a crazy way to live?

My mother struggled, and she always preached about how much easier raising me would've been had she had a man. She couldn't keep one either, which was why we had a revolving door in our house. I saw man after man and watched my mother suffer disappointment after disappointment. Sort of what I was doing to myself now. I once went to a psychic who told me I would have all of my heart's desires one day, including a good man. I wanted to slap that bitch and ask for every dime of my money back. How could she possibly believe that I was worthy when even I didn't believe it? It was crazy. I was crazy. But that didn't change shit. I was still on every dating website, dating app, and social dating scene around.

"I just do it for fun, LeLe," I lied, snapping out of the sad memory of my childhood. Fuck it! What did I have to lose? Self-dignity had been long gone. When you're a big girl, everyone (women included) will make you feel like you don't deserve shit in life but a tub of chicken and a girdle.

"Whatever. Just keep my number on speed dial in case your speed date is a serial killer," Leitha half joked.

"They only kill skinny bitches, remember," I joked back. We both laughed and eased some of the very real tension in the room.

I cannot lie, my heart slammed against my chest bone like the beater inside of a bass drum. I smoothed down my bright yellow Ashley Stewart sundress to make sure my Spanx weren't rolling in the middle, and I shimmied my ample hips over to the next table. *Oh, God!* He was ugly as hell. This was the second table in the speed-dating cycle, and I was already ready to run for the door.

You ain't pay a hundred dollars to waste it. Stick with it, Keisha.

The pep talks I gave myself were real at that point. I had to keep my head in the game. What if this place held my diamond in the rough?

As I moved from table to table, looking in the face of man after man, I had to really ask myself again why I was there. At this point, I had received more than one gawk and gasp at my size from the shallow bunch of stuffed suits who were there trying to find dates. And then finally . . .

I plopped down in the chair in front of a beautiful chocolate warrior. Instead of gawking or acting disgusted, he smiled. Not only did he smile, but he smiled like I had made his whole day.

"Hi, I'm Wilson," he said, still smiling. His teeth were beams of light they were so white against his dark skin. His accent was noticeable right away. Nigerian? Ghanaian? Senegalese? I couldn't place it right away, but he definitely wasn't American.

"Keisha," I said, parting an awkward, half-hearted smile. I had a general distrust of foreign men. The explanation would take a whole other book, but let's just say I grew up wary of men with accents.

"Queen Keisha. You look beautiful tonight," Wilson said, still smiling like his ass was half silly.

I cringed a little bit at that accent. I told myself I could make it through it, though. He was the first friendly face I had encountered, so that had to count for something. Wilson snatched his speed-dating number from the little holder on the table and nodded at me so I'd do the same. I was already tired of the pace of looking at man after man, so I followed his lead.

"Can we go someplace for a drink?" he asked. That shit was fast and forward, but who was I to question fate? Right?

"Okay," I said. But I was thinking, *a drink? Don't think you're getting away without feeding my ass, Prince Akeem from Zamunda!*

I can't lie, after I got past Wilson's accent, I was impressed. He said he was in the United States on a school visa. He sounded like he was a hardworking student, and I was here for all of it. Shit, I had met American men who were born here with a million opportunities to go to school and weren't doing shit but squandering their lives away.

Wilson asked me what I liked to do. I had to look at his ass twice. *What the hell it look like I like to do? Eat!*

"These are so good," I mumbled as I cracked another snow crab leg in half with my bare hands and brought it up to my mouth so I could suck the sweet juice out of the middle before devouring the crab meat.

"In my country—" Wilson started.

"Errp." I threw my hand up in front of my face. "Let me stop you there, Wilson. I want to enjoy this good food you're paying for, so please don't keep telling me how bad the food in America is compared to your country," I said flatly. I had already had enough of that talk. It always killed me when people from other countries talked badly about America, especially when not one damn American soul had asked them to come over here. I always thought, *if your country is so much better, why the hell are you here?*

Wilson smiled and shook his head. "Okay, Queen, I understand."

Dinner was great. I couldn't say the conversation was any good because I had to keep asking Wilson to repeat himself with that accent, but he was someone I might see again. And I did.

Two weeks later, I sat in Wilson's apartment in the one chair he had, looking around at the shabby furnishings. He kept apologizing and explaining that he was just a student with "meager" earnings, as he put it. It fascinated me how he could barely speak English but he used such big vocabulary words. Amusing and funny.

In any case, I put Wilson at ease. Shit, he was broke and so was I. I was just happy he hadn't friend-zoned me yet, like most of the dates I had gone on.

"You look ravishing today, Keisha," he said with that accent and his usual big-vocabulary word added.

"Thanks." I smiled politely.

"I'm going to get ready. Make yourself at home," he said.

He left me alone and went to the bathroom to finish getting ready for our date. Of course my nosy ass couldn't just sit and be a normal good-girl date. I got up and started snooping. I picked up a picture frame and saw Wilson in a picture with a woman, two kids, a man, and another woman. I scanned the photo trying to figure out who was who. Maybe the woman sitting in the center was his mother? Maybe the other woman was his sister? I couldn't tell.

I put the picture down and scanned his desk. My hand accidentally, yes, accidentally touched the keyboard on his laptop and the screen lit up. Of course my eyes were drawn to the bright light of the screen. There was a half-written email showing. I squinted and craned my neck so I could read it. I knew that might've been out of order, but oh, well, once I started reading it, there would be no turning back.

Dear Adjua,

I am missing you like crazy. I hope your experience at home is not as stressful as mine. I will be sending money as soon as I can. Please kiss Odjo and Bakari for me. I am missing them so much. I am still working on my plan to citizenship. I have met someone who seems easy to trick. Adjua, she is not beautiful like you, and she is so fat. Fat like the rhinos in the bush. I hope that made you laugh. She is nice, but again, very fat. At home, she would have only been someone's house maiden. No man would choose her for a wife for fear that he would not tell whenever she was with child. I purposely picked her because I could see the desperation in her eyes. She doesn't love herself, and she is almost begging for love. It will be easy to fool her into thinking I really like her and even love her. I can tell it will not take me long to get her to marry me for my citizenship. I will have to deal with her until the time comes, and as soon as I can fool her, I will get the citizenship and send for you and the boys. It won't be long. She is easy. Easier than any American girl I have met so far.

Anyway, enough about my fat fool. How is Maman? Is she

I heard a noise behind me but not over the whooshing sound of my boiling blood rushing through my ears. My chest heaved up and down, and my fists curled on their own.

Desperation in her eyes? Begging for love? Easy to fool? Fat fool? The words played over and over in my head until both of my temples throbbed painfully. I didn't think I'd been that mad in years.

"Hey, are you ready to go?" Wilson asked with that stupid, disgusting accent and one of his dumb, goofy smiles.

"Fuck you!" I hissed. "I'm not so desperate and fat that you could fool me into marrying you so you can become a citizen, you piece of shit," I snarled and stormed toward the door.

"Keisha! Wait!" Wilson yelled, grabbing my arm. "Let me explain."

"Get the fuck off of me!" I barked, pushing him so hard he stumbled backward and landed on his ass with a hard thud. I was nothing to play with when I was hurt and felt backed into a corner. I had learned long ago how to defend myself.

"Just wait!" I heard Wilson yelling at my back as I slammed out of his apartment and raced down the stairs of his old-ass building. "Keisha!"

"Fuck you!" I screamed. "You'd be better off staying the fuck away from me if you don't want to end up in a box back to Africa, you piece of foreign shit!"

I raced around the corner from his building and summoned an Uber. I didn't know why the hell I didn't drive! My blood was still boiling, but as soon as I sat in the back seat of my Uber, the tears came fast and furious. I couldn't tell if they were sad tears or mad tears. I was so sick of this game with men. What about me screamed "desperate fat girl who will take any shit off of any man"? I mean I carried myself with dignity. I knew

I was beautiful, in the face at least. Why? Why was God constantly punishing me with these scenarios? I tried to be a good person. All of my friends always went on and on about how I was the life of the party. I had tried it all: dating apps, blind dates, and even meeting men in the clubs. Nothing had gotten me further than tricky, using-ass niggas. Oh, and then there was the "I like you as a friend" niggas. Oh, and don't let me forget the "you're like a sister me" niggas.

"Have a good evening."

"What?" I snapped, quickly realizing I was barking at my Uber driver for no reason.

"I . . . I just said have a good evening."

"Oh. Sorry," I apologized. I had been in another world thinking about my failures. I hadn't meant to snap. "You too."

When I got into my apartment, I quickly shut the door, locked it, put my back against it, and slid down to the floor. The tears came fast and furious, and I just let them.

Chapter 3

Better to Be Born Lucky

I groaned and slapped at my nightstand for my phone. As soon as I cracked my eyes open, pain rocked through my skull. "Fuck," I hissed, finally locating my phone. "Hello," I grumbled into the phone, my own breath threatening to kill me.

"Keisha!"

Ugh. I moved the phone from my ear quickly. My head was pounding too hard for the damn screaming.

"Keisha! You there?" I could hear Leitha even with the phone away from my ear.

"LeLe, what the fuck? Why are you screaming like that?" I rasped, my voice heavy with sleep and hangover. I had polished off a whole bottle of Hennessy the night before. Drowning my sorrows in liquor was better than trying to find the next stupid nigga to fill the void.

"Girl, listen to me! Somebody won the lottery last month at the store around the corner from your damn house! They haven't claimed the prize, and they just showed the shit on the news!" Leitha yelled.

I sucked my teeth and shrugged my shoulders. She had to be fucking crazy. "So?" I grumped.

"So? Bitch, it was the same day you fell in the mall, met your Prince Charming who you let disappear, and were told by me to buy a gotdamn lotto ticket. Which I fucking hope you did!" She went on with so much feeling that I was all the way awake now.

I finally sat up, scrubbed my hands over my face, and wiped the sleep out of my eyes.

"Well? Keisha? Did your ass get a lotto ticket that day?" Leitha pressed.

"Ugh. Yes," I grumbled. "But I don't know what the hell I did with those damn tickets. That shit was weeks ago," I said, looking out into my apartment like the tickets would just appear out of thin air.

"Bitch, I'll be there in twenty minutes to help you look. You must be crazy," Leitha said before hanging right up on me.

Leitha was not playing. As soon as I stepped out of the shower, I had just enough time to wrap myself in my terry-cloth robe before she was pounding on my door.

"Oh, my God, this girl," I mumbled as I padded to the door. I snatched the door open, and Leitha rushed inside so fast a swift wind passed my face from her movement.

"Okay. Let's start with what you were wearing that day," Leitha said, wasting no time.

"Um, hello to you too, bitch," I said, shaking my head at her. "Damn."

"Bitch, you know I love you already. We don't have to waste time. I'm telling you Keish, I got a feeling about this. That same deep gut feeling I had when I told you I knew my ass was pregnant before I had even missed my period."

"LeLe, that shit is totally different. You ain't have a deep gut feeling about that shit. You had your guts dug out and knew your ass ain't use no condom, so you knew you were pregnant," I corrected.

Leitha waved her hand in front of her face. "That's beside the point. Dammit, we need to find those lotto tickets! Now, what the hell did you have on?"

Of course I remembered everything about that day, especially my encounter with Andre. I had replayed his face, his scent, his body, his mannerisms over and over in my head so many times that I felt like I actually knew him now.

I moved around my apartment and picked out the dress I had on. I grabbed the purse I carried and the jean jacket I had on over my sundress. I dumped it all into the middle of the floor. Leitha tore through the pile like a madwoman but came up with nothing. She looked up at me with pure terror in her eyes.

"Think, Keisha. When you cleaned out this purse, what did you do with all the stuff?" Leitha asked, her voice quivering.

My heart sped up. She and I were both thinking the same thing, and we both opened our mouths at the same time.

"I hope you . . ."

"I hope I . . ."

"Didn't throw them away," we said in unison.

Leitha ran to the small garbage can in my bathroom. Empty.

I ran to the garbage can in my bedroom. Empty.

"I take the kitchen garbage out way too often for anything to be in there a month later," I said.

"Where else?" Leitha waved her hands frantically. "Fuck."

Shit, she was acting like she'd lost a potentially million-dollar ticket. I mean, she was my BFF, so technically if I won, she won, but still.

"Let me check one more place," I said, trying to have a glimmer of hope shine through my words.

I walked to the corner of my living room where I had a glass-top computer desk set up with my printer and a small file cabinet. Essentially, this was my "office." I sat down in the office chair and filed through every piece of paper atop the desk. Nothing. I looked at the printer desk and filed through those papers too. Nothing. Then, with my last-ditch hope fading, I bent under the desk and grabbed the little silver shred bucket I kept under there for months and months before I ever decided to shred shit. I pulled it up to my lap and dug through it. Leitha was hovering over me like a buzzard over a dead carcass. I didn't even think she realized that her ass was pacing like a crazy person.

"Just dump it out already, Keisha," Leitha urged.

I turned the chair around and turned the little bucket over onto the floor. It seemed like a ton of papers fell out. Who knew that little-ass bucket held so much shit?

Leitha bent to her knees and started sifting carefully through the pile. At first, it seemed so hopeless.

"Here! They're here!" Leitha screamed triumphantly.

I swear, between the still-lingering hangover and the excitement of what might be, I almost had a gotdamn heart attack. I actually had to clutch my damn chest to keep myself from fainting and spilling out of that chair.

"Okay. Okay," Leitha huffed, fanning herself with one hand and clutching the lotto tickets with the other hand. "I have the numbers. We have two tickets. How we going to do this?" she continued, huffing and puffing like she was about to hyperventilate.

"Girl, give me these damn tickets and let me check the numbers. You acting all dramatic, and for all we know, these shits are duds. Got me all riled up," I said, flustered. I snatched the tickets and Leitha pulled out the paper she had with the winning lotto numbers on it.

"Call out the numbers," I demanded, "slowly."

"Okay," Leitha replied. Then she blew out a breath.

I rolled my eyes and chuckled. "Bitch, you missed your calling. Actress."

"Shut the hell up and listen," she said. "Two, three—"

"Hold on. Give me time to check both tickets." I put my hand up. Leitha blew out an exasperated breath.

"Okay. I have both of those on the second ticket," I said. "Go ahead."

"Six, seven, thirty-three," Leitha continued.

I was silent, because suddenly, as I ticked off those numbers on the same ticket I had the previous numbers on, my stomach knotted.

"Well, bitch? What is the word?" Leitha said, craning her neck over my shoulder.

I swallowed hard. "Ye . . . yeah. I, um, I have those," I stammered.

"Wait? What?" Leitha asked, her voice going up ten octaves.

"Wh . . . what's the Meg . . . Mega Ball?" I asked, barely able to speak. I closed my eyes and waited to hear her read the number. Everything in the room was spinning off-balance, and trust me, it wasn't the Hennessy this time.

"Bitch, it's eleven!" Leitha said, almost screaming. "Bitch! Tell me that fucking ticket don't have eleven as the fucking Mega Ball number!" She started bouncing on her knees and fanning her hands in front of her.

I swear I felt like my soul had left my body. I don't know how else to describe the crazy out-of-body experience I had in that moment.

"Keisha! What does the Mega Ball say?" Leitha yelled at me.

I couldn't speak. I stared down at the ticket clutched in my trembling hand.

"Keisha! Let me see!" Leitha urged frantically.

I held out my quaking hand. Leitha snatched the ticket.

"Agghhhhhh!" She belted out the most ear-shattering scream I'd ever heard. Her scream snapped me out of the catatonic shock. I jumped up from the chair so hard I sent it slamming into the wall.

"Oh, my God!" I screeched, and believe it or not, all 320 pounds of me jumped so high off the floor I knew my neighbors under me thought an earthquake had hit. I continued to jump, too. Leitha and I jumped and hugged and screamed and cried and danced and went 'round and 'round until we were finally exhausted and collapsed on my floor, heaving and out of breath.

"Bitch," Leitha breathed out each letter.

"Biiitttccchhh." I dragged mine out on a long breath, hardly able to breath anyway. "Agh!" I screamed and kicked my ham-hock legs in the air.

Leitha turned her head to the side and looked over at me. "Agh!" she screamed too and kicked her legs. We busted out laughing. It was the kind of laughter that said we were set for life and would never have another care in the world. I had hit the motherfucking lottery, all off of using Andre's name as my numbers! My mother always said it was better to be born lucky than rich!

Chapter 4

More Money, More Problems

My entire body shook as Leitha and I walked into the New York State Lottery office the next day so I could come forward as the winner. We hadn't slept at all from the time I found out I won until that moment. I didn't even remember Leitha calling her man to say she was staying at my house. We were both so blown away we didn't know what to do. First we jumped around, screaming and cheering and falling down with joy. Then, we fell into a stunned silence for a few hours, shock I guess. When the realization that I'd won had set in, I suddenly got so paranoid.

"Bitch, we can't tell anyone," I had whispered, holding the ticket up against my chest. "Shit, somebody might kidnap my ass." I had looked around all crazy.

"I'm not telling anyone, but you know in the state of New York you have to come forward publicly, so everyone you know will know, eventually," Leitha had told me.

"Can I help you?" the woman behind the window asked pleasantly.

"Um, I, um . . ." I couldn't even speak.

"She won. She's the winner from a month ago with the unclaimed ticket," Leitha blurted, filling in for me. "The one worth sixty million dollars."

The woman smiled. You know, the wicked kind that said she heard this same story every day and it was bullshit. "Okay, sweetheart. Be sure to sign your ticket first and then you have the right to stand here and watch me verify it," she said in that perfunctory business way.

My hands shook so damn hard my signature looked like I signed while riding a roller coaster. I pushed the ticket toward the skeptical woman and watched as she punched in some numbers with a blank face. I heard the computer ding and something blue lit up on her screen. I also saw her eyes stretch wide.

"Right, she's the winner, so let's get this popping," Leitha said with a hint of shrewd satisfaction in her tone.

Everything after that moment seemed to be a whirlwind. I felt like fairies had whisked me away to a new lifestyle, one of the rich and famous. There were tons of papers to sign. There were pictures and fingerprints. I met a ton of people from the New York State Lottery Commission. To me, they all looked like godfather mafia types. It was definitely an eye-opening experience.

"I'd like to stay anonymous if possible," I told the group.

"In New York, you have to do press, Ms. Long. That's just part of the process when you win," a greasy-headed stuffed suit told me.

Leitha and I eyed each other. I could tell she was playing the same song in her head that I was playing: "More Money, More Problems."

Bloomingdale's, Neiman Marcus, Bergdorf Goodman, and Nordstrom were just a few of the stores Leitha and I hit up before the money even hit my account. We were spending what was left of our "poor man" money like it wasn't an issue. Which it wasn't anymore.

I'm a big girl, so it wasn't easy finding high-end name brands to fit me in clothes, but that didn't mean I couldn't shop for shoes until my head spun. Gucci sneakers, Balenciaga sneakers and shoes, Aquazzura boots, and Sophia Webster pumps were just a few of the brands I purchased during the trip.

"You ain't getting no Christian's?" Leitha had asked as she modeled a hot pair of Christian Louboutin So Kate pumps that looked smashing on her feet.

"Girl, you think my fat-ass feet can fit into those shits? I refuse to walk around looking like I got some pigs in a blanket for feet. No thanks, boo," I said. We had a good laugh off of that.

Leitha and I stayed the entire weekend in a suite on the top floor of the Waldorf Astoria hotel in the city. It was my idea, because as a child I just always associated the Waldorf Astoria with being rich. Now that I was rich, I figured, why not?

Honestly, Leitha didn't care where we stayed, so long as she was sticking close to me. She'd been a great friend, and she was the reason I had played the lotto in the first place. She had nothing to worry about. Every time I thought about winning, I thought about Andre, too. Love and happiness were always what came to mind when I thought of him, and I didn't even know him.

"Leitha, you up?"

Of course her ass was knocked out. She groaned. We had partied all night and gotten back to the hotel room at three in the morning. We hadn't had a good club night in a long while. We rolled like the rich and famous. But today was press day. I would have to go forward and collect the big check while on television. I was nervous as hell, too.

"It's almost time to go to the press conference," I said, nudging Leitha again.

Leitha finally sat up and rubbed the sleep and hangover from her eyes. "Are you ready for this?" she asked, her voice so gruff with sleep it sounded like a frog had gotten lodged in her throat.

"I mean, what choice do I have?" I murmured. "I just don't want all these people coming out of the woodwork asking for shit. I don't want a bunch of suddenly new friends and family members. You know how that shit goes," I continued.

Leitha shook her head in the affirmative. "Let's just make a promise that we won't change up on each other. I know it's your money, and I get that, but let's just make sure our friendship stays the same no matter what," she said.

I looked her in the eyes and raised my right hand. "I promise I won't switch up on you as long as you don't switch up on me. Money ain't got shit on our friendship."

"Swear?"

"Swear," I said, putting my right hand over my heart.

Leitha and I hugged to seal the promise. But neither of us really knew what the future held.

After the press conference announcing that I'd won the $60 million jackpot and taken home over $40 million in the end, my cell phone began ringing nonstop. It got so bad I couldn't keep up. Call after call. Of course my mother was first. I hadn't told her anything when I first found out. It wasn't like she and I had the best relationship over the years. Honestly, I couldn't stand her deep down inside. She was the reason I overate and grew to this voluptuous 320 pounds. She always blamed me for everything that went wrong in her life, including the fact that she didn't have a man. I had all intentions of hitting her off with some cash, but more so to buy her a one-way ticket out of my life than to mend our relationship.

I hadn't decided where I was going to move to yet, so I returned to my apartment for a few days. I needed to gather my keepsakes and some other sentimental things, but I was leaving all the rest of that cheap-ass IKEA furniture behind. I had so many ideas about how my new life would be.

Keith was the first dude who tried to make a move after I'd won the money. What can I say about Keith? Hmmm. He was my foray into the older-man arena, and he'd proven to be a damn controlling-ass mess. He'd tried his best to lock me down. He had wanted me to cut off Leitha and all of my friends. He didn't want me to hang out. He wanted to have me when he wanted me. I had quickly grown tired of that bullshit. So, after I won the money and found my front door flooded with dozens of long-stemmed roses from Keith, I had to laugh. He'd also called my phone a dozen or so times. But it wasn't until he showed up at my house that I knew he had definitely lost his mind.

"Keith," I said when he appeared out of nowhere holding yet another bouquet of roses.

"Keisha, I've missed you," he said in that proper way older men speak.

"Well, I—" I started.

"You don't have to say that you missed me. I know you did. We had something good," he went on, trying to step inside. I was quickly reminded of why I had broken up with Keith: that control and him always trying to tell me what I was thinking.

The day I met Keith, I had literally run into him.

I had been banging the steering wheel of my boss's Mercedes-Benz impatiently. Traffic had been at a complete standstill, and I was late with his dry cleaning and lunch. "Shit! He's going to kill me!" I had exclaimed, realizing I was powerless over the bumper-to-bumper traffic on the FDR. I had been personal assistant to Orin Brouzin, a millionaire tycoon, and he hated when I was late.

I had laid on the horn. "Drive, people!" But traffic had only inched forward.

I slammed my fists on the steering wheel. But I had needed the job so quitting wasn't an option.

Finally fed up, I had swerved the car out of the lane to try to maneuver through the gridlock. I hit the gas, accelerating the car forward. A horn sounded from somewhere to the right of me, and I hit the gas again, just as my boss's car collided with another.

I screamed as my body flew forward against the steering wheel, causing the airbag to deploy. I remember feeling like someone had punched me in the chest. The dusty smoke from the airbag caused me to cough, and it covered my face with white dust. I heard three loud bangs and felt the whole car shake again. I blinked my eyes, trying to get them to focus. I couldn't seem to locate the source of the noise.

"What the fuck was you doing? You ran right into me!" a big hulk of man had barked. He had come up on me. His features were etched into a scowl. The man had started pounding on the hood of the car.

My heart leapt into my throat.

The driver's side door of the Mercedes suddenly flew open, sending a gust of humid summer air into my face. Before I could react, I felt myself being forcefully dragged from behind the wheel. I tried to hold on to the steering wheel, but even with all my size, the bump to my head had made me too weak to hold on. I was pulled forcefully from the car. The man had been hell-bent on kicking my ass.

"Get off of me!" I shrieked, swinging my arms wildly. I had tried to duck back into the car, but the man gripped me too tightly. I kicked my feet and caught him in the gut.

"You little bitch!" the man had snarled, grabbing a fistful of my hair.

"Don't touch me!" I growled, punching the hulk somewhere close to his chin. I couldn't believe the man was really assaulting me. I had tried to stand on wobbly legs. I smoothed down my rumpled dress with my trembling hands and reached up to my hairline, where I was bleeding. The impact of the accident still had my head spinning.

"What the fuck were you doing coming over to my lane?" the man growled, jutting an accusing finger in my face. "You should fucking learn how to drive!"

With sweat beads running a race down my back, I stood my ground. "First of all, you hit me!" I said indignantly, not letting the man's size intimidate me anymore.

I watched as the man curled his huge hands into fists. He moved toward me like he was about to pummel me to the ground. I kicked off my sandal and steeled myself, waiting for the man's powerful punch.

"Wow, so beautiful and feisty as hell." Another man had stepped from behind the menacing hulk, pulling the hulk's arm down before he started to rearrange my face.

"I got this, Mr. Jones. You get back in the car out of this heat. She's going pay for the damage to your car," the hulk stammered, his voice a low murmur. It was a much softer tone than he had used with me seconds before.

I rolled my eyes at Mr. Jones. Shit, I was ready for him too. It was clear that the hulk was Mr. Jones's driver. I wasn't in the mood to deal with either of those bastards.

"I apologize for my driver. He is just protective. I'm Keith Jones." The suit extended his hand toward me. "Pleasure to meet you."

I stared at his hand. I had to admit Keith was handsome for an older man. He reminded me a bit of a cross between Idris Elba and Lance Gross with a splash of salt and pepper. He was dressed in a three-piece suit that was perfectly tailored to his form. Whether he was gorgeous or not, I still didn't like what had happened.

"Look, I really don't have time for this chitchat. Your driver needs to learn how to drive. It's people like him who make this kind of traffic worse," I had spat, folding my arms over my chest defiantly.

Keith shoved his hand back into his pants pocket and then laughed. He laughed so hard I started to question his sanity.

"What's so funny?" I had asked.

"How amused I am by you. I don't think I've ever met a woman so beautiful yet so unrefined. You're an original, that's for sure," Keith said, still chuckling.

I threw my hands up, thinking he was trying to insult me. *Unrefined? You haven't seen unrefined!* "Look, mister, I really have to go," I had said, annoyed. I'd wasted enough time arguing with these men.

"It doesn't look like you can go anywhere," Keith said, nodding toward the front-end damage on the Mercedes. I pushed past Keith and surveyed the damage. The front of the car was a mass of twisted and gnarled metal.

"I'm dead!" I muttered, letting out an exasperated breath. The car was going to need to be towed. My shoulders slumped with defeat. All I could see and hear now was my boss's reaction. I shuddered. "I'm fired for sure. Now what will I do?" I gasped, cupping my face in my hands.

Keith had touched my shoulder, sending a cool chill down my back. I had shrugged away from him, feeling uneasy. I didn't trust anyone, especially men.

"I'll take care of it. I'll take care of everything. But first, I need to know your name," Keith had said. That was the start of it all. He had taken control of the situation and had never really let the control go.

I blinked away the memory of how Keith had come into my life. I wasn't going back to him that time. I had forgotten how fast and easy it had been for me to lose myself with him.

"Actually, Keith, I didn't miss you. I have moved on, and I know you're only here because you saw me on the news as the jackpot winner. No thanks. I can buy my own flowers," I said and slammed the door in his face.

I turned around and danced a little bit. It felt so liberating to do that. I wasn't always strong enough to stand up for myself like that. I felt proud.

A week later the trail of dudes and deliveries of "I'm sorry" flowers hadn't stopped. It was kind of amusing how many boyfriends I suddenly had pounding down my door to be with me. These were the same dudes who had friend-zoned me or called me their sister. Or worse, had just downright dissed me because I was a big girl. I wasn't hearing it. That was, until I got caught off guard.

I was dancing around the apartment, gathering things to box up, when someone knocked on my apartment door. I grumbled as I made my way to the door, thinking it was Leitha. She wasn't really letting me out of her sight since I'd won. I snatched back the door, ready to curse at her ass because she had a damn key, and when I looked up and saw who was standing there I almost fainted.

"Mmm . . . Malek?" I stammered with a mixture of shock, delight, and "nigga, what the fuck" all rolled into one.

When I pulled back the door and found him standing there flashing that megawatt smile, I truly almost gagged on my own tongue and suffocated my own damn self.

"Keisha," he sang, licking his lips in that LL Cool J way I remembered.

"Malek?" I huffed, exasperated already, and he hadn't even said more than just my name. He was the last person from my past dating life I'd expected to show up. I was sure my mouth hanging open sent that very message, too. I blinked rapidly, not believing that he was at my door. Suddenly, everything about him came rushing back to my mind. I closed my eyes and remembered. Damn, I had been soooo in love with Malek.

The night I met Malek was one of those friend hookups. A friend of ours named Danielle had decided she was tired of seeing me lonely, and her boyfriend had a friend, blah, blah. You know the rest. Malek initially didn't seem interested in me, but as the drinks flowed and my bubbly, "life of the party" personality shined through, he had warmed up to me.

Before I knew it, he and I were off in a corner laughing and talking into the night. We had exchanged numbers at his urging, which was a first for a fat girl like me. I had always been the one begging for the number. The next day, I had shrugged off my interaction with Malek. I just knew he was going to sober up, remember the fun fat girl he'd had a good time with the night before, and rip my number to shreds. In other words, I didn't expect him to call me at all.

So you can imagine my surprise when my cell phone had lit up that fateful day with his name and number. From that first call, I just knew Malek was different. We would speak for hours, laughing the whole time. He seemed interested in finding out everything about me. We had fun dates, the kinds that were stress free. Once, we went out and I didn't even wear makeup, and trust me, that is a big no-no in my book. Shit, I wore makeup to go to the corner store on my block.

Malek didn't have a lot by way of material things, but he made me feel like I was dating a rich man. He was definitely charming. He was also a gentleman, which at that point I hadn't been used to. Before long, Malek and I had been spending so much time together that Leitha and our other friends had begun to refer to Malek as my "boyfriend," a term I had never really had attached to me and any man I'd dated.

Things seemed perfect, and maybe they were too perfect. It was a nice fall day, and Malek had asked me on yet another real date. Up to that point, I had never turned him down. Back then, I didn't care if Jesus Himself was going to be somewhere; if Malek wanted me to meet him in the opposite direction, I'd be going that way. Malek and I sat across from each other that day, and he kept staring at me.

"Why you looking at me like that?" I had asked, breaking eye contact because I was trying to mask the fact that my damn face was on fire.

"Why you think?" Malek had replied, chuckling.

"I don't know, but you're staring at me. Real hard, I might add. Shit, you better tell me if I have bird doo-doo in my eyes," I had joked, swiping at the cracks of my eyes to make sure I didn't have anything in them.

"I don't have to have a reason to stare at you, Keisha. I just like staring at a pretty woman who I admire a lot," Malek had said, reaching across the table and putting his hand on top of mine.

My entire body jerked. Malek's touch always set off electric currents that I hadn't felt before, but something about that particular day was different. It had been in that moment that I had started to question whether it was really love. True love. I didn't know what that meant, but I'd always heard people say that when true love happens, you'll know.

There was nothing Malek couldn't get from me at that point. Right there at that little Brooklyn café table, in my mind, I had surrendered it all to him. There had never been another man who had come close to making me feel like that.

Malek and I had taken our time and enjoyed each other's company. We'd sat across from one another at a small table in the back of the restaurant with sexual tension and maybe love buzzing around us like bees over a pot of sweet honey.

"Penny for your thoughts?" Malek had said.

"Hmmm," I'd answered, giggling. "I'm not even thinking right now." It was a dumb answer, because there were so many things I could've said since I'd been thinking about how damn in love I was with him.

He put his hands under his chin and made a sad puppy-dog face. "So you have no thoughts? Dang. We are sitting in this little sexy spot. I'm smelling all good, you're looking all beautiful, and nothing?" Malek had responded.

I hung my head but was still smiling. I had never ever told a man my real feelings and thoughts this early. I'd been hurt so many times. In that moment, I swear it was like someone had cemented my tongue to the roof of my mouth. I wanted to speak, but I just couldn't.

"Okay. Okay." Malek threw his hands up. "Maybe that's a loaded question and it's a bit too much pressure for you."

I inhaled deeply and lowered my eyes to the delicious plate of whole fried snapper sitting in front of me. There I was again, turning a pressure moment into an opportunity to overeat.

"I, um, I . . ." I started, but again I was tongue-tied.

Malek put up his hand. "It's all good, Keish. No pressure," Malek had said, flashing his pearly whites. "How about you give me a penny for my thoughts instead?"

Why is this man so perfect? I had screamed in my head. My stomach felt like it was sitting in the center of the table and someone was hitting it with a meat tenderizer.

"Okay, penny for your thoughts," I had replied.

Malek opened his mouth and started to speak, but his words seemed to get caught too. I also noticed that his eyes had stretched wide and suddenly he looked as if he'd seen a ghost. His expression was so horrifying that I had whipped my head around and peered over my shoulder to see what the hell was happening.

That was when I saw her. Her: that's how I still refer to her to this day. She was storming toward Malek and me like a tornado set to destroy everything in her path. At first, the shock of what was happening had kept me glued to the chair. I literally couldn't move. My heart felt like it was going to jump loose from my chest, and I could feel the instant rolls of sweat falling in lines down my back.

"Malek!" the girl barked before she could even make it all the way to the table. "What the fuck, Malek?"

I turned my bulging eyes back to Malek and noticed that his eyes were also almost popping out of his head.

"I can't fucking believe you!" the girl boomed. She was so close by then that I could smell her perfume, see the whites of her eyes, and feel the heat rising up off of her body.

Malek shot up from his chair like a jack-in-the-box. I moved my eyes from Malek to the girl and back to Malek again.

"You out here with this fat bitch when I'm at home waiting for you?" the girl spat, thrusting an accusatory finger in my direction. She was fairly cute, not fat, but not skinny. I think I was way prettier and I'm not just saying that, because I'm one who gives bitches credit where it's due.

I stood up once she called me a fat bitch. I didn't know if I wanted to slap her first and then Malek or vice versa, but I was immediately steaming inside.

"Who the fuck is this fat pig, Malek?" The girl pointed at me again and spoke like I wasn't even there. "Who the fuck is this?" she repeated.

"I'm Keisha," I answered, rocking my neck from side to side. Shit, I was tired of her asking and Malek's dumb ass acting like he was stuck on stupid.

"Delia, what the hell are you doing here? You fucking stalking me?" Malek asked through his teeth.

"You just going to try to flip this shit on me, Malek?" the girl Delia said, sounding like she was about to cry.

"No. No," I said, throwing my hands up. "I've seen enough." I started grabbing up my jacket and purse.

"All of the work I put in and you turned around and cheat on me with a fat girl?" Delia spat, her bottom lip trembling.

"I ain't going to be too many more fat girls and fat bitches," I retorted.

"You can't do this to me! I loved you even when you didn't have shit! I have put in years and years with you, Malek." Delia finally let her tears burst through the dam.

At that point, I had seen my own heart lying on the floor between Malek and me, and I envisioned him stomping on it with his Timberland boots. I had wanted to scream, "I knew it was too fucking good to be true!"

Malek looked at me and sighed and shook his head. "It's a long story."

"Seems like a short story to me," I snapped. I had seen and heard enough. I dug inside my purse and tossed a couple of twenty-dollar bills onto the table. And trust me, that was just so I didn't get arrested for theft of service.

"You're lame," I grumbled at Malek. Then I turned my attention to his little woman. "As for you, I'm no fat bitch, or fat girl, or nothing of the sort. I'm a big, beautiful woman, or BBW as the real men like to call us," I had spat. With that, I sauntered my fat ass toward the exit.

"Keisha! Wait!" Malek had called after me.

I couldn't resist. I turned around with such a scowl on my face. I was sure Malek saw the devil flashing in my eyes at that moment, but he also probably saw the tears rimming my eyes.

"You know what, Malek? I thought you were different. I thought this was real, everything. I actually almost said some words to you today that would've made me go home after this bullshit and off myself. You're the kind of man who makes women like me regret the day we were born. You get off on hurting others. You're a fucking loser, and I really regret the day I laid eyes on you," I had said through gritted teeth. With that, I had stormed away and couldn't help the tears that finally spilled from my eyes once I was out of his sight.

Now, at my front door, he repeated, "Keisha." This time the hint of urgency in his voice snapped me out of my daydream or nightmare, whichever way you looked at it.

"Malek, what are you doing here?" I rasped, actually feeling like someone had their hands around my throat.

"Can I come in and talk to you?" he asked, craning his neck to look over my shoulder into my apartment.

I stepped aside so he could enter, but I immediately scolded myself for that. I closed the door, turned around with my back against it, and stared at Malek. Everything came rushing back. I was fighting a losing battle combating the memories of what we had, even if it was a brief few months. I knew I loved him.

"Well?" I said, smirking as if to say, "Get to the point, nigga."

"I, uh, um . . ." Malek stuttered. He swiped his hands over his face roughly. "Damn. Seeing you again makes this so hard all over again. I just, well, I never got to apologize for everything that happened back then," he said.

I felt like I could hear sincerity in his voice, but what did that mean to me now? He hadn't come to my apartment to apologize those ten days I'd stayed inside crying myself to sleep and binge eating until I vomited. He damn sure wasn't the one who'd finally come and lifted me up out of the bed, made me shower, and took me out so I wouldn't linger in a depression so deep I'd eat myself into being stuck in the house. That was Leitha who'd done that.

I twisted my lips and swallowed hard. "Soooo, you suddenly thought of me after all this time and decided now was the perfect time to apologize?" I asked. It was a rhetorical question, but I wanted to know.

Malek sighed loudly. "I know how this looks. It has nothing to do with you winning the lottery, Keisha," he said, holding up his right hand. "When I saw you on the news, I was just reminded that I had chickened out of coming to apologize too many times to count. I figured if I didn't come now, you'd be long gone soon. I'm sure with forty mil in the bank you ain't staying around here," he said. He tried to chuckle at the end with his joke, and I didn't flinch, crack a smile, or even breath hard.

"And you would be correct," I answered dryly. "I only came here to get my keepsakes: pictures, diplomas, shit like that."

"Wow." Malek shook his head like he was in distress. "I guess I always thought I had time to get back the one girl I actually loved, but fucked up and let get away," he said sadly. He let out another long, slow breath. "And here she is about to be gone for good, off somewhere in the world and I'll never get her back. I'll never get that chance." He dropped his head and shoved his hands deep into his jeans pockets.

My whole heart almost exploded. Malek was saying all of the right things. I wasn't over him. I knew that now. I shifted my weight from foot to foot. I was antsy because I was still desperate for something I knew money wasn't going to buy: love.

"Did you, um, say 'loved'?" I said, almost whispering.

Malek crinkled his eyebrows as if I'd asked him something strange. "Yes. Keisha, c'mon, you had to know that I was . . . am . . . I mean, um, I love you," he fumbled.

I couldn't speak. I pushed past Malek. He tried to grab me, but I yanked away and tore into my bedroom and slammed the door. I put my back against it, slid to the floor, pulled my knees to my chest, and buried my face. Why was this happening? Why after all those lonely months that turned into a year would he come back now with this when I was supposed to be my happiest?

Malek softly tapped on the door. "Keisha? Let me just talk to you. I just don't want you to disappear and we never get to say what we had to say to one another. That's all. Nothing else."

I shook my head, disgusted with myself. But still, I stood up and let him in. And that is not just what literally happened. It is a metaphor for everything happening.

We stood almost nose to nose for a few long minutes. My pulse quickened, and my head felt swimmy. I felt almost the same as I did the day I found out I'd won all that damn money.

Malek used the edge of his pointer finger under my chin and urged my head up to meet his gaze.

"Why now, Malek?" I gasped, barely able to get the words out. Fuck! I didn't realize how weak I still was for this dude. The room was literally spinning around me. I felt like I had just downed a gallon of Hennessy straight. "What about—"

Malek put his finger on my mouth before I could say anything else. My entire body (all 320 pounds of it) was ablaze.

I moved my face away from his finger and closed my eyes. My instinct was telling me to push Malek in the chest, curse, and push him some more until he was at my front door and out of my life. But my weakness for men and my need to be loved kept me there. I felt a stab of hurt in my gut. My mind, again, flashed back to that day with his girlfriend or whoever she was. I wasn't over what had happened.

"We don't have to speak about the past. I'm here for you right now. To make sure that you know everything that we had back then was real to me, Keisha," Malek said softly.

I hiccupped a quiet sob. He had me. I was all in now. Weak.

"How could it have been real when you had her all along? I just don't understand that concept. If you loved me, then why not tell me to wait for you until you had that situation handled? You left my heart broken in a million pieces. I had never been with anyone who made me feel the way you did," I said, barely able to keep it together.

"I know that now, Keisha. I swear, in my head things between me and her were over. When I met you, I felt, like, alive in so many ways that I hadn't in a long time. You were fun, sexy, serious when you needed to be, and most of all your heart was made of gold. She was still there but just in theory. I never loved her. We had fallen out of like long before I met you. I just hadn't taken care of the business of breaking up, and that was my fault. It was definitely all my fault," Malek said sincerely.

I felt his words. By then I was sobbing until my ample cleavage shook. This shit was crazy. I wasn't supposed to be crying unless it was tears of joy about this money and this new life I was about to start.

"That day, I was stuck, Keisha. I was caught between telling you how I really felt and risking that you didn't feel the same way and telling her I wanted to be with you and risking her making an even bigger scene. I've regretted that day ever since. I kept telling myself there was so much more I could've done. So many ways I could've changed things and the outcomes," Malek said.

I shifted uncomfortably under his touch. The heat from his body, the load of his words, everything was making me crazy. "I don't know, Malek. I just don't trust you. You could still be with her and here only because, you know . . ." I replied.

"I never saw her after that day in the restaurant. I had had enough of her and the antics. I never went back to her. I just suffered without you because I kept trying to get up the nerve to face you, to tell you how I always really felt about you. Right hand to God," he said, raising his right hand.

Why was God playing this trick on me? That's all I could think about. After all these months I spent lonely and serially dating all of these losers, God waited until now, *now,* when I won the biggest jackpot and was heading into a new life, to reveal to me that I'd always had a man who loved me out there? This had to be some sick fucking joke.

Nonetheless, I hung on Malek's every word. I didn't want to see him go, but I wasn't sure he was going to be able to stay. How could I trust him? Something deep down inside of me said that he was there just for my new-found riches, but something else said that he didn't have to come back to tell me all of this either. I was definitely stuck on stupid and caught up in the moment.

"I know you don't trust me, Keisha. You don't have to. I just wanted you to know. You always told me how you didn't believe in yourself and believe you were worthy of a good man. Listen to me," Malek said. He urged my head up again until I was looking in his eyes. "You don't ever have to settle for less. You're beautiful inside and out. Never let any man, woman, or child tell you otherwise, you hear me? Keisha Long, you're the most beautiful woman I know."

"Thank you," I said, my tone low and soft.

"You don't have to thank me for telling the truth," Malek said.

I stared deep into his eyes. I was trying to see if I could detect any deception or an inkling of game. I didn't. His eyes told the story. He did love me. I believed him.

I suddenly felt something inside of me pop loose. I wanted this man so badly it was like an itch deep down inside that I needed to scratch. I couldn't take it another second. His words, his scent, his gorgeous face, and the feelings I had been stifling inside for him for so long all bubbled to the surface like a hot well spring of lust.

I grabbed his face and crushed my mouth on top of his. It was not my usual habit, but I couldn't help it. It was as if some unknown force was moving me. Our tongues intertwined, performing a soft, sensual dance. Malek groaned into my mouth and pressed his body into mine. I moved backward toward my bed. What was I doing? I didn't know, but it felt damned good.

We moved together, kissing, touching, feeling until finally, he forced me down gently onto my back. The sounds coming from us—grunts and pants and hisses— were almost animalistic. Malek's hand ran a race over every inch of my body. I held on to him tight, feeling things happening to my body that I hadn't felt in a long time. My head got swimmy and so didn't my panties.

"I need you," Malek whispered in my ear. That sent an explosion of heat into the center of my chest. That was that love feeling again. Damn! I couldn't resist him. He kissed me deeply, and his hands roamed in places no one had touched in a long while. I didn't fight it. I wanted it. I wanted him. I wanted all of this.

Malek moved his mouth from mine and hovered over me until he was staring down into my face. He looked me in my eyes. "I'm finally going to tell you the truth. I love you, Keisha Long. I always have and I always will."

I swear fireworks went off in my head. I saw red, blue, white, yellow, and maybe even purple bursts of light erupting. I heard loud booms inside my head. Malek had made my whole life with those words.

I reached up and pulled his face back down to mine. I opened my mouth and accepted his tongue. With that, he entered me, and I totally surrendered to him, again.

"Keisha! What's going on here?" Leitha screamed from my bedroom doorway.

I almost jumped out of my skin. Her yelling violently yanked me out of my sleep. I thought my heart would leap through my mouth. Malek and I had made the sweetest love and fallen asleep with our bodies intertwined. That was the last thing I remembered.

"Oh, my God, Leitha!" I exclaimed, popping up in my bed and grabbing for the comforter frantically.

"No, I should be saying oh, my God, Keisha," Leitha retorted with her hands on her hips like a mother who'd just busted in on her teenager having sex.

My heart was racing, and I was red with embarrassment. "LeLe, c'mon, girl, step out. I'll come talk to you. Just let me get myself together," I said, my voice still thick and gruff with sleep.

"Oh, yeah, you need to come talk to me right now. Shit, because I surely want to know what the hell this nigga is doing here," she said, her heated gaze falling on Malek.

I could tell he didn't know what to do. Probably because his mind was also clouded over with sleep.

"Girl, if you don't . . ." I said, tilting my head knowingly.

Reluctantly Leitha stomped out of the doorway of my bedroom and back into my living room.

"I'm sorry," I said to Malek. "She's super protective of me. Oh, and she really hates you."

"I get it. No need to be sorry. I fucked up, and she's your friend. Got to love it," he said understandingly. "I better get out of here. I'm really going to miss you, Keisha."

"Wait, is this it?" I asked incredulously. "Again?"

"No. Well, I, um, I didn't know if you'd want to see me again. I didn't want to jump to any conclusions. It's your call," he said.

"Keisha!" Leitha yelled out from the living room.

"Oh, God. Let me go talk to her," I said, flustered. I wrapped myself in my robe and stormed out of my bedroom to face this crazy friend of mine.

Leitha was actually tapping her damn foot. I rolled my eyes and put up my hand. "No lectures, LeLe," I said, closing my eyes and shaking my head.

"Oh, no, you're going to hear me out, Keisha," she said.

Just then, Malek walked out of the room, wearing an awkward smile. "I'll talk to you," he said, his voice quivering.

"Okay, I'll call you," I said, smiling nervously.

"Oh no the hell you won't, and oh no the hell he won't," Leitha said, pointing at me first and then at Malek.

"Just let yourself out," I told him, embarrassed.

As soon as he was gone, I turned on Leitha. "Listen—" I started.

"No, you listen, Keisha," she interrupted. "I watched you make yourself sick over that dude. You were around here crying and eating yourself into hell. He never, ever thought to come back until now? 'Now' meaning after you're forty million dollars richer? That doesn't seem suspicious to you?" she ranted. "Please, if you can't see it, then you're all the way blind."

"Look, I know you have my best interest at heart. And I thank you for that. But I'm grown, and I'm far from stupid. He isn't asking me for anything. He just wanted to come and finally explain the whole situation with the girl. He wanted to tell me once and for all that he was always in love with me, but he just didn't have the balls to come before," I replied.

"Oh, but he all of a sudden grew a pair after you hit the lotto?"

"No, Leitha," I sighed and rolled my eyes. She knew I was serious because I hardly ever called her by her full name. "He came because common sense told him I wouldn't be living in this tiny-ass apartment for much longer. He wanted to catch me before I was gone for good."

Leitha twisted her lips and rolled her eyes. "Whatever you say, Keisha. I just don't trust him as far as I can throw his ass. And you shouldn't either. Of course he's going to talk a good game now. You're a fucking million-aire. He wouldn't care if your ass kicked him and spit on him every day so long as he could get his hands on your money. I'm just saying, everything that glitters ain't gold."

Leitha was right and I knew it. I couldn't trust a soul. I didn't admit it to her, but I was thinking that "more money, more problems" had never been more of a true statement than in that moment. I needed to brace myself because I was going to either lose a bunch of friends or gain a bunch of friends. Either way, I knew it was all going to be because of the money. All because of the money.

Chapter 5

Everything You've Been Missing

Despite Leitha's protest, Malek didn't disappear, and I didn't make him. In fact, I decided to spend more time with him.

"I missed you," Malek said.

I smiled and melted against him. My heartbeat sped up so fast I could see the material of my shirt moving. The throbbing between my legs matched my heartbeat thump for thump. Damn, I'd forgotten how good it felt to be in Malek's arms. With all of the time that had passed, I had totally lost sight of how deeply I'd felt for him in the first place. I had to wonder why God was blessing me with one thing after the other. Maybe God finally decided that Keisha Long was a good person who'd sacrificed her own happiness for far too long. Yeah, that was it! I deserved every minute of how my life was going right now. I closed my eyes, inhaled Malek's cologne and listened to the thrumming of his heart. I could've sworn it was matching mine thump for thump. Malek and I were in sync.

"Promise you're here to stay this time," I said, letting my vulnerable side show through. "I don't want you to prove my best friend right. And I'm scared to death that you will."

"I won't. I'm not going anywhere. Trust me," Malek said, pulling me closer. "It has nothing to do with money. I'll never let you get away from me again, Keisha."

I can't lie. My mind raced in a million directions. I was thinking about Leitha being mad at me. I was thinking about who I was going to bless with money. I was thinking about who I wasn't going to bless with money. My mind mulled over whether I should have plastic surgery to look like an Instagram model. But most of all, I was preoccupied with fear of Malek not being sincere. I so wanted this to be real. I wanted his love, and I had for a long time.

With thoughts of being abandoned again plaguing my mind, I decided to show Malek why he couldn't leave me. Fuck money. I was going to be all the woman he needed.

I reached up, grabbed his face, and pulled it close to mine. He chuckled. "What's this about?" he asked, but he didn't hesitate to follow my lead. He put his sexy lips on mine. I sighed and exhaled. Then I parted my lips and allowed his tongue in. Malek sucked on mine softly. That drove me wild.

"Shit, Keisha. I really missed you, ma," Malek whispered without even moving his mouth from mine. We kissed so passionately I was soaked down below. I could hear myself moaning, and I moved my body against his, but I felt like I was floating. It was like an out-of-body experience. My nipples were so hard, every moment sent electric pulses of passion all over my body. I was so alive with human electricity I probably could've lit up the entire room. Within a few minutes, it was apparent Malek was enjoying the same feelings I was. His dick was so hard I felt it pressing into my meaty flesh like a metal rod.

"I need you," I huffed. I moved my hands below his belt line and took his girth into my large palm. He was so big even my big-ass hands couldn't close around that monster.

"Fuck," Malek whispered in my ear. A hot feeling sizzled through my body. Fuck it. I gave up. I was all in. I wanted to be all his, forever. Most of all, I just wanted to be wanted. Malek was fulfilling my needs in more ways than one. He knew I wanted to be loved and wanted. He knew everything. I stop fretting about whether I could trust him, and I surrendered to him.

"You ready?" Malek asked softly.

I didn't know exactly what he was asking me I was ready for, but still I said, "Yes. Yes. I'm ready."

I can't lie. I was lost in lust, and even thoughts of Leitha and my mother had faded out of my mind for that moment.

Malek slipped my dress over my shoulders, down my waist, and past my wide hips. Then he told me to wait as he slid out of his shirt and wife beater, exposing his six-pack abs and slim but muscular chest. I licked my lips and smiled. This was like a dream come true. Malek's perfect caramel skin seemed to glow. Why was this man so perfect? Honestly, in that moment if he'd asked me for every dime in my account, I probably would've given it all to him. Every cent. That's how gone I was off of Malek. It was like he was a new drug.

"You sure you ready?" Malek asked as he climbed onto the bed.

"Stop prolonging this shit and come here," I said, finally tired of all the foreplay.

Malek laughed. He kissed me again, deep and passionate like before. "Okay. Okay," he said.

"Shit," I huffed. "You're so perfect."

My thighs trembled, but I didn't let that stop me from taking control. Malek was playing around, and I was over-the-top horny at that point.

"Take this pussy," I demanded.

Surprise flashed in Malek's eyes. I could tell he was little taken aback by my newfound confidence. What did I have to lose? I let my inhibitions fall away. I wanted Malek, and that was that. Shit, we had already missed out on a lot of time that we couldn't get back. Besides, there was a still part of me that didn't believe it all.

"I love you, Keisha," he whispered. It was the second time he'd said it, and each time it had really pulled something inside of me to the core. My stomach quivered at the sound of those words. When I'd first opened that door for him two weeks ago, us being all in love was the furthest thought from my mind, but I couldn't help it or hide it anymore. Fear and reservations were all tossed away at that moment.

Without another word, I hoisted my big ass up and climbed onto Malek and straddled him. I leaned over his face and looked right into his eyes. "I have never felt like this before, so you better be telling the truth." With that, I didn't give him a chance to respond. I just started licking his neck then moved a little farther down, trailing my tongue down to his pecks and gently biting each one.

Malek breathed out through his mouth heavily. I loved having that type of effect on him. With every noise he made, I gained more confidence. I let all my self-esteem issues fade away. I guessed it was true what I'd always heard: that we are all the same size once we get in bed. Malek was handling all 320 pounds of me, and he didn't even wince.

I continued down his abdomen, taking special care to run my tongue over every ridge on his sexy, firm six-pack. He was so damn sexy. I got to his snake-long manhood and wasted no time. I looked up at his face then parted a mischievous smile. With expert skill, I grabbed his thick rod, opened my mouth, and took him inside.

"Keisha." Malek sang out every syllable of my name. The sound came out as one long puff of air. Hearing him call my name just propelled my actions forward even more. I could feel his muscles tense each time I lifted my head up and then pushed back down and flicked my tongue over the tip of his dick. I ran my hands up and down over Malek's throbbing love muscles every time I moved my head. I knew all about that friction trick.

Malek was making noises that sounded like growling, grunting, and snorting at the same time. He couldn't take it any longer.

"I need to feel you. I want to feel you now." He pulled up abruptly, and as big as I was, Malek flipped my ass over onto my back before I could even react.

"Malek!" I called out, scared he was going to drop my ass on the floor.

"You good. I got this," he assured me.

"What you going to do with it?" I whispered. A pang of anticipation flitted through my chest. I had tried it, but I liked it better when Malek was in command. I was on my back watching him now. I could tell where he was taking this, so I put my hands on the top of his head.

Malek kissed my stomach, my fat rolls, and every inch of my ample body. He kissed and licked like I was the best meal he ever had. My chest rose and fell in anticipation of what was coming. I felt lightheaded. I guessed this was what they called swooning. Malek moved back up and kissed me again.

"Open those legs," he demanded.

The sound of his voice made goose bumps crop up all over my body. I lifted my knees and willingly parted my thighs.

"I'm not going to say it again. Stop playing and give it to me," I huffed.

Malek smiled wickedly. "A'ight, you asked for it."

Malek used his hand and guided his manhood into my soaking wet pussy. I clutched handfuls of the sheet and let out a song of soft moans and groans as he ground into me with so much fluid skill. Malek moved his hips like a male exotic dancer. It was lustful, skillful, and nasty all at the same time.

"Gotdamn," he growled, his eyes closed and his nostrils open wide. He planted his hands on the bed at either side of my head for leverage. I was a lot of woman, and he definitely needed the stability. I lifted my pelvis and fucked him back, stroke for stroke.

"Malek," I cooed. It was my turn to call out syllables. Malek's dick felt so good. I'd forgotten how much of a perfect match he was for me. He filled me up just right. He was made for me, and this was proof.

The more I moved, the faster Malek picked up speed from the excitement of feeling me. I turned my head to the side so Malek would see that I had tears in my eyes. They were definitely tears of joy.

"Get on your knees," Malek commanded. I had always been self-conscious about the doggie-style position. I figured that no man wanted to see all this ass up in the air, especially because all of it wasn't tight.

"Fat girls can't go doggie," I'd always heard in high school. Shit, who said so?

Before I knew it, Malek was hitting it from the back. He slammed into me so hard I swore I could feel his dick in my guts.

"Agh," I yelled as his pole penetrated my insides. Malek put his hands on my ass cheeks for leverage and started grinding into me. Within minutes, he picked up his rhythm, and I felt my entire body vibrating with each pump of his hips. The sound of our skin hitting together made a beat. We made our own beat. It was music to my ears.

"Aghh!" I yelled. "Fuck! Mal . . . Mal . . ." I was stuttering because I had never felt the fireworks exploding in my ass like what I was experiencing. I had had some decent dick in my dating days, but this, this was some next-level shit. This orgasm had me trembling like I was about to go to the other side. I felt like I was having an out-of-body experience, and the feeling was otherworldly for real.

"Keisha, baby. Your pussy is the best," Malek growled, clutching his handfuls of my ass cheeks even harder. I was feeling good now. I had him and I knew it. I twisted my hips and pushed back on his dick.

"Ahhhh!" Malek belted out. It was his turn to bust a nut. He pushed me down onto my stomach and stayed mounted on me from behind. I guessed he needed to get deeper. I fell down onto my stomach, letting him go as deep as he wanted. I squeezed my ass checks in and out. I knew that would make much more friction. Malek pounded me harder and faster now. Another explosion erupted inside of me.

"Malek!" I belted out. For the second time, my entire body shook until I was too damn weak to move. My legs trembled fiercely. A few seconds later Malek's body tensed up and he busted his nut deep inside of me. I didn't even care.

Malek collapsed on my back, and we both tried to calm our rapid breathing.

"Promise me that you'll be with me for good," I said. I knew I had already said it earlier, but I wanted to be sure. I needed to hear it. I closed my eyes, and for a few seconds, Malek was silent. His silence sent a wave of cramps trampling through my stomach.

"I already told you, I promise," he said softly. "What about you? Promise me no matter what people say, you'll stay with me."

"I told you, I will be with you. I swear, I promise."

Malek slid off of me and lay next to me on the bed. He stroked my hair gently. I closed my eyes, let the happy tears flow, and told myself that no amount of money could buy what I had in that moment.

Instead of Leitha, Malek was the one who went with me to see the brand-new luxury loft apartment I had purchased in the swankiest part of Brooklyn. I had commissioned two of the best interior decorators in New York to outfit the place to match our tastes. Malek and I spent hours picking out the furniture, fabrics, colors, and artwork. We spent hours kissing and canoodling while we chose customized black hardwood floors for the loft, our oversized, tufted gray suede headboard with its rhinestone accents, and the one-of-a-kind silver and black Italian-silk window treatments. I can't lie. I missed Leitha. She couldn't say that I hadn't taken care of her with money, but I was sure she felt like she was missing out. Leitha had her man, and now I had mine. That was all I wanted her to understand.

"So, I have a surprise for you," I told Malek.

"I don't need a surprise if it's not you," he said.

I felt a warm feeling envelop my body and an involuntary smile spread over my face at his words. "Well, it's not me. It's a surprise," I replied.

"But I hate surprises," Malek protested.

I wasn't listening to him. "Come here," I commanded. I covered Malek's eyes with a blindfold and led him off of the elevator that opened into our new loft.

"Are you trying to peek?" I joked, guiding Malek by his hand.

"Nah, I can't see shit," he laughed as he stumbled forward.

I guided him until we reached my intended destination. "Okay. We're here. You ready?" I asked.

"Man, if you don't get me out of this blindfold," Malek joked.

I chuckled at his playful impatience. I had stopped him at a doorway.

"So, we are not walking anymore," Malek said, stating the obvious. He reached both arms out and touched either side of the doorway frame. He inhaled deeply. "Smells like brand new," he said.

"Brand new? Is that a scent now?" I joked back. We both laughed. "You sure you ready?" I teased, feeling palpable anticipation.

"Baby, c'mon. You dragging this out for real now," Malek said, in this whining voice that he knew made me horny.

"Shit, you know how much that voice turns me one. Maybe I have to get something before I make the big reveal," I said, still stalling. It was fun.

Malek let out a long breath. I moved in front of him. My stomach quivered with nervousness. What if Malek thought my surprise was stupid?

I slowly and gently pulled off the blindfold. Before Malek could see anything, I kissed him. Our tongues danced. Still kissing him, I walked Malek backward into the bedroom. Abruptly, I ended the kiss and stepped aside.

"I want to give you this and more," I said honestly, opening my arms wide. "I want to share everything I have with you."

Malek's mouth fell open. He looked strangled, and I saw the tears rim his eyes. He turned around and around like a kid inside a candy store.

"Yo, I never had anyone do shit for me," he said as he stared in amazement at the huge professionally commissioned portrait of him hanging behind the bed.

"I just wanted you to know that it wasn't all mine. I wanted to let you know that everything in the room belongs to you, including me," I said, fighting back my own tears.

"This shit is boss, and I love it," Malek gasped.

"It came together much better than I expected," I said.

Malek pulled me into him. He just didn't know how badly I needed his love. Growing up hand-to-mouth, this was more than I ever expected out of life.

"I love you," Malek whispered as he pulled me down to the gleaming hardwood floors. Overwhelmed with emotion, we held each other tight. Breathing heavily, Malek moved on top of me and ground his pelvis against mine. I immediately clawed at his shirt buttons.

"I want you, now!" I urged.

Malek let out a gust of breath, turned on by my assertiveness. It worked every time. I leaned up and forced my tongue into his mouth, grinding into him harder.

"I like when you take charge," he moaned into my mouth.

"Take off your clothes," I ordered, my voice throaty and harsh. Honestly, I didn't know what had come over me. "Hurry up," I demanded, my eyes going wild roving his body.

Malek smiled as he unbuckled his pants and slid out of his boxers. He was aroused. Thrilled. Taken aback. I licked my lips and grabbed Malek's manhood roughly and tugged on it.

"Whoa! That thing is connected to me." He winced at the rough handling.

I didn't care. I was possessed as I took him into my mouth.

"Shit!" he hissed. I was ravenous as I moved my mouth up and down on him. I could feel the swell of blood rushing through his vein. That made me work my jaws harder, faster. The slurping sounds were driving Malek crazy. He grunted like an animal. Sweat glistened on my temples, and saliva trickled down the sides of my mouth. I moved to his balls and took them into my mouth. It was deliciously daring and kinky as hell.

"Damn, this is something new," Malek murmured, his legs beginning to shake. I gently sucked then blew air on them. I did that over and over as I moved my hand over his shaft.

"You fucking me up, baby girl," Malek gasped on the verge of exploding. I knew I had him now. I stopped on purpose. Malek's eyes popped open incredulously.

"Lie down," I instructed seductively. Malek did as he was told. The cold, hard floor stung his back and ass cheeks, and he let me know it. I didn't care, and he didn't either. We wanted each other. We needed each other.

I got completely naked in front of Malek. I didn't hide shit. I straddled him, skin to skin.

I lowered my body onto his, throwing my head back as he filled me completely. I rocked my hips, feeling his girth take up all of my space.

"Cum for me," I growled as I ground into him so hard he lost his breath. Malek gasped for breath as I swirled, rocked, and ground on his dick. My insides throbbed with every inch of him.

I glanced down at Malek to find his eyes tightly shut. "Look at me," I instructed, lifting his face to meet mine. "Look into my eyes." Malek's eyes opened wide. It was like he was under a spell as I pumped up and down fast, slamming my big body into his.

"Are you all mine this time?" It was an important question. Malek couldn't catch his breath to answer. I stopped moving, but I squeezed the muscles inside of my pussy around his manhood.

"Shit! Oh, God!" Malek huffed.

"Answer me!"

"Yes! I'm all yours, Keisha," Malek proclaimed just as he exploded inside of me. I smiled and followed his lead, wetting him with my juices. I collapsed on top of him, my body rising with each heave of his chest. Silence enveloped us. This was the life, I hoped.

Chapter 6

Fate or What?

Leitha whirled around and opened her arms, resembling an enchantress in the batwing black designer dress she was modeling.

I giggled. "Okay, Morticia from *The Addams Family*, cast a spell on my ass why don't you."

Leitha laughed.

It was so good to be hanging out with my best friend again. I had been spending all my time with Malek for the past three weeks. Having money was still new to me, to us. I had called Leitha up and demanded that we do an all-expenses-paid shopping trip on me. She tried to have an attitude at first, but you know me, I didn't give up. Leitha could never resist my bubbly personality.

"Let me see yours," Leitha said.

I mimicked her Bride of Frankenstein movements and opened my arms wide and spun around. I could feel the dress hugging me in all of the right places.

"Bitch, now that dress is on fire," Leitha complimented me.

"Are you sure?" I asked, letting my arms fall at my sides as I turned to the mirror and looked at myself in the deep maroon gown one last time. "I've never worn anything this damn fancy. Now I have to make sure I have a place to go in it," I said.

"First of all, you're rich now so you can just wear that shit to walk down the street. Second of all, that shit was definitely made for you," Leitha replied, rolling her head like she did when she was making a point.

"Okay. I'll take your word for it," I said, walking back into the fitting room. "Come get it. And add your stuff to mine."

Leitha sighed and snatched the dress over the fitting room door. She tossed it on top of the huge pile the salesgirl held on her arms.

"What about shoes and bags?" I called out as I got dressed.

"You know what? We are playing ourselves really. When you have the kind of money you got, you're supposed to hire a damn personal shopper. They bring everything to your house, and you can sit in your shit and pick out what you want. We definitely acting like new money," Leitha preached.

"Well, bitch, we are new money. Shit, I ain't scared to admit that," I said as I emerged from the fitting room. "You're also the one dressed up like we were going someplace fancy just to come shopping. If that ain't some new money shit, I don't know what is," I joked.

Leitha looked at her perfectly placed makeup and slayed hairstyle in the mirror. "Shit, you're right. I wasn't about to come in here and be profiled like I'm some broke bitch."

I raised a brow and nodded at Leitha as if to say, "I know that's right."

"I missed you," I admitted.

"Yeah, right. Your ass been giving me the shaft for weeks. That dick must be great," Leitha chuckled.

"Lord, you sound like my mother." I rolled my eyes.

"Well, if we all saying the same thing, then it must be true," she said, moving her hips like she was humping the air. "Good dick will make you lose your damn mind."

We laughed.

"Let's get out of here. I'm starving." I signaled the sales-girl, who by then had a sweaty upper lip and quaking arms. "I'm ready to check out."

The salesgirl craned her neck to see behind the pile of clothes we had stacked on her, and she smiled. We followed her to the counter, lost in conversation.

"Wait a minute." I stopped Leitha. "Girl, I have always wanted a Chanel bag. You have no idea how I've dreamed about one day buying one," I said, pulling her into the Chanel salon inside of Neiman Marcus.

"Eww, girl, five thousand dollars or more on a bag makes my stomach hurt," Leitha said. "But it ain't trick-ing if you got it."

"And I definitely got it," I said dreamily.

Another saleswoman walked over to us as we stood in front of the glass showcase literally gawking at the beautiful Chanel bags. I picked up on her little suspicious eyes, but I ignored her. I wasn't about to feed in to her "shopping while black" silent stereotyping.

"I'll take two of those classics. The aqua green and the red caviar leather." I leaned into the counter and pointed at two bags on the shelf behind it.

"Whew," Leitha huffed, playfully fanning herself.

"Girl, stop. I think you should get two too. Let's start our collection together," I chimed. If this saleswoman was going to act suspicious, I was going to act over-the-top. I could be a snob too. I was getting used to it.

The tight-faced white saleslady widened her eyes at me, but she tried to keep that fake smile on her face. I could tell she was probably secretly judging and she more than likely instantly thought I couldn't afford these expensive-ass bags. It was amusing to me to watch her struggling to keep it professional, because she also knew just as well as I did that my purchase of these two $5,000

Chanel bags would be a payload of commission for her. And if Leitha took my advice and got her bags, she'd get even more.

As the ugly saleslady worked to retrieve my items, I kept shopping with my eyes. Now I felt like I had a little point to prove. I smirked to myself, and for spite, I decided to make her feel like she might need to call somebody. I bet when I walked in she had immediately looked at my race and my size and pegged me as a window shopper or credit card scammer. I was about to show this bitch a thing or two about judging books by their covers.

"Wow, these are beautiful too. Hmmm, I think I should take every color of these as well," I said, pointing down into the counter at the Chanel brooches. "Oh, and give my friend one of each too, please. Why not? You only live once."

"YOLO!" Leitha belted out.

We both busted out laughing. The saleswoman almost dropped the pocketbooks as she clamored over and grabbed the merchandise I was asking for with the quickness. I could hear her cursing in her head, probably green with envy about how two chubby black girls could afford all of this high-end shit while she was an old white bitch waiting on us hand and foot for the commission she would make from our sales. I chuckled to myself with satisfaction and eyed Leitha knowingly.

"Is that all?" the saleswoman asked me, barely able to get the words out clearly.

"I think I've done enough damage for one day," I said snobbishly.

Then I slapped my American Express Plum Card down on the counter. Can you believe that bitch of a saleswoman had the nerve to squint at my card like she couldn't tell what it was? She picked it up and looked it over like it was a piece of shit. I could the questions glinting in her eyes: *is this really hers? Is she stealing someone's identity? How can she afford to have a plum card?*

I quickly began feeling indignant. *How dare this bitch!*

"Do you do that to all customers or just the black ones?" I asked through my teeth.

"Yes, please tell us," Leitha added. "Because it's real obvious that you're profiling us."

The saleswoman's eyes popped open like we each just dashed a cup of cold water in her face.

"Oh, don't act surprised by the question, now. You've been acting suspicious of us since we walked in here," I said. "Why is that?"

"Correct. I'm sure if we were of any other race, you would have picked up my friend's card with a smile and run to the register without a second thought. I'm just wondering what all the extra examination of the card is all about," Leitha said through gritted teeth.

"I don't know, do you think we need to speak to your manager?" I asked, the underlying threat readily apparent.

The saleswoman's cheeks flushed deep red, and she shifted her weight from one foot to the other. She parted a halfhearted, embarrassed smile and broke eye contact with me. "No, ma'am, and I apologize if you feel that way," she replied meekly.

"That's what we thought. Now I think you can stop scrutinizing the card and ring us up, or this store will be all over the news when I'm done speaking to the media about the blatant discrimination we experienced here," Leitha snapped.

Leitha and I laughed as the saleswoman raced to the small area in the Chanel suite where they rang purchases over a certain amount. We laughed, but it wasn't really a laughing matter. As someone who'd dealt with discrimination based on how I looked all of my life, it was ridiculous to keep going through the shit. Honestly, being fat and discriminated against was a lot, but being fat and black was worse. Oh, and the fact that I was a fat black woman didn't help the situation any, either. This incident just served to show that it really didn't even matter how much money you had. The world was a cruel fucking place.

I could tell Leitha and I had scared the holy shit out of the saleswoman, which was what we wanted to do after her disgusting behavior.

As we stood there waiting for her to return with our nicely bagged and wrapped items, my cell phone buzzed. I looked at the screen and bit down into my jaw. It was Malek.

Should I answer? Should I answer? I contemplated. I didn't want Leitha to feel like I wasn't into spending time with her. A cold sweat broke out over my body.

Leitha rolled her eyes. "He better not even come between our time together today, Keisha. I mean, I've hardly seen you in weeks. You can't throw money at me and think I'm just going to stop being your damn best friend. Only fake bitches would do that," Leitha said, noticing the struggle playing out on my face.

"He really likes you, LeLe," I said, pressing IGNORE on the call.

"Whatever." Leitha waved me off. "He likes me now, but he ain't like me when he left you all fucked up back in the day and I had to be there."

"Oh, God, are we going to keep bringing that up? I forgave him. I think you should too at this point," I said pointedly.

Leitha sucked her teeth. "Look, I just want the best for you. Hate it or love it, I got your best interest in mind, no matter what."

"Your total is $16,256.33," the saleswoman interrupted us all of a sudden with a smile.

"Thank you," I said, matching her phony smile.

"That was some damn damage," Leitha said, shocked. "I take my wig, hat, and my whole damn scalp off to you. I hope you don't go spending like that too often and damn sure not on that nigga Malek."

"Stop!" I shot back. "You're starting to sound like a nagging mother instead of my damn best friend. I know I am a fat girl who you think has to buy a man, but I'm not. Malek loves me."

"All of a sudden, though?" Leitha asked. "Why all of a sudden? That's all I want you to see. Where has he been? Why did it take until everyone found out you hit the lottery for him to show up? Why? What? I just can't wrap my mind around it, Keisha."

I knew Leitha had been waiting for the opportunity to ask me all of these questions. Ever since the day in the apartment with Leitha, I'd felt like I was torn between my man and my best friend, each tugging me in a different direction.

"Listen, I love you, but this is on me. We're just fine. It's like nothing has changed. Malek has been so attentive. He's been at my side and with me every minute, of course except now while I'm with you."

As I said the words, a cold chill shot down my back. The truth was Malek had disappeared twice, and I had been afraid to ask where he'd been. He'd come back with flowers or some of my favorite food each time. Malek and I had been living like nothing had happened, and since I didn't want my new lifestyle to change, I didn't press him. I was actually afraid to lose him again.

I knew Malek still had things to take care of outside of our relationship, and that's what I told myself. No, I convinced myself. That was it. He was just out taking care of business. If I pressed him, I might push him away, and I refused to do that.

"Just be sure, Keisha. That's all I'm saying," Leitha said.

I waved my hand and chuckled nervously. "Girl, that man is never going to let anything come between him and his Keish Keish ever again," I joked.

Leitha shrugged. "His Keish Keish better be smart smart and not dumb dumb when it comes to her coins coins and niggas trying to use her," she said.

"Ugggh, please stop. Enough. This is supposed to be a happy day, right? We are together. We are shopping. And I ignored my man's call all for you. Let's make the best of it," I said.

Leitha had always had an unwavering protective streak when it came to me, ever since we were kids. She was like my cheerleader, protector, mother, and advisor, and even when I was wrong, Leitha would always stick by my side. She'd always be right though, so I was slightly uneasy about the things she'd been saying about Malek.

But I could always count on my mother's sick logic to give me an excuse. My mother would always preach, "Remember, good men are hard to find, and they all have faults. When you get one, you better hold on to him. Somebody else would gladly snap him up."

That's how I rationalized things in my head, until I couldn't any longer.

"You know, all of my years living in New York, and I've never come to this place. Heard about it, couldn't afford it," Leitha said as we walked into Mr. Chow's, a well-known celebrity haunt in the city. Leitha and I both loved Asian fusion food. Mr. Chow's was as fancy as everyone made it seem, too. The white tablecloth service, glass bar tops, and expansive ceilings gave the inside of the restaurant a bright and inviting but rich feel.

"I love it in here. I love to be able to just get up and go anywhere I want to go without counting pennies," I replied.

"I hear you, girl. Life has definitely changed for the better," Leitha agreed.

We were seated at a prime table. It seemed like the perfect spot: not too far from the door, so we could see the comings and goings, not too far from the bar, so we could have drinks faster, and close enough to the restaurant's center so our new-money-groupie asses could snap pictures of celebrities if we spotted any.

"So what's good on the menu?" Leitha asked as she scanned her leather-bound menu. The scent of roasted garlic, fresh seafood, and newly authentic Chinese food made both of our stomachs growl.

"Girl, you asking me? I don't know, but I've heard that everything is good here. I think I want to try every entrée," I replied without looking up from my menu. "I'm going for anything spicy that goes over white rice and is enough to fill up my big-ass stomach." I laughed.

Leitha nodded her agreement. "All of that sounds good to me."

"Good evening, ladies." The waiter approached, taking a quick little bow in front of us. "I'm Khan, and I'll be serving you this evening."

"Even the waiter looks expensive," Leitha joked. "He look like he only serves millionaires." Leitha eyed him up and down. We giggled.

"I'll start with an order of dumplings," I said.

"The spicy ribs for me," Leitha said.

"Any drinks, ladies?" Khan asked us.

"For me, something sweet and potent." I winked. Khan nodded, smiled politely, and rushed from the table.

"It feels like we've been missing out," Leitha said.

"What do you mean?" I asked.

"Like, we used to spend more time together when we were broke," she said solemnly.

She was right, but I didn't want the mood of our day out to change. "Let's move past that. Let's promise to make sure we do this more often. As long as you don't beat me up about my relationship every time we are together," I said, kind of on the defensive. Leitha's eyebrows arched in understanding.

"LeLe . . . Oh, shit," I whispered, abruptly changing the subject. I squinted and stared past Leitha. I was suddenly clued into someone near the bar. Leitha had opened her mouth to say something but quickly snapped her lips shut and turned slightly to see what had me so caught up.

"LeLe, th . . . that's him," I stammered, unable to break my gaze.

"Him who?" Leitha questioned, confusion evident in her tone.

"The knight. The guy," I said.

"Who? Girl, you got me confused as hell," she said.

"That's Andre. The mall . . . The lottery number name dude," I huffed excitedly. Leitha wore a blank look.

"Remember the guy who helped me up in the mall and then I used his name to play the lottery numbers that helped me win?" I prattled off.

"Oh. Hiiim," Leitha said, suddenly recalling.

"Yes. Oh, my God. Is this fate or what?" I whispered, kind of flabbergasted since I never thought I'd see him again in life.

"Are you going to go over and say something?" she asked while I dreamily kept my eyes glued to Andre and his company, which was all dudes.

"Yes. I have to go over and introduce myself. This has got to be fate," I said excitedly. "What are the chances of us coming to this exact spot and the hottest Good

Samaritan I never thought I'd see again in life being in the same spot at the same time?"

"Yes, fate," Leitha declared. "And maybe a new man in your life to boot."

"Your ass never stops, do you?" I said, shaking my head at her slick comment. "Mama LeLe never stops trying. I got to give it to you, bitch."

"I know. I know," she said, laughing. "Enough about me. Go make your move. Shit, I ain't offended. I know what it is like to see destiny right in front of your face," Leitha continued. "Just make sure you get the damn phone number this time, silly ass." She winked.

I smiled gratefully. "You're the best. I'll be back before the food comes. Promise," I said as I eagerly slid from behind the table. Malek flashed through my mind, but I couldn't help this urge. It was like something else had come over me when I saw Andre again. I stood up, took a deep breath, fluffed my hair, and started confidently toward the bar.

Hi, remember me? The fat girl you helped up in the mall? I rehearsed. "No, you can't say that, stupid," I scolded myself. *C'mon, Keisha. You got this. He will definitely remember you. Shit, not like you're some forgettable skinny bitch. You got this.*

"Hi, Andre." I walked right up to him with the confidence of a sexy model. "I don't know if you remember me. Keisha, Keisha Long," I boldly said, smiling all goofy.

Andre furrowed his brows, his eyes scanning mine as if he was trying to place my face.

"Atlantic Terminal Mall, the floor, Target flip-flops," I said for clarification, feeling kind of stupid for approaching him now. "You helped me up after a bad fall and a bad high heel that wanted to do its own thing."

The creases in Andre's forehead eased with understanding.

"Ahh. Right! I remember now. How are you?" he said, his voice going up a few levels. He turned all of his attention to me. My heart jerked.

Damn. Now what? I don't even know what else to do. I fiddled with a stray string hanging from the bottom of my dress. "I'm well. Thanks for asking." I beamed.

"That's good." Andre nodded.

"I was out with my best friend and saw you and figured I'd come over and buy you a drink," I said levelly, trying to stave off my nerves.

Andre chuckled. "I'm usually the one buying ladies drinks," he said.

"Well, I figured since you helped me out and I never got to say thank you, it's the least I could do," I replied, smiling. Without another word, I tapped the bar to get the bartender's attention. "Two of whatever he's been drinking. Bill to my table over there," I instructed, pointing at the table where Leitha sat staring, curiosity playing all over her face.

"This is a nice turn of fate," Andre said, facing me. The left corner of his mouth curled upward with intrigue.

"And if I told you the real turn of fate about our first meeting, you might not believe me," I said, climbing onto the bar stool next to him. Andre's friends exchanged looks with him and moved aside to make room for me. As I got closer, I immediately picked up the scent of Issey Miyake, my favorite men's cologne. Malek flashed through my mind for a quick second again. A wave of nausea followed. I swallowed hard and pushed the thoughts down. I wasn't doing anything wrong. I just wanted to make sure Andre knew how he'd changed my life.

"Well, try me and see if I believe you," Andre said, touching my hand softly. My body warmed up. I watched him examine me as if he were making an assessment, but I can't front, I did the same.

*This man is as fine as I remember him to be. Damn!
Stop it, Keisha. Stop!*

My stomach fluttered. Andre moved his hand. I fiddled
with that string on my dress again. Of course I had seen
Andre before, but I didn't think I remembered nor was I
prepared for how gorgeous he was up close and in person.
Andre had the most gorgeous eyes and full, kissable lips. I
blushed. I could feel it.

"Well, that day you helped me, I was so thankful I went
to the store and used the letters of your name to play the
lottery," I said.

Andre chuckled. "Nice. Well, I hope you won."

"That's the thing. I did," I said, smiling wide.

Andre choked on his sip of drink. His eyes went wide.
"What?" he wheezed.

"I sure did. You were my lucky charm. So now you
understand why seeing you here today was like . . . I don't
know how to explain it," I said.

"Damn! That's amazing. Glad I could help out," he
replied with his perfect smile painting his lips. This man
was so hot my underarms itched with sweat.

"I'm glad you could too," I said. "It was totally unex-
pected, but you've changed my life in a lot of ways, Andre."

"Wow." He flushed. He reached into his pocket. "I tell
you what, Keisha. Let's stay in touch," he said smoothly,
extending a card toward me.

I took it. I was kind of disappointed he made it like a
business transaction, but still, I happily took the card.

"Please call me," he said.

"Okay." I smiled, the butterflies batting around in my
stomach making me sway a little bit.

"What about you? You got a number for me?" he asked.

That made me happy, and without thinking about
Malek or the consequences, I rattled off my number as
Andre punched it into his cell phone.

"Got it," he said.

"Well, make sure to use it," I blurted without thinking, letting him know I hoped to hear from him.

Andre nodded and grinned. "For sure. Can't keep fighting fate, right?"

"Right," I agreed. My whole face was on fire. Whew! Something about this man. Mmmm!

"I guess I will see." He winked.

"You won't have to look far," I said with a rare self-assured smile.

"Looking forward to hearing from you." With that, I walked away, knowing that he was following me with his eyes.

"Well?" Leitha asked before I could sit down.

"Girl," I huffed, trying hard to keep my cool.

"Mmm-hmmm. Sure looked like you got up close and personal," she said, leaning into the table like she was looking for the tea.

I waved her off. Couldn't have her getting all excited for nothing.

"I'm just saying. Nothing wrong with moving on from the other one," Leitha said, twisting her lips. "Especially with that fine one."

"Girl, stop. Let's eat, drink, and be merry. I'm going to act like I never saw Andre at all," I said. But I was definitely lying through my teeth.

Chapter 7

Revelations

I groaned lazily and stretched my arm out, blindly feeling around on my nightstand for my ringing cell phone. I finally placed my hand on top of the noisy nuisance, slid it off the nightstand, and clumsily raised it to my ear. "Hello," I grumbled without opening my eyes.

"Keisha!" Leitha shouted. "I need to speak to you right away. Are you alone?" she continued, rushing her words out on waves of panic.

"LeLe, what the hell?" My eyes popped open at the sound of my friend's frantic voice. "What's the matter?" I squinted across the room to my floor-to-ceiling windows. It was still kind of dark outside. Malek was not in bed. I didn't even have time to question where the hell he would be so early in the morning, or so late at night, whichever way you wanted to look at it. I moved my cell phone from my ear and looked at the time. 5:10 a.m.

Leitha was speaking so fast. With the fuzziness of sleep still clouding my mind, I couldn't understand anything. "LeLe. You're . . . I can't understand." I finally sat up.

"I, um . . . He . . . he was . . ." Leitha stumbled over her words.

"Okay. Okay. Slow down," I said.

I could finally hear Leitha take a deep breath and blow it out. "I need to come see you right now. I can't explain over the phone," she said.

My heart began hammering so hard it took my breath away. I could tell Leitha was crying.

"Do you want me to meet you?" I gasped. This wasn't like her at all. She was the strongest person I knew. "Is it you? Bobby? Who?"

"Malek," Leitha said. "I saw him, Keisha," Leitha said through tears.

"This again, Leitha? You scared the shit out of me," I said, gripping my phone so tight the veins in the top of my hand ached.

I was out of bed, pacing now. My stomach swirled with waves of nausea, and my head throbbed from being woken up in a panic. I stopped for a few seconds and pinched the bridge of my nose.

"Are you there?" Leitha asked.

"I'm here," I replied, moving aimlessly on my feet again.

"I'm sorry, Keisha. I have proof," Leitha said, sobbing heavily. "I know you wanted this to be real this time. But I can't let you get hurt again. I am worried about you."

"I'm fine. I guess we need to meet up. I have no idea what's going on," I said calmly, although my heart was knocking against my chest bone.

"You going to be okay until I get there?" Leitha asked.

"Girl, I'm fine. I swear. I'll be fine. I don't even know what's going on, but whatever it is, you're real upset over it," I said.

"I'll see you in a bit," Leitha said uneasily. She took a shaky breath. "Keisha?"

"Yeah, girl?"

"I'm so sorry," she said in a low whisper. As the words left her mouth, I felt all the air in the room swirling around me, and I think I fainted.

Leitha came barreling into my house about an hour later. I didn't even know what to say, because I didn't know the extent of the information she had. "Hey, girl," she said all solemnly and gave me a hug.

I returned a dry hug. "You have me on pins and needles, LeLe. What's going on?"

Leitha shook her head. I knew her well, and she was totally undone. Her hair was frazzled, her eyes were swollen from crying, and she was just sad.

"Just tell me," I said.

"I know this will be hard to hear and see, but I have to tell you as a friend," Leitha said, delaying.

I shifted my weight from one foot to the other, listening intently. "Go on," I huffed impatiently.

"I don't want you to be mad. But I never trusted Malek, so I had him followed by a PI," Leitha relayed, her words dropping like bombs in my ears.

"What the fuck are you talking about, Leitha?" I exploded, calling her by her full name, which I never did. Leitha put her hands up as if to halt me. I folded mine across my chest in defiance.

"Keisha," Leitha said, sympathy lacing her words, "I just had your best interest in mind. I want what's best for you, and I just didn't trust him at all. Something about him just didn't sit right with me."

Before I could say a word, Leitha reached inside her pocketbook and removed a big business-sized envelope. Instinctively, I took a few steps back, not sure what to expect. Leitha kind of did the same. She tossed the envelope onto my glass coffee table and stared at me expectantly.

My shoulders slumped, and I inhaled deeply. My heart pumped so hard and fast it hurt. I swallowed the fear forming into a ball in my throat. *What the fuck is this? Why would she have him followed? Why is she doing this to me?* My mind raced. I already felt like my worst fear was coming true.

"Proof," Leitha said calmly, folding her hands in front of her. I sucked in my breath and hesitantly reached for the package. But something inside of me was just angry.

"This is bullshit, Leitha. You just don't seem to want me to be happy, and I don't understand it," I exploded.

My best friend was not fazed. I guessed she could see that I was struggling with the truth and my feelings. A royal battle was going on inside of me.

"I want you to be happy, that's it, and that's all. Period. All this extra shit is not needed. The truth about that bastard is what's needed," Leitha shouted.

I was visibly nervous about what might be in the envelope. I stepped around Leitha and lifted the envelope. *Proof. Proof.* The word played in my mind like a scratched CD as I tore at the sealed envelope. I felt an uneasy tightness in my chest as I dumped eight four-by-six photographs into my hand. My mouth hung open slightly as I scanned the first picture. I squinted to make sure my eyes weren't deceiving me. My head moved from side to side involuntarily.

"No," I whispered breathlessly. Heat rose from my toes up to my face. I knew my face was beet red. I bit down into the side of my cheek as I flipped from one incriminating photograph to the next. I looked over at Leitha then back at the pictures. My nostrils flared as I tried to keep my breathing under control.

"When did you get these?" I asked Leitha through my teeth.

"Over the past month or so, I had the PI on the case. I wasn't trying to hurt you. I was hoping the PI would come back with nothing and we could all live happily ever after. I just wanted you to know everything, Keisha," Leitha said gravely. "So like I always suspected, Malek came back so he could get some of your money. He doesn't love you, I don't care what act he put on. If you don't believe what I am telling you, I have more proof that this is true," Leitha said, pulling out her cell phone.

"What?" I asked.

Leitha made a call. "Yeah, you can come to the door now," she said and then disconnected the call.

In shock, I watched as Leitha walked my expansive hallway to my front door and pulled it open to allow someone inside.

At that point, I was shaking. "What the fuck is this?" I growled, my voice unsteady. I was on edge, to say the least.

"Come in," Leitha instructed.

"I'm not feeling this shit right here, Leitha. In my own house," I complained. I still clutched the pictures against my chest as if that could make what I'd seen disappear.

A tall, dark-haired woman sauntered into my house. She was gorgeous, slim, and tall. She was like a model. And she was everything that I was not!

I sucked in my breath at the woman's beauty. She had an air about her that exuded confidence and beauty. I wanted to faint and run away. My legs went weak and shaky. She wore a simple pair of jeans and a fitted top, but to me, she looked like she was wearing a beautiful gown. Everything about her made me feel as if I should just bury myself now. I felt like a fat pig compared to her. I felt ugly. I felt trapped. I felt betrayed. I simply felt like dying all over again. Malek had done this to me again.

"Tell her," Leitha said, urging the woman forward.

I looked at the woman's beautiful face: almond eyes, perfectly clear radiant skin, and her perfect teeth. She looked at me sympathetically, but she didn't speak at first.

Leitha stepped between us. "I think you both got played. But you need to talk. It's important that he doesn't get away with this," she said.

"Malek didn't tell me about you," the beautiful woman said, seemingly barely able to form the words. "He told me he had to travel for work, and he would always come back with money. He would be gone days, sometimes for a week, but never longer than that," she said.

The sound of her voice made my insides feel like they were going through a meat grinder. It was like nails on a chalkboard. I stared at her, dumbfounded.

"He, um, he bought me things. He would show up with beautiful bags and jewelry. He, um, he took me on a trip. He would give me money, and he treated me well," she said like she was already sorry.

I didn't know how much Leitha had told her or what Leitha had told her that convinced her to come to my house. My mind screamed as her words hit home. It hadn't even been three months, and Malek had already been caught out there in a web of lies. To say that my heart was broken was a total understatement. I felt like my entire world had just caved in on me. I felt like the shit under this woman's shoes. He had actually used my money to wine and dine the next bitch. It stung so badly. I flopped down onto my couch.

"I'm sorry. I never knew about you. I want you to know that I would never date a man who was using another woman like this," the woman said.

My head pounded. Everything around me seemed to be spinning. I didn't care about her explanation. I didn't need her fucking sympathy either. The embarrassment I felt made me feel like I had just taken a mouthful of glass and tried to chew it. I was cut deep. So deep I didn't know how I'd recover. Fuck the money. Fuck the fancy car and house and all of the things. My heart was shredded.

"You can leave," I rasped. "I don't need to hear any more."

"I'm sorry," she said.

Leitha let her out and found me with my head in my hands. "Believe what you see in those pictures, Keisha. Malek is the same person he was back then," Leitha said calmly.

My body was engulfed in heat now. Something ticked at my core, like the timer on a bomb.

"Why?" I shouted. The room was spinning. I felt sick to my stomach. My ears rang. I felt like a hamster on a wheel.

"It's not your fault, Keisha. You're beautiful inside and out. You can't take the blame. You have plenty of people who love you. You don't need him," Leitha comforted me.

"It's not fair!" I exploded, tossing the pictures back onto the table. "I can't keep being the bitch who gets used and left! I thought having money would change that! Why me? Why can't someone just love me for me!" I slammed my hand on top of the pictures, spreading them out like a sick artwork display.

"I guess this makes you satisfied," I huffed, pushing the photographs in Leitha's direction. She was silent. My eyes went into slits. I hated nothing more than liars, thieves, and traitors.

"This can't be life," I said, placing my hands on either side of my head. I took another close look at the pictures. "Nah, this fucking can't be life!" I croaked, my words getting caught in my throat. "Something has to be wrong with me. God is punishing me over and over again." I lowered my voice into a growl. My body went cold like someone had pumped ice water into my veins.

"I'm so sorry," Leitha said. "I'd rather you know now than let him use you any longer. I know this hurts, but it was for your own good. Trust me, God is going to send you someone, Keisha. God is going to bless you."

I knew that Leitha meant well, but I wanted to scream at her and tell her she should've minded her business. It wasn't like I didn't suspect Malek of doing something with all his recent disappearing acts, but maybe I just needed to believe that for once I was worthy of a man who looked like him. Either he'd really seen me as a weak woman, or he knew he was a weak fucking man. Either way, I was done with him, and he was going to feel my wrath.

I felt vomit creeping up my esophagus. Fire burned in my chest, and huge sweat beads raced down my back. With my lips pursed and nostrils flaring, I picked up my cell phone and dialed Malek's phone number. I wrapped my hand around the phone so tight I felt like my bones would break. With my adrenaline rushing so fast, I was waiting for his ass to answer the phone. Of course he didn't. When his voicemail came on, I threw my phone across the room. Leitha jumped.

"Are you going to be okay, Keisha?" she asked, her brows furrowed.

"I just want to be alone," I said, attempting to halt my own fury.

"I don't think that's a good idea," Leitha said.

There was an angry hornet's nest of buzzing in my ears. I felt like screaming as loud as my voice could go. I shook all over. "I just want to be alone," I repeated, this time with grit. "Please leave."

Leitha opened her mouth to say something, but the fire in my eyes told her not to. She saw herself out, leaving me alone with those pictures of Malek with several women in several compromising positions. I was all alone with my thoughts and my broken heart.

With trembling hands, I poured a full glass of Hennessy and drank it straight. I winced as it burned my chest going down. I was going to need to be drunk when Malek finally came home, or he might find himself dead in here.

It was moments like this when I wanted to call my mother and curse her out for how she raised me. My mother was the one who made me weak like this for men. I was raised to believe I was fucking nothing without a man. When I was younger, being a wife or someone's woman was the only thing my mother talked about. She would actually say a woman without a man was like a human being without a face. As if I couldn't be seen in the world without a man. I'd fed into that all of my life. I'd been spending all my years unhappy because I had never learned how to make myself happy.

"Keisha, Keisha, Keisha," my mother would say. "You're so pretty, but that weight is going to keep you from having a man. You better stop eating or you'll never be wife material."

When I was in elementary and high school, my mother obsessed over my weight, but more importantly over which boy liked me and whether I had a boyfriend. That kind of pressure made me eat and eat and eat. I hated myself. I hated her. I hated boys. I hated life. I never let my mother know how much the constant badgering about having a boyfriend had affected me. And my mother certainly acted as if she didn't notice how big I was getting and how sad I was all the time. It was a fucking mess growing up. Honestly, I didn't know how I didn't just off myself. I didn't know how I always managed to stay so bubbly and happy around the friends I did have. I guessed they were my escape.

With tears racing down my face, I stared into the bottom of my empty glass. I filled it with the last of the Hennessy and took it to the head again. "Agh," I growled from the hot liquor stinging my insides.

There was something real harsh and sobering about realizing that I'd lived my entire life chasing a dream that would never come true. I was never going to be someone's wife or loved for who I was inside. Men wanted to be my friend or use me, that was it. Nothing more. I had been so stupid! Everything I did in life had been in furtherance of finding the perfect man. Even now, with $40 million in my bank account, I still couldn't be happy!

"Who are you, Keisha? Do you even fucking know who you are?" I murmured, speaking to the empty glass. My insides were warm, and my head swirled, but I didn't feel better at all. Tears slid down my face. I had let this happen to me. It was my fault.

I fell into a fitful sleep waiting for Malek. I heard when Malek into the loft, taking care not to make too much noise. In the darkness, he didn't see me until it was too late and I was on his ass.

"You lying bastard! You piece of shit! I gave you my heart, again! I hate you! You piece of shit!" I blacked out, screaming and pounding my fist into his face and on his head.

Malek was clearly caught off guard. He stumbled back a few steps and tried to grab my wrists, but I was too much for his ass. "Wait, Keisha. What . . . Wait."

"Fuck you! I hate you! I know everything!" I screeched as I swung my arms wildly and my voice cracked with anguish. "You used me! You fucking used my money to care for another bitch! How could you?"

"Keisha, wait." He tried to keep me from hitting him by ducking and weaving, but I was too enraged to care. "Keisha, calm down." He struggled with me, but I wasn't one of his skinny bitches. I wasn't ever going to be one of his skinny bitches.

"Get off of me. Don't touch me, you fucking liar!" I said through gritted teeth, fighting against him.

"Calm down. Let me talk to you," he said, winded and out of breath.

"How could you? How could you do this to me again?" I huffed and finally collapsed, worn out. "Why, Malek?" I whimpered.

"I know you're upset, but I can explain everything," Malek said in a smooth, calm voice. He guided me over to the couch. "Sit down for a minute. Let me talk to you."

The liquor in my system made him look distorted. Even the words coming out of his mouth were garbled to me. "Why did you do this to me?" I asked, my words slightly slurred.

"In the beginning, I was on some shit, Keisha. But I do love you. I had a lot of things to work out, but I wanted to be with you. I just had to take care of the things I had going on out there," he said and hung his head. "I told you that I wouldn't hurt you or leave you, and I meant it. I meant every word of it."

My head shot up. "What? Are you fucking kidding me? You didn't mean any of it. You're a born fucking liar, and you're a selfish user," I spat.

"I know that's what you think, but I'm telling you, I love you. I just had a lot of baggage, and I didn't want to drag you into it. I didn't want you to be hurt. I should've just been honest with you. I was too scared I would lose you to the money and you'd disappear for good."

"Liar," I croaked. I lowered my face into my hands and sobbed. He sat next to me and tried to hug me.

"Get out," I said in a low growl.

"Keish," he started.

"Get out!" I screamed this time. "Get out! Get out! Get out!"

Chapter 8

Redemption

The night I put Malek out, I cried and cried until I made myself so sick I was throwing up nothing but my stomach acid. I didn't even have enough energy to go up to my bedroom that first night, so I had slept curled up in a fetal position in the living room. It wasn't until a day and a half later that I was able to even drag myself to the bedroom. I lay in bed, tossing and turning, replaying Malek's betrayal in my head over and over. My emotions ran the gamut from sorrowful to all-out full of rage. Finally, after days of a mentally debilitating roller coaster, an unnerving calm suddenly came over me like a warm blanket. Still, I didn't leave the house. I ordered food in, ignored my cell phone calls, and secluded myself from the world.

I stayed in bed three weeks before Leitha used her key, stormed into my house, snatched my bedroom blinds open, and told me I had to get my ass up out of the bed and stop feeling sorry for myself. I had tried to fight her at first, but there was no use. We all know when Leitha had something in her mind, she wasn't going to back down.

When I stepped into the shower, the water felt like needles. I had been laid up so long my hair was a matted mess. It was like I was bringing myself back from the dead.

I wrapped myself in my robe and padded into the living room where Leitha sat tapping her foot while waiting for me. "This is just ridiculous," she said, pointing to all of the delivery food boxes and cartons strewn all over the house. "You're fucking rich, and you're laid up in here depressed and hiding over some no-good nigga?"

"I don't want to talk about it. I'm up and out of bed. Take that victory and leave it at that," I scolded her. Truly, I didn't want to dwell on it any longer.

"Here." She tossed my cell phone at me. "Your damn voicemail is full."

I rolled my eyes and punched the voicemail button. Leitha was right. It was flooded. There were messages from every dude I'd ever dated. I had to laugh when I heard Wilson, Darius, Wilson, Tony, Keith, and Malek on my damn messages. Were they serious? I guessed the word was finally all the way out that I'd hit the lottery. Each and every one of those niggas were losers. Not one of them had ever really cared about me. I sighed loudly, remembering when Malek told me I was like a sister to him after we had fucked. How many dudes you know fuck their sisters? I shook my head now thinking about them. Tony had a whole wife who came to my job showing out. What in all hell was he doing on a damn dating website while he was married? I'd had some nightmarish dates, I tell you. I deleted message after message, but I got to one and I didn't recognize the voice.

"Hey, Keisha, this is Andre. I was calling to speak to you. I hope you're well. I thought I'd hear from you by now. I hope I dialed the right number. Let's chat soon."

My eyes went round, and I clutched the phone so tight my knuckles turned white. I pressed the phone harder against my ear and listened to the message again to make sure my ears weren't deceiving me. It was Andre for sure. I never expected in a million years to hear from him.

Leitha looked at me strangely. "What? What is it?" she asked.

"Andre, the lottery name guy, left me a message," I said.

She rushed over to me. "Call him. Maybe that's what you need to pull you out of this funk: a real man. You said it yourself. He was a gentleman."

My hands trembled just thinking about going back out into the dating world. I didn't think my heart could take another devastating heartbreak like the ones I'd suffered. I also didn't trust any man at this point.

"Wow," I gasped, holding my phone against my chest. Andre had left three messages. I closed my eyes and could see his gorgeous face. But then sadness cropped up in my mind.

"I'm not calling him," I said. "It's too soon. I'm not ready, and I'd just be fucking up his life."

"Well, I don't care if you call or not. We are going out tonight. No more of this feeling sorry for yourself shit," Leitha said.

"I'm definitely not going out. Do you see me?" I snapped, irritated as hell.

"C'mon, I'm going out tonight, and you are too," Leitha demanded. Then she let a warm smile spread across her face. "It has been a minute since we went out together. We wait until we get money to actually afford VIP to decide we're going to turn into old ladies and stay in the house all the time. Let's go have a celebrity-style night out," she urged, giggling. She was just trying to get me out of my slump. I appreciated it, but I just couldn't even imagine washing my ass, much less going out around a bunch of strangers.

"I am not going out," I snapped.

"Your ass is going out. I'm your best friend, and I'm not about to let you sit in this house and drive yourself crazy," Leitha said. I was quiet. She sucked her teeth.

"I'm going right upstairs to find you something to wear. Drake is going to be in the city tonight, and we are going, and we are doing it big," Leitha said, knowing that Drake was my favorite.

"I'm too depressed, LeLe. I swear I won't be good company out there," I said apologetically.

"Well, going out is the perfect cure for being depressed. You'll enjoy being out with people. I can picture it now. We finally get to hang out in VIP with all those ballers," Leitha mused like she could picture it.

"Ugh. I don't know why you can't just ever take no for an answer."

"Just c'mon and let's go pick out something to wear so we can hit the damn town," Leitha replied.

I followed her to my bedroom. I wanted to just hug her ass over and over again. She had no clue how grateful I was to have her at a time like this.

When Leitha and I stepped into the club, I could feel all eyes on us. It was the effect of the outfits we had managed to put together. Leitha had chosen a royal blue Michael Costello dress for me. When I put it on, the shit looked like it had been tailor-made for all 300 and more pounds of me. I grabbed a pair of Jimmy Choos to top the outfit off.

Leitha wore a Bobbi Fields dress with a plunging neckline and some Aquazzura pumps. The turquoise color of her dress complemented her skin so well she seemed to glow. We were a pair of fine-ass sisters if I did say so myself.

Once we were inside the club for a few minutes, Leitha was finally able to unwind. It had been a long time. I actually felt like a fish out of water at first.

The music in the club was hitting. It made me want to move my body, but I was still feeling like I shouldn't be there, so I just sat down and struck a pretty pose. As Leitha yapped on about nothing, I had a fleeting thought about Malek. It was like he just popped into my head. I bit down into my jaw and closed my eyes for a minute. I popped my eyes open real quick.

"Keisha, what you want to drink?" Leitha screamed in my ear, breaking up my thoughts. I shrugged. "You're so damn boring! Liven up. We out there like VIPS, finally," Leitha chastised me. She took the lead and ordered us our first round of drinks. As the night wore on, I wanted to just scream. Being out had not helped.

"I'll be right back," I told Leitha. When I stood up, I could feel myself swaying. I was feeling the liquor coursing through my system. I can't lie, I was starting to feel a little like I had no cares in the world. I stumbled into the bathroom. Inside, I looked at myself. If only Malek, Wilson, Darius, all of the dudes I tried to have something with could see me now: moving on, rich as hell, having fun, and totally different from the unsure fat girl they'd dumped.

After a few minutes, my face changed. Who was I kidding? I wasn't happy. Money didn't matter. I was still a million dollars' worth of fat. The thoughts had me boiling inside. I balled my hands into fists and bit down into my jaw. My chest rose and fell with anger. "All of y'all wasn't worth it anyway!" I said through gritted teeth under my breath. My head was swaying with anger, sorrow, and liquor.

I rushed out of the bathroom still wobbly as hell. I just wanted to go home now. I couldn't stand being out anymore with all of the recurring thoughts.

"Ugh!" I grunted as I ran head first into someone. I almost fell I had hit into the person so hard.

"Oh, my God! I'm so sorry!" I slurred. I put my hand over my mouth. I had run into a guy and spilled his drink all over his crisp white shirt.

"Don't worry about it," the guy said smoothly.

My heart felt like it had seized in my chest. I recognized that voice anywhere. I swallowed and looked dead in his face.

"Andre?" I gasped.

"Keisha?" he replied. "Wow. We just literally keep running into one another."

I felt hot all over. He was right! What was the universe trying to tell me? This was absolutely crazy and insane.

"I'm so sorry for ruining your shirt," I said apologetically. I wanted to reach out and try to clean it or just reach out and touch him period.

"Aye. Don't worry about it. This old thing ain't nothing new," Andre assured me, his deep voice making me warm up inside.

I shifted my weight nervously and partly because my damn feet were killing me in those heels. You'd think I would've learned my lesson wearing skinny bitch shoes by now.

"So how have you been? I called you," Andre said, right to the point.

I looked into his face. I felt slightly flushed. *Damn!* He was still just as fine as I knew him to be. I was immediately aware that I was blushing like hell.

"I've been okay. You know, just trying to find my purpose in life," I lied.

"Your purpose? Isn't it to just be beautiful?" he replied.

I batted my eyelashes and exhaled. Damn. He was so fucking smooth. "Thank you. You're not too shabby yourself," I joked.

Andre smiled, and we both laughed. I took in all of his features. They were just like I remembered. The things that stuck out the most, and that I guess I'd been too bashful to look and notice before, were the deep dimples that he had in both of his cheeks.

"Well, since my drink is gone, come to the bar and let me replace my drink and get you one," he said, placing his hand on the small of my back. It was a bold move. It also made me even more attracted to him. His touch was as electric as I remembered. I smiled and followed his lead. I didn't even think about Leitha and some of our friends in VIP. Money or not, that wasn't really my scene. Hanging with the pretentious didn't do anything for me.

As we slid onto the bar stools, I watched Andre order our drinks. His swagger was undeniable, but there was also something very gentleman-like about him. In that moment I felt like I could be okay being his friend if nothing else. I was over fighting to make someone all mine. I felt like I genuinely liked Andre as a person and wanted to get to know him before I just tried to lock him down. That was my past mistake, and I wasn't going to make it over and over again. Not when it seemed like God kept putting this man in front of me over and over again.

"So, I know you can't be here alone," Andre turned to me and said as he handed me my drink.

"Oh, no, my best friend dragged me out," I answered, nodding toward the VIP section.

Andre laughed. "You party in VIP? So your lottery story was true?" he asked, kind of chuckling. I almost choked on my drink. He had called me after I told him the story in Mr. Chow's but never believed me? That meant maybe he wasn't just calling for the reason the other assholes had been calling and creeping back around. Maybe Andre just really wanted to get to know me.

"Let's just say I don't make up stories," I said.

"Okay, okay. That's something. I would think you'd run out of New York and live someplace exotic," he said.

"Nope. This is home and all I know. Money or no money, I just want to be happy and live a regular life. It's nice to be able to buy things or to hang out in places like this and be in VIP once in a while, but honestly, my entire goal is to just be settled and happy," I said with feeling.

"Aw, man. That just touched me. A lot of people wouldn't be honest like that. Most would pretend that money was all they needed in life," Andre replied.

I chuckled at his "aw." I could feel the liquor completely taking hold of me. I wanted to play it cool though. "What do you want out of life?" I asked.

He took his drink to the head and smiled at me. "You know, no woman has ever asked me that," he said.

That surprised me, and my eyebrows shot up. "Really?"

"Really. I think a lot of women just see me as a handsome face and nice body. I actually haven't found a woman who could hold a conversation the way you can, Keisha," he said.

Wow. My heart did something when he said that. I kind of felt the same way about him. "Well, how else will I get to know my lucky lottery number knight in shining armor savior?" I joked.

Andre laughed. "True. True," he said through his laughter.

"Well? Answer the question," I pressed. "What do you want out of life?"

"Honestly, I want to love and be loved. I want to build a family and be a regular husband and father. The total opposite of what I grew up with," Andre said honestly.

I felt like this man was speaking to my heart directly. I could feel tears welling up in the backs of my eyes. I refused to cry. That would've just made me look like a straight nutjob. Crying in the middle of the club? Oh, my goodness, could you even imagine that dumb shit?

"Same here. I just want to do the opposite of what I grew up with," I agreed. It was the damn truth. I raised my glass and sipped my drink.

"There you are," Leitha said, suddenly materializing out of nowhere at my side.

"Leitha, this is Andre," I said, widening my eyes at her so she got the hint. "Andre, this is my best friend Leitha."

"Nice to meet you, Leitha," Andre said, extending his hand and shaking hers.

Leitha smiled at me wickedly. "Andre, why don't you join us in VIP?" she said with a cocky tone.

Andre put up his hands. "I don't want to intrude on your good time."

"It's not an intrusion," I blurted. I didn't want to part from him. I felt like I couldn't let him just get away this time. Something about this felt like a last chance.

"Yeah, no intrusion. Now come on, we have the whole section to ourselves, and I can tell my girl is feeling you," Leitha said boldly, grabbing Andre's arm and damn near yanking him off the barstool.

Yeah, she was definitely tipsy as hell. I shook my head, but I didn't protest. I knew Leitha was always going to do whatever she thought was going to make me happy, and for that, I was grateful.

Andre and I had a good time. We danced, we laughed, we drank and laughed some more. It was a lot of fun. As the night went on, I felt closer and closer to Andre. I wasn't hard-pressed to make him my man. He didn't appear to be pretending to like me. With the liquor completely taking over all of my senses, I whispered in Andre's ear that I promised to call him. He whispered back that he hoped so.

I actually didn't want our night to end. Leitha had come over once they started calling last call at the bar. Leitha grabbed my arm and held on to me. "Time to go, lovebird," she had whispered.

I was feeling too good to let her break it up. I just laughed at her. "Don't be a party pooper," I slurred, snickering like a schoolgirl.

"No, seriously, girl, it's time to go," she said.

I introduced Leitha and Andre again and instantly they both started laughing. Leitha rolled her eyes. Andre chuckled.

"You already introduced us, silly," Leitha said.

I looked at Andre and giggled. Of course, that was the liquor.

"You're gorgeous," Andre said boldly.

"No, you're gorgeous," I told him.

"Time to go," Leitha interjected.

We all headed out of the club. Andre held my elbow to make sure my fat ass didn't fall. I was seriously tipsy. I hadn't had a thought about Malek after I saw Andre.

He walked us to Leitha's Range Rover, which we had valet parked. I didn't know what made her drive, knowing we would be drinking. Andre seemed worried about that.

"Maybe you ladies should take an Uber home," he said.

"We're good," Leitha proclaimed. "I'm not drunk. Tipsy, yes. Drunk, naw."

"How about I drive you all home and you come back tomorrow for the car?" Andre insisted.

"Don't you just love how much of a gentleman he is," I whispered to Leitha. Well, I thought I was whispering, and we all know drunk whispering is just speaking like you're out of breath but loud enough for everyone to hear.

"Trust me. I don't mind driving you all home. In fact, I'll drive your car and then Uber back to mine. How does that sound?" he insisted.

"If you insist," I giggled. "You are just too good to be true. Let me pinch you and see if you're real." I pinched his arm.

"Oww," Andre belted out. "You know I'm real. Really feeling you," he said.

"Oh, my God. I'm in heaven," I slurred as Andre helped me into Leitha's car.

"Me too," he said.

I smiled so wide I was sure all of my teeth were showing. This was too good to be true. I was loving every minute of it. I was definitely feeling this thing called fate. Shit, I wasn't that drunk.

When we got to my luxury high-rise, Andre helped me out of the car. I just kept a lazy, alcohol-induced grin on my face.

"When will I see you again?" he asked.

"When do you want to see me again?" I said seriously.

"Keisha, I don't want to lose touch with you. I really want to get to know you," he said.

I rolled my eyes. The self-doubt was creeping back in on me.

"How come you want a fat girl like me, Andre? You can have all the beautiful girls in the world out there," I asked, my tone serious.

"I think you're the most beautiful woman I know, inside and out," he said. "I don't think I've ever constantly thought about a woman after I've parted from her like I have you since the day in the mall. Some things just can't be explained. Sometimes in life we just have to go with it," Andre said.

I wanted to break down, but I think the liquor saved me. He was saying all of the right things, but so did Malek and all of the others.

Perfect! Just what I want! He is so damn perfect! I screamed inside of my head. I remained silent. I could feel Leitha looking at me.

"I'm going to call you," I said sincerely. I closed my eyes, leaned up, and kissed Andre on the lips. "I'm definitely not going to let you get away from me again."

***

After a twenty-four-hour hangover, I finally got up
the nerve to reach out to Andre. Even in and out of my
hangover sleep, I couldn't stop thinking about him.
Leitha kept asking me when I was going to call him. She
was annoying sometimes.

Finally, I scrolled through phone until I came to his
number. Without thinking too hard about it, I hit the
CALL button but hung up after the second ring. *Is it too
soon for all of this? I am not even ready. I can't do this
again. Maybe he is just being nice and we can be friends.*

I chewed on my bottom lip as I contemplated my next
move. I could feel Leitha watching me, but I wasn't going
to be pressured. I had made up my mind that I would live
for me and not for everyone else.

I was kind of mad at myself that I'd lost the nerve to
call him just that fast. I massaged the sides of my head.
My mind raced. I didn't want to jump right into dating
after all that I'd been through. That would've been stupid.
But I didn't want Andre to think I was blowing him off.
He had been nothing but nice to me.

*It's just a friendly call. I'm not trying to date him or
anything. This is strictly platonic.*

I took a deep breath and courageously hit the CALL
button again. I closed my eyes and waited for Andre to
answer.

I didn't even realize I was holding my breath when I
heard Andre's deep voice filter through the phone. It was
just as sexy as it was the other night. Andre was definitely
an unforgettable man who I just so happened to keep
running into, literally. Fate was a strong bitch. She didn't
give up for nothing.

"Andre? Hey, it's Keisha," I said, trying to sound non-
chalant. If smiles had a sound, Andre would've surely
been able to hear mine.

"I'm glad you called," Andre replied. "I was starting to think I had pissed you off or something."

"No. No. Just been hung over," I said, hiding my angst.

"Ah, I understand. Look, I thought about the other night, and I didn't want you to think I was coming on too strong. I didn't want you to think I was some creep," Andre said.

I laughed. "You a creep? The man who picked me up from the floor of the mall and got me the right size flip-flops in Target? A creep? No way," I joked. We both laughed. It felt so good to laugh again. Talking to Andre, I always had the best laughs. That was important to me.

"Okay, I won't lie. I am attracted to you. I have been from the first day," Andre said honestly. "Keisha, I really want to get to know you on a deeper level."

My stomach lurched. I was attracted to Andre as well. But how would it look if I started dating again so soon after everything with Malek? The whole idea of dating made my stomach hurt to the point of nausea.

"How does drinks and dinner sound?" Andre asked when he didn't get a response from me.

I cleared my throat. "I'm okay with that so long as we keep it friendly. I'm just not looking to date right now. I've been through a lot in the past year," I said honestly.

"Totally understandable. Let's start out slow. Give me a chance and maybe I can change your mind over time," Andre replied.

Wow! I smiled so wide all of my teeth were showing. "You're right. Slow and steady wins the race, right?" I said.

"How about this evening?" Andre blurted.

"Uh, sure," I answered, immediately feeling panicked about my hair, nails, everything.

"I'll come by and grab you around eight," he said.

"Friendly dinner and drinks at eight," I clarified.

"Friendly dinner at eight," Andre repeated with a hint of joy in his voice.

"I'll see you later."

"Can't wait."

I didn't realize how wide I was smiling until my moment was interrupted by Leitha pressing me for information as soon as I got off the phone. My mouth quickly flattened into a straight line. I didn't want my friend to think I was rushing to the rebound date.

"It's nothing. Just going to get some drinks. No more crying over spilled milk," I said evenly.

"Good for you," Leitha said. "Now you gonna have to do something with that hair if you're going out."

I ran my hands over my hair. "You damn right about that," I agreed.

After going through my entire closet, I contemplated canceling my dinner date with Andre. Nothing seemed perfect enough to go out with Mr. Perfect. Leitha would not hear of it.

"Listen, I'll call Gail and Deidre. Shit, they will make house calls as your glam team if you paying, and you damn sure can afford to pay. I will go grab you something cute to wear since you probably need all day for that head and lots of makeup for them bags under your eyes," Leitha said.

She kept her word and returned to with a gorgeous Gucci smock-style dress. I didn't know how Leitha always pulled shit off, but she did. Shit, I didn't even know Gucci made shit in my size. She also copped me some very cute booties. Almost five hours of work later, I was dressed and sweating and nervous as fuck. I felt like I was going on my first date ever. What the hell was it about Andre that always made me feel so, I don't know, alive, I guess you could call it?

"How do I look?" I asked, stepping back into the living room after I finished getting dressed.

Leitha, my hairdresser, Gail, and the makeup artist, Deidre, all turned around to check me out.

"I don't know why you even have to ask. You know damn well your ass is fine with a capital F," Gail announced, waving her hands for emphasis. I felt fat as usual. I walked over to my floor-length mirror and tugged at the dress and adjusted it.

"Ugh! Y'all don't think I look way too fat in this?" I groaned.

Leitha rolled her eyes. Deidre sucked her teeth. Gail made some kind of noise that sounded like a groan.

"Fat? Girl, please. We've been telling you that your ass is pleasantly plump and far more beautiful than you think for years," Gail said. "Shit, I wish I had that gorgeous skin you got."

"I'm just not feeling how I look. And I'm nervous as hell about this. The whole 'trying to impress someone' all over again. I hate starting over and the whole pressure of first dates and then getting to know someone again," I said, flopping down on the couch. "Fucking tired of this."

Leitha rushed over to me and shook my shoulders. "Stop it. It's not starting over. You not trying to marry the dude. He has been nothing but nice to you every time you've seen him. You said you were going to take things slow, but I say do whatever your heart tells you to do. You can't always count yourself out. Sometimes you have to just let things happen and not force it. There's a reason he keeps popping up. I mean, maybe he's your redemption song. Shit, his name did make you a millionaire. You can't get no better than that," Leitha said, giving my shoulders a playful shake.

We all laughed, and they sent me on my way. I didn't think I had ever been as nervous as I was in that moment. I took one last long look at myself in the mirror before I stepped out of my door. I exhaled and prayed for the best.

Chapter 9

Love's Got Everything to Do with It

My first date with Andre was like nothing I'd experienced before. His conversation was authentic. His manners were ever present. And although he knew I was the millionaire, he still paid the bill. This man was amazing in so many ways it scared the shit out of me.

"So did you enjoy yourself?" Andre asked as he walked me to his car. Of course I blushed. Plus my cheeks were already aching from smiling so much throughout the night.

"I sure did. You're the best company I've had in a long while," I replied, being totally honest with him. "I don't think I've ever talked to a man about my childhood, much less about my dreams and the things I want to see happen in the world. I think the quality of the conversation was the best part of this night."

"I agree," Andre said. "I still don't believe you were bullied in school, though," he laughed.

"What? Please believe it," I said, laughing too. "It was the worst time of my damn life." I shook my head.

"Damn. Well, at least you don't have to go through that ever again. Not with me around," he said sweetly.

I blushed again.

"I just don't want this night to end," Andre said, making a playful sad face.

I tilted my head and smiled bashfully. "There's always tomorrow and the next day and the next day, and all of the days of the future," I said, boldly letting Andre know I definitely wanted to see him again.

"For sure. So where to tomorrow?" he asked and winked at me.

"Hmm. Let me see," I joked, tapping my pointer finger against my forehead like I was thinking hard.

Andre and I stood outside of the restaurant talking. The night breeze wrapped around us like a love cocoon. It was the most perfect date I'd ever been on.

"You know, we've spoken about everything except what you do for a living," I said.

"I was waiting for you to ask me that," he replied. "I am an investment banker and financial planner. I never said, because you never asked. And honestly, after you told me about your windfall, I didn't bring it up because I never wanted you to think I was interested in your money. I don't need to be," Andre said sincerely.

I smiled. I was too dumbstruck to speak.

"Is that going to be a problem for you?" Andre asked.

"No. Definitely not. I was just . . ." I was saying when suddenly my voice caught in my throat. I sucked in my breath as I saw Tony, a blast from my past walking toward me, smiling.

"Keisha!" Tony yelled, walking fast straight toward me. "Keisha, my love." I couldn't react fast enough. I couldn't move. I couldn't believe it either.

"Keisha, Keisha! My little freak-a," Tony called out.

Andre stepped in front of me, shielding me with his body. I was dizzy and embarrassed. I'd done things with Tony that would make my mother hide under a bed.

"Aye, man. She's out with me," Andre said levelly. Tony had stopped directly in front of Andre.

"What? Who the fuck are you? That's my girl," Tony spat, standing almost toe-to-toe with Andre.

Andre put his hand up in front of him, palm facing Tony, to halt him. "Your girl? I don't know about all of that," Andre said evenly and then turned a little toward me.

I couldn't speak. All sorts of shit played out in my mind about Tony. He could ruin this for me. I was mortified but stuck. I wanted to chase him away, but it was like I'd lost my voice.

"Keisha!" Tony called out, trying to look around Andre at me. "You really going to stand there and let this nigga keep me from talking to you? After all the shit we been through? After all the shit I got on you?" Tony shouted.

The home porn movie we'd made immediately popped into my head. I shuddered. Suddenly my teeth started chattering together loudly.

Andre bit down into his jaw. He took a few steps forward, moving closer to Tony. "Look, as you can see, she don't want to speak to you. Move around," Andre said, pushing Tony forcefully in the chest. "Leave her alone."

"Fuck you." Tony swung his fists toward Andre's face. Andre pivoted smoothly, causing Tony to miss.

"You asked for it," Andre said, his voice still calm. He grabbed Tony's shirt collar with his left hand and raised his right fist.

"No! Don't!" I suddenly came alive. I didn't know why, but I grabbed Andre's arm, preventing him from punching the shit out of Tony. "Stop!"

Andre flexed his jaw and exhaled loudly. He looked at me strangely.

"Let him go," I whimpered. "It's my fault anyway. Just let him go. I don't want nobody fighting over me."

Andre and Tony both looked at me with confusion painting their faces. Andre shook his head and released Tony with a hard shove.

Tony started laughing.

"You thought she was going to choose you over me? She still wants me. I know she does. She always will," he yelled out.

Andre turned to me with a pained looked on his face. I covered my face with my hands and sobbed. I was embarrassed, mortified, and devastated all in one. Needless to say, my date with Andre ended terribly. He didn't say another word to me all the way back to my house. He was still a gentleman about things and walked me inside, but I just knew I had blown my chance with the only man I felt genuinely cared about me.

I spent the next ten days calling Andre and leaving apology messages. I had really messed things up for us. On day eleven, Andre finally stopped sending my calls to voicemail.

"Hello?" Andre answered, his tone flat.

"Hey," I sang, my nerves erasing everything I had rehearsed to say.

"Is there something you needed? You've been calling a lot," Andre said hesitantly.

Damn. He wasn't feeling me. I closed my eyes and slumped back onto my bed. "Andre, I'm really sorry about what happened," I said sincerely.

Andre didn't say anything.

"It wasn't like I was choosing Tony over you. I just got caught off guard by his presence. He was someone from my past who, um . . . I don't even know how to explain it. I don't want him and I never will. I just didn't want to see anyone get hurt. You have so much to lose. I didn't want to be the cause of that. If you had actually punched Tony . . ." I was saying.

"Be honest with yourself, Keisha. You stopped me because you still have some semblance of feelings for that guy," Andre said.

I swallowed hard but was silent.

"That's what I thought. I have to go," Andre said, disappointment evident in his tone.

"No! Wait!" I yelled into the phone. I couldn't let him hang up. I couldn't let him get away. "I don't have feelings for Tony, but I also never had two men interested in me at the same time like that. When you grow up fat and you believe all of your life that you're not worthy, a situation like that will leave you dumbfounded. I was completely frozen with shock. Look at you: a fine, successful man. Why would I think you'd ever fight over me, a desperate fat girl? I finally jumped in the middle because I didn't want any harm to come to either one of you, but I am not in love with him. I never was. I am in love with you, Andre. I want to be with you, and I know that now," I said honestly. My voiced cracked and the tears finally came rushing down my face.

"You're the one I want to get to know better. You're the one I want to . . . to start over with," I confessed, warm relief washing over me. It was so freeing to get that off my chest. I wasn't going to play hide the ball anymore. I was going to go after what I wanted. Almost losing Andre for good like that was the biggest wakeup call I could've ever received. Fuck it! I wanted to be with him, and I wasn't going to pretend anymore. The experience with him was much different than anything I'd ever experienced with other men.

"Let's get together and speak about all of this in person," Andre said.

My eyes lit up, and I popped up and danced around my bedroom. "Yes. That sounds like a plan," I said excitedly.

Andre laughed. I did too.

That was the beginning.

***

Six months later, Andre and I were inseparable. I let out a small gasp as my body became engulfed in the heat of desire. I reached down and pinched my own erect nipples, sending an electric sensation flooding all over my body. The combination of what was going on below my belly button and the pressure I was putting on my nipples was almost too much to handle.

"Oh, God," I whispered lustfully, lifting my hips slightly off the bed toward Andre's mouth. "Don't stop," I urged.

Andre thrust his long, wet tongue deeper into my center. He used his hands to gently part my labia and carefully lapped up every bit of my juices.

I'd had plenty of good sex in the past, but with the way Andre took his time, loving every single inch of my big body, he was by far the best.

Andre moved the tip of his tongue up, putting pressure on my clit. Then he buried his face so deep my love juices soaked his lips and chin.

"Shit!" I shouted out and placed my hands on the top of Andre's head so he wouldn't stop. "Right there!" I screamed. My inner thighs vibrated from the explosion of pleasure filling my body. I could feel the pressure building in my loins just on the verge of climax.

"I'm right there," I panted, shifting against his mouth. Andre stopped abruptly and lifted his face from between my legs. My eyes popped open. "Don't stop. Please."

Andre looked at me with a grin on his lips. "Beg for it," Andre whispered, crawling toward me like a lion on the hunt. He used one of his strong, muscular legs to gently part mine. As he positioned himself to enter me, he buried his face in my neck.

I let out a windstorm of breath from the mixture of pleasure and pain as Andre used his thick, throbbing dick to enter me. My slippery walls responded immediately, pulsating and squeezing him tight.

"I fucking love you, Keisha," he huffed in my ear. The heat of his breath sent heated sparks down my spine. I arched my back in response. For a quick second, Malek's face passed through my mind. He'd said the same things at the same times. I quickly shook it off. I couldn't ruin things between me and Andre again. I wouldn't let any intrusive thoughts fuck up what we had built so far.

"Shit," I gasped, losing my breath as Andre slowed down and began grinding into me slowly.

I knew Andre loved me. Andre stood by my side every time one of my money-hungry exes showed up. After Tony, there was Keith. That stalker had been searching all over to find me. When he finally did, he'd started following me and actually stalking me. Keith wasn't even one of my memorable exes at that. He'd gotten busted by his baby's mother and dragged away like a little kid. That hadn't stopped him from pursing me, though. Andre had dealt with Keith's death threats against him. Andre even suggested that I relocate.

Honestly, Andre had been nothing short of a miracle, if you asked me. Through it all, Andre never gave up on me.

I knew that most men in Andre's shoes would have walked away without a backward glance. I had a lot of baggage, but Andre stuck around.

And I finally felt comfortable letting go and letting someone love me.

I stood at the end of a beautifully decorated aisle on the white sandy beaches of Jamaica. I shifted my weight from one foot to the other, looking down at my custom-made Swarovski-crystal-covered gown. I was still in awe that I, Keisha Long, the fat girl who everyone thought would always be in the friend zone, was getting married to the man of my dreams.

Finally, the low hum of my favorite wedding song, "You" by Kenny Lattimore, filtered through the outdoor speakers. That was my cue.

My mother grabbed my hand and smiled at me. I'd decided to let her give me away since I didn't have a father and I knew my mother's lifelong dream was to walk down an aisle at a wedding.

"Thank you for giving me away, Mom," I whispered.

"Thank you for including me," she said back. I could tell she was choking back tears just like I was. Happy tears.

I smiled, and my mother gave my hand a reassuring squeeze.

"You look so gorgeous, Keisha. I am so proud of you."

That's all she wrote. The tears danced down my face at her words. I never thought she'd say those words to me. My life had certainly come full circle.

"All right. Here we go."

I looked down at my custom-made gown. The beautiful pearls glinted in the sun. I took that as a sign of God's grace. I deserved to have this fairy-tale day. I finally believed that I deserved it.

I sucked in my breath and watched the ocean waves in the distance. The sound seemed to be calling me forward. Red rose petals dotted the path in the center aisle, and huge seashells hung at the ends of each row of guest chairs. It was dreamy. It was all I had imagined as a little girl when I'd pray and pray for a good husband.

With my hand clasped with my mother's, we inched our way down the sand, both of us smiling so hard it hurt. Gasps of amazement rose and fell among the guests. I was the happiest I'd ever been in my entire life. I saw Leitha smiling and crying at the same time as she waited for me to reach the beautifully decorated arch that would serve as our alter. She mouthed the words "I love you," and I did it back.

But nothing took my breath away more than when Andre stepped into the aisle to meet me. He wore a smile that lit my heart afire. He looked so handsome in his tan linen suit. I swear, in the light of the sun, Andre looked like a god. He was my god, and I was his goddess. Andre took his rightful place at my side. I looked over at him, and he smiled at me. He reached out and playfully touched my nose. That was our thing, our love signal. I giggled.

"Shall we begin?" the officiant said, opening his leather-bound Bible. I didn't bow my head like everyone else. I kept my eyes on my future husband. I never wanted to take my eyes off of Andre again in life.

It wasn't long before I heard the words I'd been waiting my whole life to hear. "I now pronounce you husband and wife!"

Cheers erupted from the crowd of guests in attendance.

Andre beamed. "It's time for me to kiss my bride," his cool peppermint breath whispered on my lips. I gladly welcomed his tongue into my mouth for a long, passionate seal of our vows. More cheers arose. We reluctantly disengaged from each other to acknowledge the crowd.

A perfectly pink blush colored my cheeks. Joy permeated my entire body. The bones in my face ached from grinning. I felt as if all the struggles in my life had led me to that moment in time.

Andre didn't try to play it cool like most grooms. He simply beamed with pride and happiness. That made my heart full. As we slowly made our way down the aisle, he squeezed my hand reassuringly. The guests, seated on either side of the decorated path, blew bubbles at us. Even that had come out just like I'd imagined it when I was planning my wedding.

"Wait right there. Hold that pose!" the photographer called out us. "Kiss her," he instructed, hoisting his cam-

era to eye level to ensure he captured the exact moment
our lips met.

Andre and I turned to each other on cue and again
out tongues engaged in another intimate dance. The
photographer's flash sparkled, and the crowd erupted in
another round of cheers. It was truly the perfect wedding.

"Walk slowly forward now," the photographer instructed.
I hooked my arm through Andre's. We were bombarded
by guests eager to snap photos of us. Andre waved like a
politician, and I flashed a perfectly even white smile.

"One more!" the photographer shouted, jutting his
camera forward for a close-up. We faced each other, our
happiness so palpable it hung over us like an iridescent
bubble. This time Andre kissed me on the nose. I giggled
at his playfulness. Life was perfect, just like the day.

"Here, girl," Leitha huffed as she rushed into my and
Andre's new house. "I got here as fast as I could. Shit, you
need to move back to Brooklyn. This shit here is too far,"
she continued.

"Ugh," I grumbled impatiently. "I am on pins and
needles. I don't even know if I'm coming or going," I
replied honestly.

"Well, shit, take this damn thing and get to it," she said.

I snatched the little drug store bag from her hand and
rushed into one of the many bathrooms in my house.
My hands trembled like crazy as I tried to get the package open. It probably didn't help that my heart felt like
it was about to bust out of my damn chest. My nerves
were so on edge I couldn't keep still. After struggling
with the damn package, I finally lifted it to my mouth
and bit it open. I stared at the shit for a few minutes,
swallowed the bile that had crept up my throat, and got
down to business.

This is a happy time. No matter what the outcome, Keisha, you are happy. Remember. You are happy.

I looked down at the little blue and white contraption in my hand and then at myself in the mirror. Was I even worthy? Would Andre be supportive or happy? Were we ready for this? Oh, God, here came the self-doubt. I swallowed hard.

"Here goes nothing," I murmured. I squatted and released my bladder.

I placed the test on the side of the sink and refused to look at it. Leitha kept on knocking on the door until I finally let her ass in. We both paced around. She seemed more damn nervous than I was.

Leitha looked at her watch. I could hear her mumbling and counting the time.

"Damn it," I huffed. "Stop counting. You are making me crazy," I said.

My nerves were already on edge. I couldn't wait the two minutes. I rushed to the sink and picked up the test.

I sucked in my breath and threw my hand over my mouth. Tears immediately sprang to my eyes.

"What? What does it say?" Leitha yelled, almost knocking me down to see.

"Oh, my God," I said, my words coming out on shaky breath. I handed the test to Leitha.

"Aggh!" she screamed and started jumping up and down. "Oh, my God, Keisha! I'm so happy for you! Agh!"

I collapsed to the floor, sobbing.

"Oh, girl, why are you crying?" Leitha got on the floor and hugged me. "This is the best news ever!"

I held the test in my hand and cried some more. I was scared to death. *What if Andre is not ready? Will he leave me? What will my mother say? Will I be a good mother? Can I do a better job than my mother did? What if I have a daughter and she's big like me? How will I protect her from this cruel world?* All sorts of things ran through my mind. I honestly didn't know whether to be happy or sad.

That night, when Andre came in, I was in our bathroom with the door closed. I had taken a shower and sat on the floor, staring at the test. I had rehearsed what to say to him, but every time I went over it, I thought it sounded so stupid coming out of my mouth.

"Keisha? You in there?" Andre called out.

I jumped and quickly got myself together. My stomach immediately curled in on itself. I felt like vomiting. "Hey, love. Yes, I'm in here," I answered in the best fake happy voice I could find. I hurriedly gathered the test and stuffed it in the pocket of my bathrobe.

"Well, you coming out of there so I can see your beautiful face for the day?"

"I'll be out in a minute," I answered. I went to the toilet and dry heaved. I seriously felt like vomiting. I stood up, looked in the mirror, and splashed water on my face. I took one last look at myself. I thought I looked terrible, but I knew Andre wouldn't think so. If he ever did, he never said. He made me feel beautiful even when I knew I wasn't.

I pulled back the door. I couldn't even look him in the eye. I wasn't a good liar and especially not to Andre.

"Hey. Is that how you greet your husband after a long day?" Andre grabbed me midmotion and pulled me to him.

I hiccupped a small sob. My emotions were all over the damn place. It was crazy.

"Keisha, why are you crying? Is there something wrong? Did something happen?" Andre asked, real concern lacing his words. He moved me from his chest until I was forced to look into his face.

"You can tell me anything. Is it one of your exes coming around again?" he asked. "You're making me nervous."

I closed my eyes and took a deep breath. I had already promised myself and Andre that there would be no secrets, no lies between us.

"I have to tell you something, Andre," I said apprehensively.

"You're not quitting me, are you?" he joked.

I didn't laugh. "I'm afraid this is serious," I said.

"Is it that bad?" Andre asked uneasily.

"I just don't want to keep any secrets from you."

"What is it? You're killing me right now. Just say it," Andre said, losing patience. I was sure he thought it was bad.

"This is what I have to tell you." I shoved the test into his hand. "Andre, I'm pregnant," I blurted.

"Huh? What did you just say?" Andre said, excitement building in his voice. I stared at him through wide eyes for a few long seconds.

"Did you just say I'm going to be a father?" Andre asked as he scooped all 340 pounds of me up off of my feet, spinning me around until I felt dizzy.

"Keisha! You have made my life! I love you so much!" Andre cheered. He crushed his mouth over mine and kissed me deeply.

All I could do was cry tears of joy. My life was complete. Money didn't matter as long as I had a million dollars' worth of love.

Complications

by

Katt

Prologue

It seemed like forever, but Secret finally heard the sirens in the distance. She was about to face the consequences of her decision. That meant someone had heard it all go down. Why else would the police be coming to the house? There were four gunshots in the end. Secret could still hear them. Two each. That's the punishment she had meted out. It was what they deserved.

Secret shook her head. She never expected it to come to this. All kinds of complications were what she'd gotten in the end. All she wanted was to be loved for who she was, now. She hadn't asked for much: loyalty, love, acceptance. It was too late. The sirens continued to close in on her.

Secret flinched thinking back on how the gun had exploded at the command of her fingertip. She'd dropped the gun at her feet and stood there shivering. No screaming, no hysterics, no immediate feeling of regret, nothing. Even when Secret saw all of the blood and watched the terror move across their faces, she didn't cringe and barely moved, much less screamed. She was numb. Numb from all of the physical and mental anguish she'd endured trying to please him. Numb from the way he'd treated her, his lies and secrets.

Secret's self-esteem and mental stability had taken several blows over the past year. Everything had gotten complicated. She wished she could turn back the hands of time. Do things differently. It was too late. Now here she stood, blood speckled on the front of her clothes, a burner lying at her feet, and two dead bodies in front of her.

"Police! Let me see your hands! Let me see your fucking hands!" the first arriving police officers screamed.

Secret lifted her hands slowly, but it was as if someone else had control over her body. She couldn't move her feet. Something had her rooted to the floor. Her mind was fuzzy, but she smiled at the sound of the police officer's voice. It was definitely not a smile of happiness. Instead, it was like she had begun to lose her mind. That's what he had wanted all along anyway. All of the cruelty and harsh treatment over her weight gain. Secret closed her eyes, and her nostrils flared again. Every time she thought about it all over again, that happened.

With about ten police weapons trained on her, Secret stood stock-still. One officer rushed over and kicked the weapon away from her. It skittered across the marble floors with a screechy noise that made Secret's ears move. Finally, she could feel something. The numbness had worn off. It was her blood rushing as her heart thumped wildly. Secret quickly realized life as she knew it was over.

She wanted to speak, but no words came out. She wanted the opportunity to explain herself. She wanted to tell the officers what had driven her to this. But she couldn't speak. It was only a matter of seconds before she was being manhandled and thrown roughly to the floor. Secret landed on her stomach with a thud, and the wind was knocked out of her. Several officers laid hands on her, and not with soft touches either. They were treating her like she'd just assassinated the president.

"Search her good for weapons!" one of the officers barked.

Secret struggled to breathe. She hoped they didn't beat her to death right there in her own home. She had thought about her kids, but those thoughts were too painful. She couldn't do that to herself now. She'd done enough damage.

"She's clean," a female officer called out.

Secret didn't have anything else. She had only purchased one gun: a .40-caliber Glock. It was in her despair that she'd made the purchase. She hadn't been in her right mind. Maybe she could blame it on the painkillers she'd gotten addicted to after the surgery. Just thinking about the surgery now infuriated Secret. *All of that pain! All of those complications! All for nothing!*

As she was being lifted up off the ground to be placed into the squad car, Secret looked over and stared into his eyes, the familiar eyes that she had fallen in love with years ago. His seemed to glare back at her, cold, glassy, and dead.

"You did this to us. You made me turn into a monster," Secret mumbled, staring into the dead, dilated pupils of the man who was once the love of her life, the father of her children, and most of all, her husband.

"This shit is like an episode of *Snapped*," one officer spoke loudly, forcefully pulling Secret away.

"Looks like she really fucking snapped. This is one of the worst crimes of passion I've seen in a while," another officer commented.

They had no idea just how bad it was. Secret had been through the wringer.

"I wonder what led to all of this. What would drive someone to just murder in cold blood like this, with no remorse?" the other officer commented.

Secret was forced into the back seat of a squad car. She closed her eyes and let the tears drain from the sides as she thought about the officer's questions. What would drive someone to just murder in cold blood? What led to all of this? The words played over and over in Secret's mind, and just like that, she started replaying the events that had driven her to the edge . . . to murder.

Chapter 1

One Year Earlier

"Secret, are you sure you want to do this? I don't see anything wrong with you, girl," Andrea said as she pulled her car into the airport's long-term parking lot. "This shit can be so risky. Have you done your research? How does it work? Is it that much cheaper?"

"Shh, you're rambling right now. Please," Secret put up her hand and admonished. "I'm already scared as it is. I don't want anyone talking me out of this. I told you, I have to do this for him and me. Just make sure you don't post anything on Instagram or Facebook for David to see. Remember, he thinks we are going on a girls' trip. I mean, technically we are. Right?" Secret forced out a phony laugh to break up the raw nerves coursing through her body. She could only hope this would save everything.

"Umm, going to the Dominican Republic for plastic surgery and going for a girls' trip are two different things," Andrea retorted, rolling her eyes.

"Either way, I love you for going with me. You'll see, the old Secret Johnson will be back like I never left. I will get rid of this fucking FUPA and this flab, and all will be right with the world."

"Secret, there is nothing wrong with your body. You've had two children. No one expects you to be perfect after that. Shit, Beyoncé said she has a FUPA, and even she ain't cut that shit off," Andrea said. "You're so beautiful, girl. Besides, what happened to 'beauty is in the eye of the beholder'?"

Secret pulled her oversized sun hat over her eyes to hide the tears rimming her eyes. She let out a long sigh. She loved her cousin Andrea for always being her cheerleader since they were kids. If only Secret's husband, David, felt the same way.

Secret saw things changing between them after the birth of their son. Secret had gained seventy pounds carrying the baby, and only twenty of those pounds had disappeared after the birth. Secret wasn't accustomed to having a fat belly and flabby thighs. She certainly wasn't used to the back rolls and muffin top that had become a part of her now. Secret was used to being slim, trim, and beautiful. David was used to her being that way too.

The day she met David, Secret had been rushing through a party, trying to get to her friends who were waiting for her in VIP. She was over an hour late for the runway show after-party. Secret had just walked in the runway show, which had been a great success. It had been her first haute couture show, and it turned out to be a rousing success. Secret had been the star of the show and was still riding high.

David was walking through the party. He was a guest of the DJ and looking for a good time. David and Secret had run smack dead into each other.

"Excuse me," David said as he grabbed Secret's shoulders to keep her from falling over on her high-heel stilettos.

"Damn, watch where you're going," Secret huffed.

David flashed a beautiful, straight-toothed smile and in a smooth, deep, sexy baritone told Secret he was very sorry. She had sucked her teeth indignantly. She was already late for her own celebration.

"Move. I have to go," she grumbled.

"Calm down, pretty girl," David said, holding on to her with just enough force to keep her from running off. "Let me make it up to you. C'mon, let me buy you a drink or two," David said.

Secret could tell he was smitten with her. She had to admit, she was a bit taken aback by how handsome David was too. "Just one drink. I have people waiting for me," she grumbled.

"Bet. Just one."

David and Secret walked to the bar together. At first, Secret was skeptical, as she was of all men in clubs and at bars. She had heard about more than one of her model friends who had gotten something slipped into their drinks in the club. But still, she had to admit it seemed like David was a gentleman. Something about him had already made Secret mushy inside. She never really trusted men too much. Secret didn't trust any-one really, except her cousin, Andrea, who was also her best friend.

"You didn't really have to buy me a drink," Secret told David.

"What? It's no problem at all. It's not every day an old, ugly, average dude like me literally runs into an extre-mely beautiful woman like you," David replied.

Secret blushed so hard she couldn't even look at him in the eye. She was used to people telling her she was beautiful, but something about David made her pulse quicken. Secret looked around the club, but she didn't see any of her friends. She checked her watch and shifted her weight from one foot to the other. She hated being late, but she figured her girls would understand.

"I can't keep calling you the beautiful woman who ran into me, so what's your name?" David asked her.

"Secret," she replied, lowering her eyes as if she ever had a problem looking a man in the eyes.

David smiled. Secret sighed at that lady-killer smile.

"I'm David," he said. He stuck his hand out for a shake. Secret lightened up a little bit and shook his hand. He pulled hers up to his lips and kissed the top. The kiss sent a hot feeling down Secret's spine. She couldn't wait to take a sip of her drink to take the edge off. What the hell was it about this guy?

Secret felt an instant connection with David that night. Secret never believed in that "love at first sight" bullshit, but that day she thought she could understand when people said they had fallen in love at first sight. David was tall and handsome, without the dark. He was more Shemar Moore handsome. David stood six feet four inches tall, and his skin was the color of freshly poured caramel. He had an athletic build, and he wore a low haircut that was perfectly shaped up at his forehead and sideburns. His waves were perfect too. Secret felt kind of awkward because he was so gorgeous and wasn't even a model like she was. She was used to being the head turner in her relationships. But she couldn't help but think David should've been doing some modeling of his own.

"Can I get a number to call you?" David asked as Secret's friends came rushing toward her. Secret didn't hesitate. She gave him her cell phone number. She also took his. Secret hadn't planned on calling him.

David watched as her friends surrounded her and whisked her away. She looked back at him, smiling. She hadn't realized how much she wanted to keep talking to David and how much of a distraction her friends were in that moment.

That entire evening of partying, Secret couldn't concentrate. She kept replaying the episode with the hunky stranger over and over in her head. To her great surprise, David called her the next morning. He'd obviously been thinking about her nonstop too.

"I could not stop thinking about you," he said, his voice a deep baritone that made her pulse quicken. That was the first of many conversations to follow.

For their first official date, David took Secret to a quaint, little trendy eatery in Manhattan. Being a fashion model, Secret had been to quite a few places, but it seemed like David had created this place just for them. Romantic was an understatement.

Secret and David spoke about everything from fashion, police brutality, and politics to rap music. It was more than Secret could've asked for. David was not just a handsome face. Finally, here was a man who seemed more interested in her mind than he was in her body and beauty.

That night, David rode with Secret back to Brooklyn, although he was from the Bronx. He had done and said everything right.

Two months later, Secret finally agreed to a romantic night at his place. David awakened every nerve ending in Secret's body when he touched her for the first time. He explored her body like a meticulous surgeon. Secret was rigid at first, scared to let her guard down. She had never really had what she'd considered a good sexual experience. She had been molested by an uncle as a child. She had never had healthy intimate relationships after that. Her mother had berated Secret when it came out that Secret had given up her virginity in the tenth grade to a boy who spread it all over the school and neighborhood. Sex wasn't high on Secret's to-do or to-like lists.

But when David touched her, kissed her, and whispered sweet things in her ears, it put her at ease. When he entered her for the first time, it sent her reeling into a place she never wanted to come back from. It was more than infatuation that Secret felt. She felt like she was falling in love with David.

He seemed to feel the same way about her. They started spending all of their free time together. Secret started slacking on her modeling gigs and her part-time college classes. Before meeting David, Secret had balanced modeling gigs and classes like a pro. She had never been late to a class, much less missed one, before she met David. After they started dating regularly, David would beg her to stay with him and miss classes. He would start lovemaking foreplay whenever he knew she had a gig. Secret was too in love to protest.

They were together for eleven months when David told Secret, "I want you to be in my life forever. I'm not ready to get married, but when I am, I know you will be my wife." A few tears had dropped from Secret's eyes. She was so happy that day. No other man had made that promise to her. Secret finally felt worthy of being loved.

"Oh, David, I love you so much!" Secret responded, throwing her arms around his neck and hugging him tightly. It was at that moment, although she didn't say it, Secret surrendered everything, her entire self—body, mind, and soul—to David.

"I love you too," David told her. No man had ever loved Secret. She had never known her father, and her uncles and cousins certainly didn't love her. They were perverts who'd exploited her body and made her feel ashamed of her beauty.

That night David made love to her again. It was the first time he took off the protection and the first time Secret fully let herself go. She performed oral sex on David for the first time, and he exchanged the favor. In Secret's mind, she would've done just about anything for the man of her dreams.

After David moved in with her, he came home excited one day. Secret was in bed. She had just gotten in from school and a print modeling gig that had run four hours over due to her inability to get into the shoot.

"Secret! Secret! Where are you?" David called out to her. Tired as hell, but wanting to be responsive to her man, Secret bolted upright in the bed and forced a smile onto her face. David came barreling into their bedroom, waving an envelope in his hand. He bounced onto the bed and put the envelope in Secret's face.

"What? What's that?" she asked, looking at him like he was crazy. She already felt excited for him just seeing his eyes all lit up.

"It's my acceptance! I got in to the young entrepreneurs program at The Wharton School! That shit is super competitive, but I finally got it!" David yelled, running around like he'd just hit the lottery.

Secret started clapping. As tired as she was, she pulled it out for her man. "Yay! Oh, baby, I'm so happy for you!" she sang, grabbing him for a hug and kiss.

David was too excited to kiss her. He pushed her aside and started walking in circles. "You don't know what this means, Secret. The future is bright. We will be on our way. That fucking program turns out the best company executives in the nation. Can't you see me as the VP of a Fortune 500 company? Or maybe even having my own company?" David said excitedly.

Secret was shaking her head vigorously in the affirmative. She could actually see her man exchanging his baggy jeans for a suit and French-cuff shirts.

Secret was so happy for him. She had learned over the months they were dating that David had come from rough beginnings even worse than her own. David had been left at the hospital after he was born. He'd knocked around from foster-care home to foster-care home and finally to a boy's group home until he was too old to stay. He worked odd jobs while he worked hard to get his high school diploma. *Not one family member had shown up at his graduation.*

Secret had to admit, she couldn't imagine growing up that bad. She was proud of David, and she admired him so much.

"You are going to be the best VP in the world, baby," Secret said, finally stopping his pacing long enough to embrace him. David made passionate, excited love to her right on the bedroom floor. Secret was deeper in love than she could have ever anticipated.

Three months into David starting business school, Secret stopped going to college and was barely modeling anymore. David, with his charm and good-ass lovemaking, had somehow convinced Secret that quitting everything she loved was the best thing to do. Head over heels in love, Secret gave up her dream of being a nurse just like that. She walked out of school and never looked back. Instead, she modeled when she could to get money while David studied for his business degree. Secret was really their only source of income while David went to school full-time.

In her mind, Secret believed she was doing it for their relationship and for what he had been promising her: a good life as the wife of a rich businessman. Secret believed him when he told her that once he graduated and landed a job at a big marketing firm, she wouldn't have to model or work or go to school ever again.

Secret sometimes felt neglected after David started school. He would spend a lot of time at the library or at school. Yet Secret remained loyal. She did gigs during the day, cooked, washed his clothes, bought his MetroCards, and paid the rent on their apartment in Brooklyn. Secret also helped David with his school expenses. Sometimes Secret would be dead tired after going from modeling gig to modeling gig all day long to raise enough cash to cover everything. David, when he had time, would want to make love to her or ask for her help typing up his research papers. It didn't matter how tired or how frustrated she was, Secret would never tell David no, no matter if she was tired, sick, or just really didn't feel like it. Secret gave David her all.

Sometimes he acted as if he didn't appreciate it. One night, Secret was in bed when he finally came home from studying at school. Secret heard him slamming around inside the tiny apartment, but she was too tired to move.

"Secret!" David called out, his tone angry.

Secret moaned in response.

David stormed into the bedroom. "You didn't make anything to eat or at least bring something in?" he barked.

Secret couldn't believe his nerve. How fucking ungrateful could he get? She had been going the entire day, working, unlike him. All he did was go to school. Shit, the least he could do was get food. She had gone to bed hungry herself that night.

"I didn't get anything because I was too tired. But I can get up and make you something," Secret said to comfort him, barely able to muster enough energy to get the words out loudly. She didn't think David would really expect her to get up, but he did. That night was the first real sign of selfishness Secret had seen in David. There would be many more in the years to come.

It turned out in the years they were together that not all of the promises David made to Secret came to fruition. David graduated from Wharton at the top of his class and landed a big job at one of the premier financial advisory firms in New York. He even told Secret she could completely stop modeling. Secret quit immediately. It had been hard to keep up with the younger

models coming out anyway. Secret told herself she
was content being home for David. She did all of her
duties, and then he asked her to marry him. It wasn't
a really romantic proposal. David had stopped being
sweet and romantic since he'd become a big honcho in
the finance world. His proposal came across like just
another business deal he needed to broker.

David took Secret to dinner at the famous Del Frisco's
Double Eagle Steakhouse in the city. She hated steak, but
she was still overjoyed to be spending time with him,
which up to that moment had been happening less and
less.

With little conversation that night, David slid the
small ring box across the table at her. Secret had just
lifted her glass to her mouth and taken a gulp of her
soda. The sight of the box made her almost choke.

"What's this?" she said, asking the obvious.

David tilted his head and gave her a look like, "What
do you think it is?" but he didn't say anything.

"Oh, my God, David!" Secret said, cupping her hands
around her mouth, awestruck.

"I'm telling you now, Secret, the wedding will be small.
We don't need a bunch of pomp and circumstance. We've
been together too long for that," David told her flatly.

Secret's heart sank. He had some nerve. Secret had
been noticing that David was really careful about his
spending when he was the one making money. When
Secret was the breadwinner, they would sometimes
spend money frivolously.

"That's how you're going to ask?" Secret said, still
shocked at his behavior.

David shook his head as if he had to snap out of it. "I'm
sorry. I'm just stressed out at work," he said apologetically. He got up, grabbed the box from the table, knelt in
front of her, and said, "Secret Dani Brooks, will you do
me the honor of becoming Mrs. David Johnson?"

Secret burst into tears. She grabbed David's face and brought it closer to hers. "Yes! I will be honored to be Mrs. Johnson!"

With the help of Andrea, Secret planned a small, intimate wedding. Most of the attendees were her friends and some of her family. David didn't have many friends, and he certainly didn't have a family.

After they were married, David still wanted Secret to stay home. They started a family right away. After the birth of their first daughter, David and Secret seemed to be the couple to envy. Although Secret gained some weight and dealt with some of David's cruel ways in the privacy of their own home, to outsiders they seemed to be unrealistically happy in love and living what appeared to be every woman's fantasy.

It didn't matter what it appeared to be. The bottom line was Secret wasn't happy. She hated the way she looked, and with the birth of just one baby she dieted and exercised relentlessly. Secret became like a Stepford wife: cooking, cleaning, and caring for her husband and child all while keeping a smile plastered to her face. She lost the weight—well, most of it—but that didn't stop David's cruel comments about her appearance. Fatty, Chub Rock, and Chubby Checker were just a few of the names she dealt with from him.

Exhausted by life, Secret made the biggest mistake she could never recover from. Secret gave up who she was. Her totally identity changed. Everything became about David and the baby. She even changed her style to be more "wife-like." Secret changed her style of dress. Her jeans were looser, she hardly ever wore heels anymore, and she made large sweat suits her regular wardrobe. Secret no longer worried about her hair being done or her nails being filed. She no longer cared about her fading waistline or the frumpy clothes she wore. Secret was fully focused on taking care of David and building a home. In turn, she neglected herself and who she really was. Secret couldn't even remember that when they'd met, she was a beautiful young model with a Sports Illustrated *shape, a fresh face that required no makeup, and money to burn.*

When David met her, Secret had style and class, and she always made sure she kept her nails manicured and her toes done. She worked out five days a week to keep a flat stomach and a small waist. David seemed to be enamored with her in the beginning. He was super attentive to everything about her, especially her feelings. He would often tell her how beautiful she was, and he would do little sweet things for her like leaving rose petals on her pillow. When Secret committed the cardinal sin and surrendered her own education and modeling career to help finance his business degree, she thought he would fall deeper in love with her. After David graduated and they started living "real" life, things changed. It seemed like once Secret gave up who she was to be a mother and a wife, David began to lose respect and admiration for her. It just got worse over time.

David began to treat Secret even more like shit after the birth of their second child. He was upset when Secret told him she was pregnant again. He started focusing on her appearance, and it was like they couldn't get through one dinner or night at home without him mentioning it.

Secret knew she had gained weight with the pregnancies, but she wasn't prepared for the level of betrayal she felt when David told her he couldn't bear to have sex with her because he was repulsed by her "fat upper pussy area (FUPA)" as he called it. "Look at your stomach. That thing is really disgusting. You expect my dick to get hard looking at that shit? It looks like brains with all those nasty stretch marks," David said to her one night.

Secret cried for two days after that. He never apologized to her either. It was like he thought he was justified in showing her that level of disrespect. Yet Secret didn't let David's straight cruelty and neglect deter her from trying to be a good wife. She went out and joined Curves, got her nails and hair done, and even purchased a hot little lingerie number from Frederick's of Hollywood. None of those things worked or helped. David still barely touched her, and when he did, it was so mundane and routine that Secret often buried her face in her pillow and cried afterward.

After a while, David moved up in his company, and he had started traveling and spending long nights at the office. His neglect made Secret feel alone, unworthy, and less than. Still, Secret tried even harder to please him. She would cook extra-big meals, clean the house extra spotless, and she still tried to be as sexy as possible, even though she hated her own body and herself for that matter. David wouldn't put in any effort. It was like their marriage failures were all Secret's fault.

Secret started to grow frustrated and angry. Sometimes she would express her displeasure, but that would always turn right back against her. David was a master at flipping the script. After months of arguing, Secret decided she would do something drastic about what was going on.

Secret convinced herself that all she needed to do was look how she looked when they'd met, because she'd tried everything else already. David barely looked at Secret, and when he did, it was always followed by a cruel criticism. He'd say things like, "You look like a cow in that black and white. Don't wear that again," and, "How many asses do you have? Six?" It was always *something that he'd later say was to motivate her to get into the gym. Still, Secret held fast to her wifely duties.*

Every once in a while, David would have sex with her. But the way David performed in the bed made Secret feel like he was providing her with sympathy sex. He always seemed slightly disgusted and rushed. Although they had been having problems for over six months, Secret got up one day and decided drastic measures were all that could save her marriage.

Chapter 2

Secret's heart sped up when the plane landed in the Dominican Republic. There was no turning back now. She turned on her cell phone to see if she had any messages from David. Nothing. There was one text from her babysitter telling her the kids were fine.

"Well, we are here. You sure you don't want to just turn this into a lazy beach vacation and go back home?" Andrea asked, a hint of worry in her tone.

"Girl, stop saying that. I am getting this surgery. That's final," Secret said confidently.

When Andrea and Secret cleared Dominican customs, they were free to exit the airport. There were tons of drivers holding signs with names on them.

"Dr. Mungia is sending a van for us," Secret told Andrea. "Just look for my name."

They both scanned the rows and rows of men holding signs. "There." Secret pointed and smiled. They rushed over to the driver.

"I'm Secret Johnson," she told him.

He nodded, said something in Spanish, and led the way to the van.

"He's scary," Andrea whispered to Secret.

"Scary how?" Secret whispered back and then sucked her teeth. Andrea was right. The driver seemed cold and distant. He wasn't warm and inviting at all. His van was subpar and raggedy inside, but it did have air conditioning.

"I hope the place you're going is not as janky as this van," Andrea mumbled. "I just wouldn't be letting them cut on me in no poor-ass place like this, Secret."

Secret rolled her eyes. "What's the rule, Andrea? No more talking about the surgery, right? Good." The remainder of their hour-and-a-half ride was silent.

The driver eased the van down a long, winding gravel road. The area was surrounded by trees and remotely located. There wasn't a business or beach or anything in sight. Secret could see a house in the distance. It wasn't a mansion, but it was a big house. There were two other brick buildings a short distance from what seemed like the main house. Secret assumed those were going to be the hospital-style buildings. Andrea was shaking her head, but she respected Secret's wishes, and she didn't say anything.

"Here," the driver said, pulling in front of the house. There was a plantation-style porch with several chairs on it. The front door hung open, and Secret could see a small reception desk just inside. Again her heart sped up, and her palms were soaked with sweat.

"Here goes nothing," she mumbled.

"Hello," a young woman sang, walking toward Secret and Andrea. "Mrs. Johnson?"

"Yes," Secret answered, her voice trembling.

"I'm Lucia, Dr. Mungia's assistant," she said, extending her hand to Secret.

"Hi."

"As we discussed over the phone, we will need to do an exam before your surgery. Unfortunately, your escort will not stay here. We have another location for escorts to stay," Lucia said, looking at Andrea as she spoke.

"Oh, hell no. I'm not leaving you here alone, Secret," Andrea piped up. She was tired of being quiet now.

"Shh. It's okay. We will take care of her. As soon as the surgery is done, we will pick you up to see her for recovery. It's just that we have nowhere for you to relax during the surgery time," Lucia explained.

"First of all, don't shush me. Second of all, I will not be relaxing until my cousin is through this shit safely," Andrea snapped.

"Andrea! Please. Just listen to her. I don't need this right now," Secret said forcefully.

Andrea threw her hands up. "You know what, Secret? I won't worry about you. I won't care. Do whatever you want. This shit is stupid. You're cutting on yourself and risking your life out here for a man who don't want you anymore!"

Secret's head jerked back as if Andrea had thrown cold water in her face. Tears immediately sprang to her eyes. "How dare you?" Secret rasped, her throat feeling like it would close any minute. "I'm ready to go," Secret said, turning her back on Andrea.

"Secret! Wait! I'm sorry!" Andrea called at her back.

It was too late. Secret forged ahead and never turned back. She never saw the creepy driver usher Andrea away like he was about to take her to the death chamber.

Secret's eyes roved back and forth as she followed Lucia through the expansive house turned surgery center. There were rooms with numbers on them. There were women rushing through the hallways. Secret guessed they were nurses, although they didn't wear traditional nurse's scrubs. It was eerily silent in the house, which unnerved Secret a little bit.

"You can go right in here. You will find a gown on the bed. Get undressed with the opening to the back. Dr. Mungia will be in shortly to examine your body," Lucia said.

Secret watched as Lucia left the room and closed the door behind her. Secret shivered, partly because her nerves were on edge, but mostly because the room was freezing. She got undressed slowly, and as she removed each article of clothing, she examined herself in the long mirror on the wall.

"Disgusting," Secret whispered as she bunched her stomach fat together in her hands. "Stretch marks, fat, cellulite, all of this shit has to go. David, you are going to love me again when this is all said and done," she murmured.

Secret jumped and whirled around when the door swung open.

"*Hola,* I'm Dr. Mungia," the doctor said cheerfully as he rushed into the room.

"I . . . I'm Secret," she stammered, thanks to her nervousness.

"Relax. Relax. I'm going to take good care of you," Dr. Mungia said with his thick accent. "Now let's see how much work we need to do."

Secret trembled as the doctor touched her body. She winced as he lifted her flabby breasts and grunted. She held her breath as he ran his hands down her stomach and pinched the loose skin, lifted it up, and let it go again.

Dr. Mungia hummed and humphed as he urged Secret to turn around. He whistled when he looked at her butt.

"Okay, here's what we will do," Dr. Mungia said as Secret slowly turned back around to face him. "I will take the fat from your stomach and put it into your glutes. I will pull back the skin here and make you have a waist again. Last, I will lift the breasts and add the silicone," he said.

Secret let out a long breath. "How many hours will it take? And what will be my recovery time?"

"Ehhh, don't worry about all of that. When I'm done, you will look so beautiful you won't even remember any of the work and the recovery," Dr. Mungia said, smiling brightly and patting Secret on the shoulder.

"Okay. I just want to get it over with so my husband can be happy with me again," Secret said, parting a nervous grin.

"I am going to make magic happen. Your life will change forever," Dr. Mungia said. His words had more finality than Secret could've ever imagined.

"Oh, my God, Secret. This week has been the most nerve-racking shit I've ever been through," Andrea said, grabbing her cousin so hard she hurt her.

"Ow!" Secret screamed out.

"Oh, shit! I'm sorry," Andrea said, jumping back.

She was right. They'd kept Secret in the house and away from Andrea for seven days while she recovered from the surgery. It was finally time for them to fly back, but Secret could still hardly move she was in so much pain.

"How are you supposed to fly like this?" Andrea asked on the verge of tears.

"I have a pillow, and it's just four hours. I won't die," Secret said.

"Don't say that shit, Secret. Don't even say that word," Andrea scolded her.

The hours of the flight were the longest of Secret's life. She'd taken at least six Percocet pills during that short span of time, and she still felt pain rocking through her body. Her head felt light, and her heart raced. If she didn't know any better, Secret would've thought she was actually about to die. That's how horrible she felt.

"Let everyone else get off first," Secret told Andrea when their plane landed back at John F. Kennedy airport. "I need to take my time."

"Okay, boo. I got you," Andrea said sympathetically. She could tell her cousin was not feeling well. Andrea was worried. She'd noticed that Secret's skin color looked a little ashen and a fine coat of sweat covered Secret's face. Andrea said a silent prayer that her cousin would be okay.

When they finally made it outside, Secret inhaled the fresh air. The fine sheen of sweat covering her face made the air feel cool against her skin. She swallowed hard and inched her way to a bench in front of the terminal.

"You want to just wait here while I go get the car?" Andrea asked.

"No. No. I'm okay to go to the car. I just want to get out of here," Secret huffed as if every word hurt to come out.

"Okay, whenever you're ready," Andrea replied.

Secret planted her hands on either side of her legs and pushed against the bench to get enough strength to stand up. As soon as she got to her feet, she felt like the weight of the world had landed on her shoulders. The next thing she knew, her world went black.

Secret was dead. She was sure of it. Blue ringed flashes of white light behind her eyelids, searing daggers of pain pounding through her entire body, and the fact that she could no longer hear anything except her own fading breathing all told her she was dead. Secret's body curled into a fetal position. Blood soaked the front of her white sweatpants.

Andrea screamed like a banshee. "Oh, my God! Help me! Help me!" Andrea cradled Secret's head on her lap and screeched for someone to call an ambulance. The back of her throat burned from screaming, but she would not stop until she heard the sirens in the distance.

"Secret! Please! Stay with me! Please!" Andrea pleaded through tears.

Secret's eyes fluttered open. The raging fire in her throat and pounding between her ears let her know she was not dead. No, she was very much alive, as each part of her body made her painfully aware. Secret immediately started gagging. She kicked her right foot and lifted her left hand to grab the thick breathing tube that ran down her throat. It was the culprit making her gag. It was taped in place around her mouth, making it impossible to pull out. The heart monitor next to her bed sounded off with a high-pitched scream. Two nurses seemed to materialize out of thin air as they rushed to Secret's bedside.

David jumped to his feet. "What's happening?" he huffed, panicked.

Andrea was on her feet and moving toward Secret within seconds. Not for long. David and Andrea were both pushed aside by the rushing nurses.

"What's happening?" Andrea screamed, her head moving side to side frantically.

"Please! Move away! We have to treat her!" a nurse chastised Andrea and David, pushing them back from Secret's bed.

Andrea curled her hands into fists. "Bitch, don't push me again."

David grabbed Andrea around her waist.

"No, David! That's my fucking cousin lying there." Andrea started to cry. "They can't just turn me away like that. I want to know what's happening to her."

The nurse drew one side of the curtain around Secret's bed, shutting David and Andrea out.

"Mrs. Johnson, it's okay. Shhh, it's okay. Don't do that now. You'll injure yourself," a short, chunky nurse with calm eyes and skin the color of coffee beans comforted Secret.

As she held Secret's arms down, the taller, redheaded, green-eyed nurse stuck her head out from behind the curtain and huffed at David and Andrea, "We're going to have to ask you both to step out."

"I'm not going nowhere!" Andrea boomed.

David tightened his grasp and tugged her toward the doorway. "C'mon, Andrea. If they call security, there'll be attention we don't want," David said as he pulled Andrea, heels dragging, out of the door.

"I got her arms down. You tie," the short nurse barked as her partner returned to the bedside. They finally got Secret's wrists tied to the metal poles on the bed. It was for her own good, they had coaxed. They told Secret that if she pulled the tube out, she could do permanent damage to her vocal cords.

Secret tried to speak, but it was in vain. Drool leaked out of the left side of her mouth, and it felt like she'd drunk molten lava each time she tried to say something.

"I know. I know. Breathing tubes are a bitch when you're awake, but that blood clot you had in that lung is worse, so try to relax and let the machine help you. I'll give you something to knock you back out," the nicer nurse said, comforting her and patting Secret's arm.

"They always go away for this plastic surgery stuff and come back with all sorts of complications," one nurse whispered to the other as if Secret couldn't hear them.

"Mm!" Secret moaned, trying to lift her head up. Her eyes were stretched to their limits, and she was gagging against the tube again. The heart monitors went from a steady blip to a scream once more.

The head nurse came in, hands on her hips. "What's going on in here?"

Secret kept moaning.

"Something upset her," the short nurse said as if she didn't know that it was her words that had upset Secret.

Warm tears flowed from Secret's eyes, pooling in her ears. She strained against the arm restraints. Her entire body tensed. Sharp, heated stabs daggered through her back and shoulder with every movement.

"I think she just needs to be alone for the rest of the night," the short nurse said, nodding toward the door. "She also needs a sedative."

Secret relaxed her head on the pillow.

"That's it. Just relax, and let's hope they didn't do too much damage to your body," the nurse comforted her as she plunged a sedative into Secret's intravenous line.

David followed Andrea into the hospital waiting room. "How could you let her do this?" David asked as Andrea slumped into a chair.

David could see the strain on Andrea's face as soon as the question left his mouth. Andrea wore pain, regret, and anger like a hard mask. She had tried everything to convince Secret not to do the surgery. Every time Andrea thought about the powerless position she had been put in by her cousin, all the hairs on her arm stood up. It had all been so that Secret could win back David's love, another factor that made Andrea's insides boil.

"You have some fucking nerve," Andrea said through clenched teeth, her fists curled at her sides.

"I never told her to get surgery, Andrea. She told me she was going on a girls' trip," David said, pushing his pointer finger in Andrea's direction.

She rolled her eyes at him, and her nostrils flared. "You got to be fucking kidding me!" Andrea spat, bolting up out of the chair.

David shook his head. "I've got to be kidding you? I would've never approved of her going to a fucking third-world country for plastic surgery."

"You didn't have to fucking approve, David. All of your insults and neglect and rejection is the reason she did it. You're the whole fucking reason she did it," Andrea boomed, getting in David's face.

David pinched the bridge of his nose. His mind was muddled with thoughts. Was this really his fault? David felt weak, drained from everything that had happened. He was running on only a few hours of sleep because he had just returned from a business trip himself.

David flopped into one of the small waiting room chairs, physically and mentally exhausted. He couldn't even stand to look at Andrea. She was probably right. Secret probably had been trying to impress him. David understood Andrea's anger. She had been Secret's right hand for their entire lives.

Secret and Andrea had come up together from child-hood years. As cousins, they were also best friends. They had been through a lot together. David hadn't always agreed with how much time his wife spent with Andrea, but he understood that he couldn't come between what they had. They had genuine love for one another.

David knew Andrea would never forgive herself for allowing Secret to go out of the country for the surgery. Especially if Secret didn't recover.

"I tried so hard to convince her not to do it. I begged her. I told her how beautiful she was," Andrea said through tears.

David was silent. He really felt Andrea's hurt.

"Let me ask you a question. Did you ever stop and think about how hard it was on Secret going from a size zero to almost a size fourteen after having your children? I'm just saying, you may think I'm just her bigmouthed cousin and that I'm in your business, I accept that, but I think it was so fucked up how you started acting after she sacrificed everything for you and those kids. Secret told me that you were real particular about how you like her to look, but guess what, God had other plans. Now look! Now she's lying in there fighting for her life all because you're a shallow piece of shit who couldn't love her for who she is!" Andrea trumpeted. Her shrill voice had cut the silence that hovered over the room.

David was on his feet again. He didn't have to take this. "What goes on in my house is really none of your business. Don't take it out on me because you were stupid enough to allow her to do this. We will talk about this shit among ourselves, without you, when my wife recovers," David said forcefully, although somewhere in his mind, he knew Andrea had a good point, one that he'd considered as soon as he learned about Secret's surgery.

Lately, things had been strained between him and Secret. He'd been cruel sometimes. David shook it off. He couldn't think about that now. He had to keep his mind clear so he could focus on his wife and kids.

"You can't shut me up, David. I know everything. And maybe this will teach you a lesson. I know more about you than you think I know," Andrea added.

David was growing weary of Andrea's mouth. If she weren't Secret's cousin, he would've thrown her out of the hospital. Andrea was always in the middle of their lives, and if he didn't like her before, David despised her ass now.

David's stomach knotted. He didn't even want to think about what Andrea was referring to.

"Oh, what? You think Secret didn't tell me about all those nights out? All your so-called business trips? Or about your cruel words and names you call her? I told her not to get the fucking surgery. What she needed to do was divorce your ass and take you for everything you got," Andrea snapped, rolling her eyes indignantly.

David closed his eyes, and his jaw rocked feverishly. He pictured himself grabbing Andrea by her neck and choking her until she passed out. It seemed to David that was the only thing that was going to shut her ass up.

David shook his head from left to right, trying to clear his mind for now. Andrea's words settled in his mind like newly planted seeds. Something told David that once Secret got better, it wasn't going to be life as usual. He started to think about his next move before she could move first.

Chapter 3

Secret spent two weeks in the hospital. The complications from her plastic surgery were pretty serious. She'd developed blood clots on the plane ride, and one had traveled to her left lung and collapsed it. If she had been alone or if it had traveled to her heart, she would've been dead.

Secret was ashamed to look at her botched body, too. The fake plastic surgeon had made things worse. Her stomach was not only still flabby, but it had a huge scar running across the middle. Her butt cheeks were big and lumpy from where he'd injected fat and some foreign substance. Secret spent her days depressed and high on painkillers. She couldn't stand for David to look at her, and most of the time she didn't want to talk to him or deal with the kids. Secret felt like her life was over.

The sound of the doorbell ringing roused Secret from a sound, drug-induced sleep. She opened her eyes in response to the shrill sound of her doorbell. Groaning, Secret looked over at the empty spot on the other side of her bed where David should've been lying. For some reason, she was expecting him to be there, but the neatly tucked sheets and untouched pillow quickly brought her back to reality: he was away on yet another business trip. That had become his regular since Secret's surgery mishap. It was as if he couldn't stand to be around her or look at her now. Her whole plan for having the surgery had backfired.

The bell rang again, jolting her. She rolled over with her face drawn tightly into a frown. Somebody was really ringing her damn bell like they were the gotdamn police or something. Secret squinted to look at her cell phone for the time. *Shit!* It was only eight o'clock in the morning, and she wasn't expecting any visitors. Besides, the painkillers mixed with sleep aides she'd been taking since her hospital release had not fully worn off, which left her still feeling tired and drained. The bell rang again, this time with more urgency.

"Oh, hell no. I know these Jehovah's Witnesses done lost their damn minds. This shit better be life or death. Ringing my gotdamn bell like this," Secret huffed and grumbled as she threw her legs over the side of the bed. She grabbed her favorite fuzzy red robe and headed down the steps toward the front door of her home. When she made it to the bottom of the stairs, she didn't bother to peek out of the glass. She just snatched the door open and got ready to curse somebody out. Secret opened her mouth to cuss, but the person in front of her beat her to the punch.

"Mrs. Secret Ann Johnson?" a short, fat man asked as he looked her up and down suspiciously.

"Who the hell wants to know?" she snapped, surveying the man suspiciously herself.

"Here you go, ma'am," the man said, extending his hand to give Secret a thick manila envelope addressed to her with no return address.

Secret grabbed the envelope without thinking, her eyebrows furrowed in confusion. "What's this shit?" Secret asked, surveying the sealed envelope. "And that's why you were ringing my bell like your ass was on fire?"

"It's a package, ma'am. Now if you'd just sign here," the man said, rushing her. "I'm just the messenger. Don't shoot the messenger."

Secret sucked her teeth at this stupid comment. "Whatever," she mumbled as she scribbled her name down without reading. Her mind was still fuzzy between her drugs and sleep.

"Who sent this?" Secret finally asked, turning the package over in her hands a couple of times. The man was already down the front steps of her home before she could fully get her question out.

"Ma'am, you've been served," the fat bastard called out, smirking as he squeezed his fat form into a little black Honda Civic and squealed away from the curb.

Secret opened her mouth to call out to him and ask him what he meant, but he was gone before her mind could even make a complete sentence. She noticed her nosy neighbor, Mrs. Denton, across the street, watching her.

"What the hell? Nosy ass," Secret grumbled and slammed her door.

Once inside Secret ripped the seal on the envelope. She noticed a thick set of papers. She pulled them out and began reading. Secret's heart sped up, and her entire body became engulfed in heat.

"'Petition for Divorce,'" she murmured as she read the heading on the first page of the thick stack.

Secret doubled over at the waist, and she gagged. She felt like someone had punched her in the stomach and kicked her in the chest until they'd knocked the wind out of her. Secret had to steady herself because her legs became weak.

"No," she gasped. Leaning up against the door for support, Secret scanned over the words on the paper. "Oh, my God." Secret clutched her chest as she read further. David had served her with divorce papers. No discussion. No warning. No courtesy. Just a cold service of divorce papers in the middle of the morning, seemingly out of nowhere.

A golf-ball-sized lump formed in the back of Secret's throat, and she gripped the papers so tightly the paper dug into her skin until it stung. As soon as the tears came to her eyes, she heard her kids moving upstairs.

"Mama!" yelled Bella, Secret's 6-year-old daughter. Secret could also hear her 2-year-old son, DJ, calling out for her.

Secret couldn't move. She was paralyzed with shock, and her feet seemed to be rooted to the floor. She stood stock-still in disbelief at what David had done.

"How dare he? How could he?" Secret groaned, holding her chest as if she were having a heart attack. The pain she felt was probably worse than a heart attack. This was definitely what a broken heart felt like.

After everything she had been through with David. After everything she had sacrificed for the sake of their marriage, for his career. She'd sacrificed her health and her body image. It was all for nothing. *All for nothing! All for nothing!* Secret's mind screamed. Thoughts whizzed through her brain of all she'd given up. She felt dizzy just thinking about her life in retrospect. She had literally given up her own dreams, hopes of a modeling career, college, and just her entire life for David. She had dedicated it all to him. How could he betray her like this? Was he really that shallow? Was it really all about the weight she'd gained? It couldn't be. Secret swallowed hard, but she couldn't stop the stream of tears from falling. She couldn't pull it together and fake for her kids this time. This hurt too badly.

"Mommy, why are you crying? Did you hurt yourself again? Is your boo-boo hurting again?" Bella asked, her little angelic voice laced with concern.

Secret stretched her red-rimmed eyes to look into her daughter's, whose face resembled David's down to the one dimple in her right cheek. Secret hadn't even realized her kids had come downstairs and were now standing right in front of her. Secret was on the floor by the front door, sobbing uncontrollably. She inhaled and tried to pull herself together for the kids. She could barely get to her feet. Her head swam with grief and confusion.

"I'm okay, baby. Are you guys hungry?" Secret said as she swiped roughly at her tears. She parted a phony smile and tried to sound happy and excited so she could put her kids at ease.

"Yes. Pancakes. We want pancakes," Bella sang out innocently, speaking for herself and her baby brother.

Secret dragged her feet into her gourmet kitchen so she could feed the kids, but also so she could get to her pills. She needed something to ease her mind. She whirled around in the big kitchen, confused. It seemed so much bigger and lonelier now.

As Secret went about preparing breakfast for her babies, Secret had several bouts of racking sobs each time she thought about the way David had done things. She felt so betrayed. He hadn't had the decency or respect to come and talk to her about his plans. He never told her he wanted a divorce. In fact, Secret was under the impression that David felt bad about the surgery and the complications and that he would be more sympathetic and just move past her botched body. Although he had never said it was okay that she wasn't the same anymore, Secret had held out hope that he would just accept her once and for all. But no. David had shown her just how shallow and disgusting he really was.

Secret slammed her fists down her on the granite countertop and bit down into her lip just thinking about being all alone with two kids. This wasn't how she'd envisioned her life turning out. She felt nauseous, and her legs got weak as she waited for the pancakes to brown. The thought of divorce had not fully settled into her mind yet. She could not believe David was leaving her just like that. Secret had nothing of her own except two kids. Everything was David's or theirs together. What would she do with her life now? David had been her whole life and identify for so long, what would she do now?

Secret gripped the side of the counters now as she
thought about her situation. She gripped harder the
more she felt like her life was slipping away from her.

Secret managed to pull herself together enough to feed
her kids and then put them in the bathtub, where they
usually played for about an hour. Secret sat on the closed
toilet seat to watch them play in the water. She usually
played with them or sang songs with them. Not today. She
was in a haze and stupor. Even the two Percocet pills she'd
popped didn't help ease her mind. Her head still throbbed.
Every time she thought about what was happening to her,
her mind would slip back and forth to and from the past.
Some memories were good, and some were bad. She and
David had been through so much over the years. But as
she searched in her mind, nothing stuck out that war-
ranted a divorce. What could be so bad in his eyes that he
would just abandon her and the kids like this?

While Secret sat half watching the kids, she pulled out
the divorce papers again for the twentieth time since
she'd been served with them. This time her mind was
together enough to read them carefully. As she read,
some of the words stuck out to her like, "irreconcilable
differences, and cruel and unusual treatment." Secret
could feel her blood pressure rising the more she read.
David was actually saying that she was responsible for
the demise of their marriage and his wanting a divorce.
That was just like him to blame her for everything,
another habit he had picked up over the years. No matter
the issue, Secret was always responsible.

"Oh, hell no! This bastard can't get away with this,"
Secret mumbled mindlessly, stepping out of the bathroom with the crumpled papers still wadded up between
her balled fists. She had not even thought about the leaving the kids alone in the tub, which she never did, not
even for a minute.

Too angry to remember the kids, Secret stomped
into her bedroom and picked up her house phone. She

blocked the number and dialed David's business cell phone number. He had already ignored the last twenty calls from her cell phone. At this time of day, Secret knew, he had no choice but to answer an unknown call because he would probably think it was a client. She bit into her lip as she waited for him to answer.

"David Johnson," he said, his deep voice filtered through the phone.

Secret felt a flash of nerves, but they quickly congealed into a white-hot ball of fury. "You motherfucker! I cannot fucking believe after all I gave up, after all the shit I did for your ass, you have the fucking nerve to file for a divorce without so much as a conversation! For no fucking reason, David?" Secret boomed into the phone. It was out of character for her. She was usually calm and collected, and she damn sure had taken a lot of David's shit over the years without so much as an argument. The impending divorce had sent her to a different place though.

"Listen, Secret. I will talk to you about this another time," David responded with sheer indifference in his tone.

His smug tone made Secret's blood boil even more. He sounded so arrogant and composed, while she was frazzled and a complete wreck. Secret could just picture him now, a smirk on his face and his arms folded like he was taking great satisfaction at her pain.

"You sadistic piece of shit! Don't tell me it's not the fucking time! My life is on the line! Our life is on the line! What am I supposed to do, David? What did I ever do to deserve this but try to love you and take care of you? I gave you everything I had, including my beauty, my body, my whole self," Secret shrieked, her voice cracking and tears running like an open faucet down her cheeks.

Everything was spinning around her. Secret felt like she was on one of those amusement park rides where the floor falls out from under you and you're stuck to the wall, unable to move, unable to scream, unable to control anything. She couldn't help the tears. They just wouldn't stop flooding down her face in buckets. She clenched her fists tightly, and the vein in her neck throbbed fiercely. Secret was mad at herself for letting David hear her cry but she just couldn't contain her pain. She sobbed and sobbed. Secret had not felt so off-kilter and crazed since the day she realized her mother had died.

"Secret, we have been over for a while now. You and I both know this. Don't act like there was any love left. Things haven't been the same for a while now," David continued in his smooth, calm voice.

His words were like a gut punch, and Secret flopped down on her bed, exasperated. What the fuck did he mean there wasn't any love left? How? She had loved him so much she cut up her body to please him! That was love!

She loved David with every fiber of her being. Didn't he know that? Secret didn't think anything could change that. His words were so cruel in her opinion. She felt overwhelmed with anxiety, like she'd just found out someone close to her had died. What would she do without David? Secret had admitted to herself long before this that she loved him more than she loved herself.

"Please, David, don't do this. I'm begging you. I will do anything you want. I will lose the weight. I'm sorry I had another baby. I'm sorry I got the surgery. I'll get my body fixed the right way. We can work this out. Pa-lease!" Secret pleaded, her words muffled by her sobs. Secret didn't know which of these things had caused her husband to want to leave, but she was willing to fix them all.

"Please, David, give us another chance!" Secret cried, her words barely understandable. She was a blubbering mess. Secret didn't care if it made David mad. She couldn't help but let her feelings out if it meant it would save the most important thing in the world to her: her marriage.

"C'mon, Secret. Don't do this right now," David said, his voice gruff, like he was getting choked up. "Secret, you're better than this. Pull yourself together. You have to finally be your own person. I don't see us being together ever again. It's over, but I want you to be okay. I want you to be the strong woman I know you can be," David said.

"But why?" Secret screamed, letting her raw emotion be known. The nerve of him telling her to be her own person after he had completely destroyed who she was years ago. But Secret didn't say this. She didn't want to say anything else that would piss him off. She just wanted to beg him to come back home and work things out.

"Look, we have to just face it. Both of us. I'll say it: it is over," he replied, putting emphasis on his words. "You knew this before you went and got the botched surgery. You're far from a dummy, Secret. You can start over. You're beautiful. You can surely find someone at some point. It just didn't work out for us. I have to go. I will be by to pick up the kids for a visit later this evening. Please have them ready," David said with finality.

Secret felt like someone had slapped her around, or maybe even punched the shit out of her and stomped on her head. Her body ached with an overwhelming feeling of rushing adrenaline and electrified anxiety. "No! No! David, don't do this!" Secret screamed in a last-ditch effort to convince him to change his mind. Her efforts fell on deaf ears. Nothing she did would make him change his mind.

"Get yourself together. You sound like a mess. And like I said, have the kids ready," he said.

Secret's mode switched gears like someone had put an up-and-down switch on her back. A pang of pure anger flashed in her chest and replaced her previous feeling of sorrow. Secret searched her mind for something to say or do that would make David hurt as much as she did right now.

"You will not see your kids if you do this! I'm warning you, David Johnson! You will never see them again!" Secret boomed, her emotions hanging out there like a sore thumb. David was quiet.

"Do you hear me?" Secret screamed. "You will never have my kids. They're mine! We are a package! If you don't want me, you don't want them!"

Then suddenly Secret heard something that made her heart feel like it would burst. It was like her worst nightmare had come true. Secret could hear a woman's voice in the background talking to David. Secret pressed the phone to ear harder so she could hear better. She had to be sure her ears weren't deceiving her.

"David!" Secret screamed. He didn't answer, but Secret could tell he was trying to keep the woman in the background away from the phone. Secret heard a bit of shuffling and fumbling. Secret was fully focused and homed in on the phone sounds now.

"Who is that?" Secret screamed, her voice high-pitched and jagged. "We are still fucking married, David! How could you? So that's it! That's what this is all about. Just like that? Out of nowhere! A bitch is making you do this! I can't believe you would betray me like this! After all I've done!" Secret cried out. She felt defeated and weak. He was cheating on her, and now he was leaving her for another woman.

"How could you disrespect me like this? How could you give up on what we have and our kids? Don't you think they deserve better than their father leaving them over a bitch? I guess you want your kids to be statistics just like you were, huh? No father around?" Secret said cruelly.

"Look, I have to go. Either you let me get the kids or you don't. It's all up to you, but I won't fight you," David replied.

Before Secret could formulate a response, the phone went dead. He had hung up in her ear, one of the things she considered most disrespectful right up there with spitting on someone.

"David! David!" Secret screamed into the dead phone. He was really gone. Flabbergasted, Secret dialed his number back over a dozen times, but he refused to answer his phone. After her thirteenth call, it began going straight to his voicemail. Secret threw her phone across the room in frustration and anger, sending the back cover and the battery pack flying in opposite directions from the phone itself. Secret started pacing for a few minutes.

Suddenly, she was snapped out of her own agony when she heard coughing, gagging, and splashing noises coming from down the hallway where her babies were taking their bath. A rush of heat came over Secret, and she was sprinting through the house before her mind really even registered anything like danger.

"Oh, my God!" Secret shrieked as she was spurred into action and her legs started moving. She raced down the long hallway between her bedroom and the kids' bathroom. Secret almost fainted when she reached the doorway of the bathroom. Secret's eyes grew as wide as dinner plates and her throat was desert dry as a feeling of fear and panic gripped her tightly by the throat.

"DJ! Oh, my God!" Secret screamed. With one swift move, she was at the side of the bathtub, snatching her baby boy out of the bottom of the deep porcelain tub. The tub was almost filled with water. They must have been playing with the faucets and turned the water on after Secret had walked out. She never put more water in the tub than just enough to cover their little legs.

"DJ, baby! C'mon, breathe!" Secret belted out frantically. Secret started shaking her youngest child frantically. The baby's eyes were rolling as he fought to breathe. Secret continued to shake him, and then she turned him upside down. She didn't know what else to do. She didn't even think about shaken baby syndrome or the damage she could've inflicted on her baby by jerking him so roughly. All Secret was focused on was getting her son to breath properly.

"DJ! Please!" Secret screamed, shaking the baby even more violently than before. Bella was still standing in the water, screaming and crying and calling out for her daddy. Secret couldn't comfort her other child right now. She had to save her baby.

"C'mon, baby!" Secret belted out, hitting her 2-year-old on the back hard now. Suddenly, the baby started coughing and throwing up water. Secret had never been so happy to see vomit in all of her life. A sense of relief swept over her.

"Oh, thank God! Baby! My baby! I'm so sorry! Mommy is so sorry," Secret cried, clutching her son to her chest. He was trembling, his teeth chattering. Secret helped Bella out of the tub and wrapped both of her kids in their cartoon-character towels. The close call was enough to get her back to reality.

"Mommy is sorry. It's all my fault. Everything is my fault. Neither of you deserves this kind of life," Secret said, holding her babies tight to her body. Secret and her kids sat on the wet bathroom floor for the next half hour. Secret didn't know what to do next. She didn't know how her life would end up, but she knew it couldn't be good without David.

Chapter 4

Secret hadn't slept the entire night after getting served with the divorce papers and her baby's near-drowning scare. Although Secret had calmed down a little, she was far from mentally okay. In fact, she felt obsessive, like she needed to do something about her situation. Secret literally felt like she was losing her mind. She paced. She ate a whole bag of snacks and then threw it up. She put on a full face of makeup and then washed it off. She was spiraling. She felt herself coming apart at the seams.

Secret rummaged through her closet. There were only a few things from when she'd first gotten together with David that could still fit her. Secret held up an outfit he used to like. She smiled and fumbled and twisted into the old sweat suit. It was too small and put pressure on her stomach scar. It also barely fit over the lumps and bumps in her ass cheeks that Dr. Mungia had left behind.

Every time Secret looked at her ugly scars and uneven butt-to-thigh ratio, she wanted to go back to the Dominican Republic, find Dr. Mungia, and murder him in cold blood. Nothing in her life would ever be the same anyway.

Secret combed her fingers through her long weave and tried to get it to look like something. Weaves were another of David's preferences. Secret personally had preferred to wear her hair natural and short. She'd changed everything for him. Everything.

Secret glanced at herself in the mirror and didn't even recognize the person staring back at her. She cupped her hand over her mouth and gulped back a sob. She had changed over the years so much, and she hadn't ever taken the time to notice just how much. Maybe it *was* her fault that David was leaving her. "You look disgusting," she scolded herself in a harsh whisper. She had dark rings under her eyes now, where before she had flawless, blemish-free caramel-colored skin. Looking at herself caused another wave of anxiety to come over her. She envisioned David's new woman to be gorgeous, in shape, and everything that she was not right now. David had preferred Secret as a model, not as a mother.

Envisioning beautiful women with David had driven Secret crazy all night. Today, Secret had the sudden urge to see David, to confront him, but more importantly to see who he had left her for. That was it. Maybe she could talk some sense into him if they had time face-to-face.

Secret moved through the house frantically now. "Bella, let's go!" Secret called out to her daughter urgently. The kids came bounding out of their room. Secret scrambled to dress them, and nothing she put on Bella or DJ matched. Secret was clearly not focused. The kids had on bottoms and tops that didn't go together, and she hadn't bothered to redo Bella's hair, so it was fuzzy and sticking up in places. Secret never took them outside like that, but today she was in a rush. She needed to get to David's office before he got caught up in any meetings. Secret needed him to see what he was losing, at least for the kids' sake.

"Let's go see Daddy!" Bella sang out. Secret cringed and bit down into her jaw. Just thinking about what the divorce would do to her kids caused Secret's stomach to suddenly cramp.

"Yes, let's go see Daddy," she said under her breath with just a hint of anger.

Secret strapped both kids into their car seats and slid into the driver's seat of her Mercedes-Benz G-Class. Even the car reminded her of her husband. Luxury items were always David's idea. He had bought her the SUV and told her he had chosen that particular vehicle because it was a "rich soccer mom's" car. Secret had been too overjoyed that she had a new car to even think about his words. She hadn't thought anything of his statement at the time, but now the car represented everything Secret didn't want to be: some boring suburban housewife waiting for her husband to dole out her allowance so she could go buy a pair of "mom" jeans and a cardigan. Secret felt so stupid now. She'd watched her own life unravel one piece at a time, and she was too blind to even see it.

Secret made it to Brooklyn from her ritzy Long Island neighborhood in record time. She sped through the streets of Brooklyn until she was finally in front of Metro Tech in downtown Brooklyn, where David worked. She pulled her car into the inside parking lot and drove around to where she remembered David's personal parking spot was located. Secret immediately noticed a candy-apple red Mercedes-Benz S550 with personalized plates reading, "Lady Luck," parked in the spot. Secret's heart began hammering against her chest bone. "This can't be the same spot," she whispered. David wouldn't be stupid enough to have a bitch parking in his spot or driving her car for that matter.

Secret craned her neck and squinted her eyes to make sure the number on the parking spot was the same as she remembered it. "Two-two-one-one," she whispered. It was definitely her spot. She remembered it because her birthday was February 11 and she'd remarked to him about how the numbers must've been lucky.

It wasn't long before Secret noticed David's car in the spot right next to it, and that was all she needed to con-

firm her suspicions. He had this bitch visiting with him
at work? It was yet another blatant slap in Secret's face
by her husband. Without even thinking, Secret grabbed
her car door handle and scrambled to get out of the
car. When she lifted her foot off the gas, the car lurched
forward and almost hit the intruding Mercedes that was
occupying David's real spot.

"Oh, shit!" Secret cursed and threw her car into park.
Focused on her mission, Secret fumbled with the door
handle again and raced out of her car. Secret was so furious she left her sleeping children in the back seat of the
car. She was definitely losing it. This would be the second
time her mind had gone so blank she had forgotten about
her kids.

Secret took the stairs from the parking lot that led into
the business building two at a time to the seventh floor.
While she raced through the building's stairwell, a memory of a hot and heavy petting session she and David had
had when he first started working there came flooding
back to Secret's mind. David had been so proud of himself for landing the job and couldn't wait for her to see his
new office with its glorious city view.

"You're going to be so proud of me," David had said to
her that day after stopping Secret from going up the steps
and spinning her around to face him. She understood
then why they hadn't just taken the elevator. He wanted
to get freaky. Secret had giggled and tried to pull away
from him, but David held her tight. He had forcefully
placed his mouth on top of hers and forced his tongue
between her lips.

Secret had relented, like always. She gave him what
he wanted. She let herself go and kissed him passionately. Then David lifted her shirt, pulled up her bra, and
took mouthfuls of her breasts right there. "Oh, my God,
David," Secret had gasped. But still, she had let the hot

feeling overtake her. She had wanted David to fuck her right there. David had gotten her so hot and heavy that by the time they reached the door to his office, she was already half naked and she didn't care who had been watching them.

It had happened in that very stairwell. The memory threatened to send Secret's heart into convulsions and her emotional stability into overdrive.

Secret's anger was fueled all over again like someone had doused it with a fresh set of gasoline and thrown a newly lit match on it. Flinging the exit door open violently, Secret raced through it. She sped down the carpeted hallway, bypassing the empty desks and cubicles. Finally, Secret reached the familiar door: David's private office. It didn't matter if Secret was welcome, David would have to see her whether he liked it or not.

Secret tried the doorknob, and it was locked. She banged on the office door like she was the police. "David! Open this fucking door!" Secret screamed. She didn't care about the noise or other employees or security for that matter. "I know you're in there with that bitch! Open this fucking door! I am your wife! I'm still your fucking wife!" Secret boomed. She had completely lost control now. She could hear the other employees moving out of their cubicles and offices to see what was going on. It was still too early for everyone to be at work, but the early birds were surely getting a show.

David pulled back the door wearing the most evil scowl Secret had ever seen. Secret knew he'd opened up the door because he hated to be embarrassed. David was always worried about what his white and other ritzy black coworkers thought of him. Secret knew where he really came from though. She knew the real David Johnson, a former foster kid who'd grown up with nothing!

"What are you—" David started, but Secret didn't allow him to finish. She pushed him so hard in his chest he stumbled backward into his office. He wasn't expecting her brute force. Therefore, he was unable to brace himself in time. He landed on his ass. Secret barreled into the office like a heat-seeking missile.

"Why, David?" Secret growled as she stormed in circles around his expansive office. Secret whirled around like a crazed madwoman, looking in every direction for the bitch responsible for breaking up her marriage.

"You need to leave," David said, grabbing Secret's arm roughly. "This is not the time or the place."

Just then, a young, beautiful woman came sauntering into the office. Secret was stopped cold. The woman's beautiful butter-colored face, long, dark, silky hair, and slim, shapely legs made Secret feel horrible. The woman looked just how Secret used to look when she was still modeling. Secret felt like dying right there on the spot. She felt so ugly and fat compared to the sexy vixen in front of her. Secret wished she could blink herself out of there now.

"David, is everything okay?" the beautiful woman asked, her face crumpled in confusion. Secret's eyes hooded over when she recognized the voice as the same one she'd heard on the phone. All of Secret's feelings of insecurity quickly converted to blind rage. Secret's vision became clouded, and she began seeing red spots in the corners of her eyes. Her chest began heaving in and out. She viewed the woman as the enemy now. Not only had this bitch ruined her marriage, but she was taking Secret's place in David's life.

"Is everything okay? You're asking my fucking husband if everything is okay? You got some nerve, bitch!" Secret barked, moving in the woman's direction with her finger pointed menacingly. "No, everything is not okay.

Did David tell you about me? Huh? You home-wrecking bitch!"

"Secret, you just need to leave," David said through gritted teeth, trying to pull her toward the door. The woman looked Secret up and down and smirked like she was better than Secret. That was enough to send Secret over the top.

"Agh!" Secret screamed, breaking free of David's grasp. Secret charged into the woman with full force. The woman screamed, but it was too late. Secret was too thick and too strong for the puny, little woman to handle. This was the one time Secret appreciated her new weight. The woman fell backward on her ass so hard she let out a little squeak when she hit the floor. She was unable to break her own fall or put her hands up in time to block Secret from getting at her. Secret was on top of David's new love within seconds. Secret was like a wild animal just let out of captivity. She wound her hand up in the woman's beautiful hair and began punching her in her pretty face. Secret wasn't going to have any mercy on the bitch taking everything from her. Secret felt like she was at war fighting for her territory.

"He's married! I'm his fucking wife! You home-wrecking whore!" Secret growled from some place deep within. She sounded animalistic, and she acted just as bad.

David rushed over to the two women's tangled bodies and tried to pull Secret off of his beautiful new woman. Secret was relentless. She had a grip on the woman's hair so tight that each time David pulled her, the woman screamed out because Secret was pulling her hair almost out by the roots.

"Secret, you are going to jail! Security! Someone call security, now!" David belted out as he was finally able to pull his scorned wife off of his lover. Secret had a handful of the woman's hair, and she had blood from the woman's nose all over her sweat suit.

David dragged Secret over to the door kicking, scratching, and screaming. He pushed her out into the hallway, but it was no easy task. Secret took some of the skin off of David's chest and arms with her nails. Secret could hear the woman speaking to the building's security. They started heading in her direction.

"This shit is not over, David Johnson! It's not fucking over!" Secret screamed through tears as the security guards surrounded her. David slammed his office door. With the sound of the door slamming, Secret was brought back to reality.

"Get off of me! I'm leaving!" Secret growled. "Oh, my God, my kids!" she yelled, her body quaking with fear and anxiety. She had forgotten all about them again.

Secret took off running back toward the stairwell and the parking garage. When she got downstairs, she noticed more security guards standing by her car, shining a flashlight inside and peeking through the windows.

"I'm here! I just had to get something quick!" Secret called out breathlessly, trying in vain to straighten out her mangled clothes and hair.

The guards looked at her strangely. They noticed the blood on her and her wild hair. "The police are on the way, miss. I can't let you leave," one of the security guards said.

"I didn't do anything. Move the fuck out of my way," Secret growled.

The guard stood his ground. He was going to be a tough guy with no gun, no handcuffs, and just a flashlight. Secret could hear sirens in the distance. Desperate to leave before the police arrived, and totally out of control of her emotions, she punched the security guard in his face. Her blow caught him off guard, and he doubled over.

"Ahhh, bitch, you crazy!" he belted out, holding his cheek. The other guards rushed at her, but Secret pushed them to the floor, hopped into her driver's seat, and screeched out of the parking lot just in time. The police cruiser whizzed right past her. With tears running down her face and a sense of relief that she hadn't been arrested, Secret drove far away from the building. She slammed her fists on her steering wheel.

"Aggh!" she screamed. "Why? Why did he do this to me?" Secret cried.

Feeling lost and dejected, Secret drove straight to Andrea's house. "Please be home. Please be home," Secret said over and over as she pulled up to Andrea's house. When she saw her cousin's car outside, a sense of relief washed over her. Secret hadn't told Andrea anything yet, but she knew her cousin would be pissed with David. She had never really cared for David anyway.

With her hands shaking, Secret dialed her cousin's house number. When Andrea picked up, Secret just started hollering into the phone. She was crying so uncontrollably that Andrea couldn't even understand what she was trying to say. Secret finally managed to tell her cousin that she was right outside.

Andrea rushed outside to the car. "Oh, God, Secret. What the hell is going on?" Andrea gasped when she saw Secret's physical appearance. "Are you sick? In pain? What the hell?"

"He is leaving me!" Secret broke down and wailed. Her screaming caused the kids to start crying.

"What?" Andrea asked.

"He's leaving me! It's a bitch! Oh, God, what am I going to do, Andrea? I don't have anything without him! I am nothing without him!" Secret screamed some more, this time louder and with more emotion behind her words.

"Shh. Okay, calm down, girl. You're scaring these kids. C'mon. Let me take these babies inside," Andrea told Secret as she started taking the kids out of their car seats.

Secret could not stop wailing. Her body shook all over. She felt like someone had died. The grief was so real it was palpable.

Secret followed Andrea and the kids inside the house. Secret watched helplessly as her cousin fed her kids and sat them down to watch cartoons. All Secret could do was sob and sob. She looked and felt pitiful. Her kids didn't even want to be near her because she had already acted so crazy in front of them.

When the kids were settled in front of the television in Andrea's living room, Andrea grabbed Secret by the hand and led her to the kitchen. Andrea pulled out a chair and helped her cousin sit down.

"Tell me what the fuck is going on, Secret. You drive over here unexpectedly, you look a mess, you were screaming like a nut, what the hell?" Andrea asked seriously. "I can't make out what the hell is happening."

Secret couldn't even hold eye contact with Andrea. She was terribly embarrassed. Andrea had preached for years about not giving up her schooling and how Secret should be wary of giving David her whole self. Secret hadn't listened, and now she was going to have to come clean. She'd pretended for years she had the perfect marriage, but Andrea always saw through it.

Secret had no choice but to be honest about everything. The one thing she didn't want to do was lie to Andrea more than she already had over the past year. Secret broke down and told Andrea everything about what she had been going through with David. Andrea did not know that David had been staying away for weeks and months. She thought it was just more business trips. Andrea knew David was a shallow bastard, but she hadn't suspected that Secret and David's problems would've left her cousin like this. Secret always wanted everyone to think her life was charmed and enviable. Although she loved Andrea to death, Secret always wanted to be the one doing better than all of her cousins she had grown up with. She always felt like she had something to prove.

"Secret, why didn't you call me right away? Why did you hide this?" Andrea asked, a little perturbed that her cousin had hidden what was going on and only after shit had come to a head did she confess everything.

"I was sure he would stop. I was sure after I almost died getting surgery for his ass that it would work out. I just didn't want to turn everyone against him and then have shit work out between us. I hope you understand. These past few weeks since I got out of the hospital have been hell, and I was embarrassed," Secret sobbed.

"Oh, honey, I'm so sorry," Andrea said sympathetically, touching Secret's hand. She reached out and embraced Secret. She held Secret and let her cry. Andrea told her she would be there for her through everything that was happening. It wasn't any different than when they were kids. Andrea would try to protect Secret.

After about an hour of straight sobbing, Secret was finally calm. Andrea had made some chamomile tea for the both of them, and they were talking about Secret's options and the things she should ask for during the divorce proceedings. It had taken Andrea a while to first convince Secret to accept that David was leaving, and then that she needed to take his ass to the bank if he wanted to just up and leave her with two kids and a mortgage.

As they discussed things, Secret's cell phone began ringing. She looked at it, and her eyes grew wide. A quick pang of excitement mixed with fear flitted through her stomach. She looked over at Andrea like a terrified yet excited child.

"It's David," Secret said to Andrea before she decided to answer the phone. Secretly, Secret was hoping David was calling to say he had made a big mistake, he was sorry for everything, and he was coming back.

"Are you going to answer it?" Andrea asked.

Secret slowly picked up the phone and answered the call. "Hello," she croaked out, her throat desert dry and her heart beating like crazy.

"Just so you know, I have gotten a restraining order against you. If you come within three hundred feet of this building, you will be arrested. You are lucky I have a real woman who didn't press charges on you because of the kids. Now stay the fuck away from me!" David barked into the phone. He was speaking to her like she was a stranger in the streets who had robbed him or something.

Secret felt like he had just thrown a hot pot of grits in her face. She was more than shocked at how he just completely changed. She didn't even recognize him anymore. Secret's previous feelings of hope and excitement were quickly squashed by her husband's cruel words.

"Fuck you! Fuck your bitch too! You don't know who you fucked with, David. I gave up everything! I have nothing, and if I can't have it all, neither will either of you! You wait and see!" Secret screamed at the top of her lungs.

"Shh, Secret, please. This is not good for those kids." Andrea tried to quiet Secret to protect the kids from being upset all over again.

It was too late. Both kids were standing in the doorway of the kitchen, crying as their mother screamed like a maniac. They had never seen their mother act like this before, and they were scared.

Secret could feel herself changing inside in more ways than one. It wasn't a good thing happening to her. She was on the ledge, and something in her mind was telling her to jump.

Chapter 5

"Secret?" Andrea called out. The house was pin-drop quiet, which scared Andrea. "Secret? Are you in here?" Andrea called out again, pushing open the door of Secret's master bedroom and walking inside.

"Oh, my God! Secret! What the hell are you doing lying down in the closet like some crazy person?" Andrea's voice jolted Secret out of her depressed stupor. "What's going on? You sleeping in the closet now?" Andrea said softly as she stepped closer.

Secret bolted upright so fast in response to her cousin's voice that her surgery scars began throbbing. "How did you get in without me hearing you?" Secret grumbled, annoyed at Andrea's bold and boisterous interruption.

"I have a key. I mean, I've never used it, but when I called you ten times and you didn't answer . . ." Andrea said, her words trailing off.

She had been thinking the worst, Secret could tell. Secret took in an eyeful of her cousin and bestie. Andrea looked radiant, as usual. She wore flawless makeup, a professionally laid shoulder-length, bone-straight hairdo, and a bright, pastel, striped Valentino maxi dress that hugged her curves in all the right places. Secret remembered a time when she prided herself on looking as beautiful as Andrea did. Secret hadn't cared about her appearance at all lately. Not anymore.

"I'm not really up for company. I'm still in pain, believe it or not. Plus, I'm pretty tired, haven't been getting a whole lot of sleep. I have so much on my mind, girl," Secret groaned.

"I know you're not up for company, but it's what you need! Plus, I'm not damn company. I'm your damn family. Now come on. Get up. I will not take no for an answer, so don't even try to say it again," Andrea urged.

Secret groaned and rolled her eyes. Andrea tapped her foot. "Secret, you cannot, I repeat, cannot stay locked up in this house and in this dreaded bedroom another damn day," Andrea snapped, stepping to the back of Secret's closet so she could find something other than pajamas for Secret to wear.

Secret rolled her eyes and let out a long sigh. "I know you're trying, but I'm really not up to it."

"How about this little number? I always liked you in this color," Andrea said cheerfully, holding up a fuchsia Gucci mini dress with open slits on the sleeves.

Secret twisted her lips. She was trying not to be rude, although she wanted to tell Andrea to get the hell out and let her be depressed.

"Or this one. This green would be heavenly on you," Andrea said as she held up a mint green Zara strapless maxi dress.

"Whatever you pick I'll wear," Secret groaned. All of this was going to be harder than she thought.

"I can't believe getting you outside today was so damn hard. I had to practically drag you by the damn hair just to get you into the sun. Secret, you've been vamping too long. Shit, I miss you," Andrea complained jokingly with a smile. She sat across from Secret at Sweet Chick, one of their favorite spots in Brooklyn. The quaint tables and Southern hospitality theme inside was perfect. Andrea thought the closeness would help brighten Secret's mood and pull her out of the deep depression she'd slipped into over the past few weeks since David had served her. Plus, Andrea knew how much Secret enjoyed getting a taste of home-cooked Southern food when she could.

"I know it has to be hard, Secret. Having your husband abandon you out of the blue after all you've sacrificed can't be easy at all, but you can't stop living," Andrea said sympathetically, following her words up with a smile. She figured if she smiled enough, Secret would eventually catch her vibe.

Secret picked up a mini appetizer, took a small bite, and threw it back down on her saucer. The food was tasteless, like cardboard in her mouth. Her appetite was nonexistent. She didn't see it coming back anytime soon.

"Look, you're the most beautiful woman I know. Look at this whole world of men out here. How many have been staring at you since we've been in here?" Andrea continued winking at Secret playfully.

Secret huffed. She locked eyes with Andrea. Secret shook her legs under the table. She wanted so badly to bolt from the table and run back to her bedroom and lock herself inside. "You try losing your husband and dealing with oozing failed plastic surgery scars, a body that you're ashamed of, and being scared you'll never love again. I think you'd agree that all of that could cause a person to want to stop living, or at least to stay holed up in their own home alone," Secret replied sharply.

Suddenly, the jolly mood Andrea was trying to create dropped like a brick to the bottom of the ocean. "I was just joking about the men," Andrea said, her voice going low. She'd tried everything to cheer Secret up. She'd practically had to drag her off the floor of her closet just to get her out to eat. This wasn't what Andrea had bargained for today.

As they sat quietly for a minute, the cheerful waitress bounced over for the second time, wearing a bright smile. It was a welcome interruption of the tense moment between Secret and Andrea.

"What can I get you beautiful ladies for your main course?" the waitress sang. They placed their orders, and just like that the effervescent girl was gone again.

"They get younger and cuter, don't they?" Andrea quipped, trying to change the subject again.

Secret bit down on her bottom lip and looked at Andrea seriously. *Is she serious?* "I found out more things about David," Secret blurted. She couldn't pretend any longer.

Andrea stopped midmotion as she was about to shovel a forkful of her fried green tomatoes appetizer into her open mouth. She put the fork down and looked at Secret curiously, her mouth still open.

"Aside from this woman, David has had others over the years. He was never really faithful at all," Secret revealed, her voice wavering.

Andrea's eyebrows shot up to her hairline. She took a big sip of her sangria. "How did you find out?" Andrea asked, her mouth dipping at the edges.

"I went through some of his things after he was gone. And one by one, I uncovered these affairs. . . ." Secret replied, her voice trailing off. She turned her face away, looking out of the restaurant's big windows. From where they were seated, in front of the huge expanse of glass windows, she could see the bustling Brooklyn streets. As people rushed by, Secret wondered if anyone else felt like she felt inside. Dead.

Andrea was unusually quiet. Secret turned back toward her cousin, waiting for her reaction.

"Shocked?" Secret asked strangely. She had expected Andrea to start twisting her head homegirl style and smacking her lips, saying stuff like, "Oh no he didn't," and, "How fucking dare he!" Instead, Andrea was quiet, solemn even.

"Nah, not shocked. Because I kind of knew," Andrea whispered shamefully, lowering her eyes as she toyed nervously with the edge of her napkin.

Secret jerked in her chair, reacting as if she had been electrocuted. A flurry of emotion moved like a dark storm across her face. She felt like Andrea had just kicked her in the chest.

"I'm sorry, Secret. I found out in the most fucked-up way, and because of how I found out, I couldn't tell you, and then every time I tried to get up the nerve to say something, it was never the right time. I knew it would just come between us if you weren't ready to know, so I thought . . . I just tried . . . I thought it best to just . . ." Andrea rambled frantically, stumbling over her words.

Secret glared daggers at Andrea. Fire flashed in her eyes. "I can't fucking believe you knew something like that and never thought it was important enough to tell me. You let me just go about being humiliated? You're just as fucked up, if not even more fucked up, than he was for this bullshit," Secret hissed harshly through her teeth. She balled her cloth napkin up and tossed it onto the table. Secret pushed her chair back from the table. "I wonder what else you knew and never told me," Secret spat, her voice rising and falling like waves against ocean rocks.

"Wait! Secret, please! Let me explain!" Andrea cried out, reaching her hand out toward her cousin. Secret paused, squinting. Andrea's shoulders slumped, and she exhaled a windstorm of breath.

"I didn't want to see you like this, and when I confronted him, he told me he would never hurt you. I made sure he stopped. That's what it was, Secret. Nothing else. I would never hide anything from you, but it's just that if

I told you I knew you'd still be with him, and then you'd be mad at me. I wanted him to love you and for things to work out and not come between us," Andrea confessed, lowering her eyes.

Secret pursed her lips and shook her head from left to right as she looked at Andrea in disgust.

"I saw him one night with a girl. Oh, I lit into his ass for real. From what I understood, he was never going to do it again. He'd been drinking, and he said it was the biggest mistake he ever made. He promised me he would never let you find out and he would never do it again. I thought I was protecting you. I love you so much, Secret. I never wanted to see you hurt."

Secret closed her eyes, her nostrils flaring. The information Andrea relayed slipped into her head like the blade of a knife. She had been rendered speechless.

"I don't know who to trust anymore," Secret rasped right before she walked out of the restaurant.

A week had passed since the dustup with Andrea, and it had been a month since David had served the papers on Secret. Secret had pulled herself together, finally, and was trying her best to make life normal for herself and her kids. Secret decided to do some food shopping and then a little retail therapy for herself and the kids. Shopping had always made Secret feel better in the past, especially when all of the money was David's, like now. They hadn't separated their accounts yet or even had discussions about what type of alimony and child support she would receive. Secret knew she had to find a good attorney because with David's money, he would more than likely hire the best of the best to fight her in court.

Secret pulled into the supermarket parking lot and unloaded her kids. She put them into the shopping cart and pushed them into the store. As soon as she walked into the store, she noticed her pastor's wife. Secret tried to avert her eyes and act like she didn't see the fat hypocrite, but there was no use in trying. There was only one set of doors in and out, and Secret had practically run dead into her. *Shit.* She hadn't been to church in a while and certainly did not feel like explaining why to the phony-ass first lady. Secret plastered a fake smile to her face and proceeded farther into the store.

"Secret? Secret Johnson? Is that you and those beautiful little angels?" First Lady Alma Lucian sang out. As usual, her face was painted with so much makeup she resembled a clown, and although it was a weekday, she was dressed like she was going to church. The woman wore so much perfume Secret could smell it coming off of her even from a distance.

Secret took a deep breath and kept on smiling so hard her cheekbones ached. "Hey, Mrs. Lucian. How are you?" Secret replied, singing just as phony as the pastor's wife had.

"Oh, little ol' me? I am just fine. God knows it, too. Secret, what is going on? I haven't seen you in service in a month of Sundays. And then I turn around two weeks in a row and see David, but instead of you and those angels being his escorts, I notice some other woman who looks young enough to be his daughter with him just as proud as a peacock with all her cleavage showing up just like a heathen," Mrs. Lucia said, her words coming out rapid-fire like she had been dying to tell someone's dirty secrets.

The information threatened to make Secret's knees buckle. But she smiled. *That disrespectful motherfucker,* Secret screamed inside her head. It was bad enough she was already ashamed of her impending divorce, but now her husband was setting out to publicly humiliate her.

In Secret's opinion, it was totally unnecessary for David to take his mistress to their church when Secret could barely get him to attend with her and the kids. Secret felt her heart sink into her stomach as Mrs. Lucian kept on going on and on about how she was surprised to see him with such a beautiful and young woman. And how the woman even reminded Mrs. Lucian of Secret when she was younger and before the kids.

Secret felt like her bowels were going to release right there in the store at the first lady's feet. Swallowing the lump in her throat, Secret gripped the shopping cart rail tightly. She knew she had to play it off and pull it together. There was no way she'd let David win again by showing that she was caught off guard by Mrs. Lucian's revelations.

"Oh, didn't you know? I filed for divorce months ago. So David is free to have whomever he wants, and frankly, it's probably better for both of us. See, David and I just grew apart. David had become so cruel to me and the children. You wouldn't even believe he was the same man. I know Pastor Lucian teaches against divorce, but sometimes you have to know when to say when," Secret lied, trying hard to fight back the tears burning at the backs of her eye sockets.

"Oh, I didn't know," Mrs. Lucian said, placing her hand up against her chest like what she was hearing was about to give her a heart attack. "Well, I hope it all works out for you and those little angels," she continued, flashing a fake smile.

"I'm fine. We're fine. Just fine," Secret said, returning an even faker smile again. The kids started squirming in the cart. That was Secret's signal to get the fuck away from the lady. Besides, her stink-ass perfume was making Secret gag.

"Well, it was nice seeing you. Let me go. As you can see, the natives are getting restless," Secret said, nodding toward her kids. Secret's insides were on fire, and she wished she were a genie who could blink herself right out of the store.

"Take care of those angels now," Mrs. Lucian bellowed.

Secret nodded and pushed her cart away. Secret rushed four aisles down into the cereal aisle. It was the one with the least people in it. Once she felt the coast was clear, she stopped the cart and let her tears finally run down her face. A few passersby coming through the aisle looked at her strangely. A few looked like they wanted to ask if she was all right, but none dared to say anything to her.

Secret cried for a few minutes. She still could not believe the audacity of David to take his new eye candy to their church, flaunting her in front of all their friends. That church was where David and Secret had taken their vows, where they had worshipped as a couple and as a family. It was where Secret had drawn her strength when everything was on her while David leisurely went about his business at school. With one blow after another, Secret just didn't know how much more she could take. One thing Secret knew for sure: she could never step foot back in that church again.

Finally, after pulling herself together, Secret wiped her face and smiled at her kids. They had gotten so used to seeing her cry that it didn't even alarm them anymore. Secret walked through the aisles and started picking up things for the house. She was in such a routine and habit with what she purchased that each time she touched something, David was the first thing that came to her mind. Pleasing David was always paramount for Secret in everything she did, even food shopping. She was used to purchasing foods that he liked, like that nasty-ass glu-ten-free bread. Secret always hated that shit, but it was the only kind she purchased because David liked it. It was the same for everything she used to buy. If she ever purchased something he didn't eat, David would complain incessantly, so Secret had just learned to condition herself to eat the things that he liked. This time, with a devilish feeling coming over her, Secret picked up white bread instead of gluten-free kind. After that, Secret had to catch herself over and over again picking up things David preferred over what she actually liked. She made herself buy all of the things that she missed over the years just because David hadn't liked them. This time her shopping cart was filled with things Secret liked.

When she made it to the counter to pay for her groceries, the kids started whining and crying for the candy that was lined up at the side of the register. Feeling emotionally and physically drained, Secret didn't have it in her to argue with them or to hear their crying. Instead, she just allowed them to pick up whatever they wanted. DJ and Bella chose all types of chocolate bars, gum, and bags of chips. Secret couldn't care less. Normally she didn't let them eat junk food, but today whatever would keep them quiet was what Secret was going with. She just wanted to go back home, climb into her bed with her sedatives, and sleep away her pain.

Secret loaded all of her items onto the register's conveyor belt and watched as the cashier scanned her food. Secret looked around, hoping she wouldn't see anyone else who knew her and David. She couldn't take any more news about David flaunting his woman around town.

When all of the items were finished being scanned, Secret started placing her bags in the cart as she waited for the girl to give her a total.

"$140.25," the cashier said dryly.

Secret dug into her pocketbook and handed the girl her debit card.

"Debit or credit?" the cashier asked.

"Either or, it doesn't matter," Secret answered as she reached over to make DJ sit down in the cart before he fell out. Secret was distracted, so she didn't notice that the girl had swiped her card several times.

"Do you have another card? This one is not working," the cashier told Secret.

Secret crinkled her face in confusion and looked at the girl like she was crazy. "What do you mean, not working? That is a debit card connected to my bank account. It can't be declined," Secret replied, chuckling sarcastically and nervously at the same time. She knew there was money in the bank. David made a decent salary so there was no way their account could be so low or empty that her card would be declined.

"It's saying declined," the girl replied, annoyed.

"Swipe it again then," Secret growled, urgency lacing her words. She felt flushed as the heat of embarrassment began to rise from someplace deep, up her neck, and across her face.

"Miss, I have swiped it at least six times. It is denied," the girl snapped, putting emphasis on "denied."

There were people grumbling in line behind Secret. The kids had already bitten holes into the candy wrappers, trying to open the candy. DJ had even gotten a piece through one of his little teeth holes and started eating it, which meant Secret had no choice but to pay for it. Her heart started racing, and sweat dripped down her back as she dug into her bag, trying to scrape up enough cash to at least pay for the candy. Secret didn't have credit cards or any other bank cards. David had given her one card and one card only: the debit card associated with their joint account. This had never happened to Secret in her life. Even when she considered herself dead broke, she had always known her spending limits.

"I don't know what could've happened. I have money in my account," Secret croaked nervously as she handed the girl a bunch of change she had dug up out of her purse. The cashier looked at her like she was crazy. "That is for the candy. I don't have enough for the groceries," Secret said on the brink of tears. Embarrassed and wanting to melt away, Secret frantically took the bags out of the shopping cart and set them on the floor. People behind her mumbled and made mean comments.

When she was finished, Secret pushed her shopping cart out of the store at top speed. She raced over to her car, loaded the kids into their car seats, and got in. Flustered, Secret pulled out her debit card and examined it. On the back, she located a 1-800 number for the bank's customer service line, and she dialed it.

Secret pressed through the automated system and waited for a representative. When one was finally on the line, Secret began screaming at the woman about how the bank had wrongfully denied her charges. Secret wouldn't let the woman get a word in edgewise. When the woman finally got Secret to calm down, she said something that Secret thought would send her over the edge.

"Mrs. Johnson, your joint account owner has emptied this account and closed it. That is the reason you were unable to make a purchase today," the customer service representative said in the light, airy voice they all used when trying to keep calm with irate customers. The words seemed to explode inside of Secret's ears like small bombs.

"What? I don't under . . . understand. Wouldn't we both ha . . . have to agree to close it?" Secret cried into the phone in total disbelief.

"No, ma'am, I'm afraid not. When the account was opened, a Mr. David Johnson added himself as the sole

signature authority, and you were just an additional
cardholder. That means he had all the power over the
account, and all you had authority to do was purchase
with the card you were issued and make deposits. That
is the way Mr. Johnson set up the account," the woman
said empathetically. She could hear in Secret's voice that
things weren't going so well.

"Thank you," Secret replied, almost whispering, and
she hung up. "Why, God? What did I do to deserve this?"
Secret sobbed. She realized then that David was playing
for keeps. He had left her with nothing, literally.

Chapter 6

Secret rushed into her house and slammed the door behind her. She let the kids run around, and she raced around the living room. Sweating like she'd run a race, she stormed into her kitchen. Heart hammering, she snatched up the neglected pile of mail that had amassed since David had left. Breathing through her mouth, Secret shuffled the deck of letters. As she scanned each one, weak, she flopped down into one of her metal-back kitchen chairs.

"'Late payment notice.' 'Final notice.' 'Overdraft notice,'" Secret read off one by one. "No!" she screamed, sending the letters sailing all over the kitchen table and floor.

"How could you leave me fucked up like this? You said you would take care of me. What am I supposed to do now? You promised I would never have to worry." Secret cried out into the air as if David were standing right in front of her.

David had told her more than once he would take care of her. After he'd gotten into business school, graduated, and landed a good job, David had practically forbidden Secret from working. He gave her access to some of his accounts. Secret had never been able to stash money. It seemed to be the perfect situation. After all, everyone envied her life as the kept wife.

With her hands pulling at the hair on either side of her head, Secret spun around in circles. Her chest heaved as she pictured herself getting evicted from her home. There was no telling what David was capable of now.

"Agh!" Secret cried out again, flailing her arms, this time sending all of the beautiful glass canisters on the counter crashing to the shiny marble-tile floors. Each hand-painted glass container shattered into fine, misshapen shards, just like her life. Secret tore her kitchen apart until she was totally exhausted.

Secret jumped up with her body covered in sweat. She looked around for David, but all she saw were her kids. Secret could swear she could smell David in the room. But he wasn't there, and she soon realized he hadn't been there. She flopped back down when she realized she had been dreaming about him. David hadn't really come running back to her.

She realized she'd been woken up by knocking. Secret was so drugged up off sedatives and painkillers she hadn't even realized that Andrea was pounding on her door, ringing her bell incessantly, and blowing up her cell phone. When she finally came around, Secret looked over at her two kids, who were sprawled out on her bed sleeping soundly as well. She had given both of them a double dose of children's Benadryl to put them to sleep.

Secret reached over on her nightstand and retrieved her cell phone. She picked up the line after she noticed the screen flashing Andrea's name. Secret started not to answer, but she'd gotten over being mad at her cousin. She realized Andrea was only trying to protect her feelings by keeping that secret from her. Her cousin had never betrayed her in life, and Secret knew she wasn't going to start now. Andrea was the only person Secret had in her corner right now.

"Hello," she rasped into the phone. She felt like shit and really didn't want to be bothered, but she also knew Andrea wouldn't give up trying to get in the house.

"Secret! What the hell? You had me so worried about you and the kids! Please open the door. I'm out front, and I left my key at home! I know you're upset, but I have to see you!" Andrea gasped.

Secret closed her swollen, red-rimmed eyes. She was in no mood for company, but she knew if she didn't open up the door, Andrea would not leave. Secret felt a deep sense of disappointment that her dream that David had come back hadn't turned out to be true.

As she sat up in bed, she immediately felt severe, painful pounding in her head. She felt like she had the worst hangover ever, and she didn't even drink. She dragged herself out of bed and took the stairs one by one. Feeling slightly dizzy, Secret pulled back her front door, cringing at the sunlight she let in with her cousin.

Andrea rushed inside and grabbed Secret in a tight embrace. Andrea's shoulders slumped in relief when she saw that Secret was alive and well. She knew that Secret had had more than one suicidal incident. Sometimes Secret was impulsive, and Andrea knew those impulses could turn dangerous.

"Don't you ever fucking scare me like that again!" Andrea huffed.

"What were you scared of?" Secret grumbled. "Shit, if I were going to off myself, I would've done it by now."

Andrea didn't answer, because that was exactly what she had been thinking. Secret didn't return her cousin's embrace. Instead, she let her arms hang limply while Andrea squeezed her tight.

"Like I said, don't fucking scare me like that again!" Andrea said loudly.

"Shhh, the kids are still sleeping," Secret whispered, her voice sounding like she had a frog lodged in her throat.

"I was so scared. Shit, the last time I saw you I swore you was going to drive off a cliff or some shit. You better always let me know where you are. Anyway, I came by with some information. Look, I've called around to a few of my divorced friends. I got the names of two attorneys who are supposed to be the best in the city," Andrea said, digging into her purse to retrieve business cards.

Secret dragged her feet into her living room and flopped down on her love seat. She stared at her cousin blankly. The last thing she wanted to discuss was divorce lawyers. She wished Andrea had come there to give her advice on how to get her man back instead.

"Secret, are you listening? C'mon, you got to pull yourself together and call one of these attorneys. It's the only way you will get what you deserve for all the years you put in. You didn't fucking practically take care of his ass for him to turn around and leave you with nothing at all," Andrea told Secret.

She was right, but Secret couldn't listen to reason right now. "Andrea, I don't even have money to feed my kids. He took all of the money out of our joint account. The mortgage on this house is due. I just . . . I don't even have money to sustain us, much less pay some expensive-ass divorce attorney to fight for some shit that ain't mine to begin with," Secret confessed, tears brimming her eyes. She steeled herself and took a deep breath. She knew Andrea would probably offer her money, which would just make her weepy and teary-eyed yet again. After the incident in the supermarket, Secret told herself that she would not let any more tears fall unless they were tears of joy.

"You can't be serious," Andrea responded. "This bastard wants to play dirty I guess. Secret, I'm telling you in New York a man can't just walk away from his wife and take everything. I will be your witness in court. You gave up everything for your marriage. You depended on him solely for support. I'm sorry, but that bastard is going to have to fucking pay you. And he will have to take care of these children he made and just abandoned," Andrea spat.

Secret shook her head back and forth. She didn't know if she had any fight left in her.

"First things first, we need to go to the bank and find out exactly what's going on," Andrea said. "Get dressed. We've got work to do."

Secret shook her legs as she kept her eyes trained on the silver-haired old man on the other side of the desk. His furrowed brows, pinched mouth, and rapid tapping on the computer keys unnerved her. Something wasn't right, that much she could sense. With each seemingly frantic peck, the old man's facial expression grew graver.

Secret had never been in the corporate office suites of any bank. She knew this was where exclusive, high-balance clients conducted their banking. When she and Andrea entered the bank demanding an explanation for her declined cards, she was immediately referred to the bank's manager, who escalated her "case" up to corporate. Secret knew shit wasn't right.

Now, with his computer screen turned so Secret and Andrea couldn't see it, and his constant, fast finger movements on the keyboard, this man was probably about to tell her some shit she didn't want to hear.

"Let me just try one more thing," the old man said, popping up out of his chair. "I'll be right back, Mrs. Johnson."

Secret looked down at her watch. She sucked her teeth in disgust. They had already been there for forty minutes. *How long does it take to find out what this bastard did to lock me out?* She was having her second-worst day of the past month, second only to David's betrayal.

The old man returned with a much younger man. The tall, pimple-faced, raven-haired man stretched his hand out toward Secret and identified himself as Mr. Bland, vice president of the branch. To her, he looked more like Mr. Bland, vice president of the student council.

"Mrs. Johnson, I'm very sorry, but all of Mr. Johnson's regular and investment accounts with us have been closed and moved. We have no way of knowing why these accounts were moved. At Mr. Johnson's request, these accounts were wired out to other institutions, and because he removed your rights, we cannot give you any more information. We cannot open any type of investigations because you no longer have any rights to the information. There's not much else I can tell you," Mr. Bland said, his protruding Adam's apple distracting Secret's thoughts.

Secret closed her eyes for a few seconds, trying to keep her composure. "I don't understand. My husband had hundreds of thousands of dollars in both of our names. How can I just be removed without any notice or notification? How did you all know it wasn't all my money you let him run away with?" Secret said as calmly as her raging brain allowed. Andrea touched her arm, noticing that her cousin was on the verge of going off.

How am I supposed to live now? I gave up everything to be with him. He said he'd take care of me. Oh, my God! Secret's stomach and mind did somersaults. "What recourse do I have?" she asked, desperation underlying her words.

Mr. Bland looked at her with sympathy. "I don't really know," Mr. Bland said.

"Thank you for fucking nothing," she rasped. Secret swallowed hard, stood up as calmly as she could on her quaking legs, and allowed the young VP to escort her and Andrea out of the bank, but not before she threatened to go public with what the bank had done by letting her husband take everything from her. It had to be illegal. Judging by the time it had taken the bank personnel to tell her something as simple as David had wired all of their money out of her reach, Secret figured out that it had all been a distraction to buy time. She knew phone calls had probably been placed and that, more than likely, David would be waiting for her next move.

Chapter 7

Secret looked at herself in the mirror one last time. She looked better than she had in months. Andrea had paid for her to see two specialists who consulted about fixing her botched plastic surgeries. It was the one thing that had pulled Secret out of the deep depression she'd fallen into. Every time she looked at her scarred body she was reminded of just how much she'd sacrificed for David. Secret cringed every time she thought about waking up in the Dominican Republic in so much pain they had put a rag between her teeth to keep her screams down. She remembered touching her breasts and feeling right away that something wasn't right. She remembered the first time she looked at her stomach, which Dr. Mungia had promised to make look amazing, and seeing that he'd left a long, ugly scar across it. Secret felt weak every time she turned around in the mirror and saw the gross protrusion behind her that was supposed to be her new ass. Admittedly, sometimes she didn't blame David for being disgusted by her freakish body, but she expected his loyalty through sickness and health. Especially because she'd been so loyal to him. David knew damn well that the surgery was all for him.

Just like Secret had anticipated, Andrea had paid for Secret's hair and new clothes. They weren't the high-priced designer threads and shoes Secret was used to when she lived off of David's money, but they would serve their purpose for her court appearance. Andrea had also fronted Secret the money for her new divorce attorney.

"You damn good, cousin. I hired a sitter to keep the kids, and I'm coming with you to court. Ew, I'm telling you, I can't wait to look this bitch-ass nigga in his eyes and let him know that I know the real David Johnson," Andrea said supportively, coming up behind Secret.

Secret turned from the mirror and looked at her cousin. She was so grateful to Andrea for being there for her, even after she had cursed her out at the restaurant and made a damn scene. Secret knew that without Andrea, she would've probably fallen apart even worse than she had already. Secret looked at Andrea directly in the eyes. With a stone expression on her face, she spoke to her cousin.

"Drea, if something happens to me, I want you to be the one to take care of DJ and Bella," Secret said solemnly, not even batting an eye. "Don't let David raise them to be selfish and disgusting like him. I always wanted them to have better than I had. Make sure Bella knows that self-love is the best love, too. Don't let her be weak like me." Secret couldn't hold back the tears. Speaking about her children always did that to her. She loved them more than life itself.

"Bitch! Where you think you going to, criminal court to be sentenced to death?" Andrea joked, trying to lighten the mood. The tension and the mood in the room were heavy and thick with sadness. "You're going to divorce court to take that stupid, bitch-ass nigga for everything he is worth. Now stop talking all crazy and shit before I have you committed," Andrea laughed. "You're going to be around until those kids are old and gray. Remember, we have that whole *Thelma & Louise* shit planned for when we turn fifty, so your ass need to be around." Andrea had always been good at lightening up the mood.

Secret parted a fake smile. "I mean it though. I'd rather they be dead than to ever be with him," Secret finished, her tone serious.

"Girl, you talking mess. You're going to be around until we are both wearing Depends and dancing at Bella's wedding!" Andrea laughed. "Now stop all the dumb doom-and-gloom talking. I won't have any of that shit." Andrea grabbed Secret by the hand and walked her out of the bedroom.

The drive to court was solemn. Andrea and Secret didn't say much, just a few comments here and there about nothing significant. Neither of them dared to bring up the topic of the divorce or David. Secret was clearly preoccupied with what was to come. She felt huge birds flitting around in her stomach, forget having butterflies.

"You get out and get checked in. I'll go find parking," Andrea said when they pulled up to the courthouse building. Secret grabbed her purse and went to get out of the car. Andrea stopped her for a minute. "Just remember—"Andrea started.

"I know, I know. I'll have my day in court," Secret interrupted, finishing her cousin's sentence. They both forced a smile. Secret chanted the words in her head so that she could make herself believe it also. She knew David had a lot of powerful people in his corner. This would be a fight to the finish, one that Secret had never prepared for in her life. She just prayed she would make it through it with her mind intact.

When Secret finally walked into the small courtroom, she felt cold all over. Andrea had made it upstairs just as they were called into the courtroom. She grabbed Secret's hand and whispered a few words of encouragement to Secret. Secret nodded and walked slowly toward the end of the table her attorney sat at. Andrea had been gracious enough to retain the top divorce attorney for Secret. It was a debt Secret swore over and over that she would pay back, although her cousin had told her to stop talking about the money each time Secret brought it up.

Of course, David sat smugly next to his attorney, and his girlfriend was next to him on his other side at the opposite end of the table from Secret's attorney. Seeing the young woman made Secret stumble a bit as she walked. *This bastard has the fucking nerve to have this bitch here?* Secret bit into her lip in an effort to control her emotions. It was extremely hard to look at the man she still loved and comprehend that he had done this to her.

The family court judge said the perfunctory spiel about the parties being present in the matter of Johnson vs. Johnson, blah, blah, blah. Secret was only half listening to whatever the judge was talking about. Her focus was on David's eye-candy bitch, who Secret felt was totally out of place being at the proceedings. She was beautiful though. She was model-like in all the ways that Secret used to be. So Secret had actually risked her life having plastic surgery to look like that, and now she was left in worse condition than before. All for David. Secret wondered how fast David would leave his new bitch when age and time started to take her beauty away too.

Secret couldn't help but cut her eyes at David and his woman. Leaning in and whispering to her attorney, Secret expressed her displeasure at the woman's presence at the divorce proceedings. Secret's attorney totally agreed that the woman being there was completely inappropriate. Finally, Secret's lawyer stood up and asked the judge to have David's girlfriend removed from the courtroom, as she was party to adultery and direct party to the demise of the marriage. Secret felt deflated inside and kind of defeated when the judge disagreed and allowed David's bitch to stay. Secret felt infuriated all over again when David kissed his girlfriend passionately on the lips as a great big "fuck you" toward Secret. Andrea grumbled all kinds of things under her breath. What a bitch this judge was.

The divorce proceedings seemed to go on for hours. Secret's head pounded with all the back and forth. Secret's lawyer would ask for something, and David's lawyer would strike it down. David's lawyer would ask to be absolved of giving Secret something, and Secret's lawyer would argue its necessity. Secret and her attorney tried to argue to the judge that she had given up working and attending school for the sake of her marriage and now she was left with nothing. David's attorney countered by arguing that after David was established at the firm, Secret had numerous opportunities to return to work prior to the birth of their children, but she had chosen to be a housewife. Secret's lawyer argued that Secret had very little education after high school, aside from a few college credits, and no real skills, which made it nearly impossible for her to find gainful employment that would benefit them as a family. Basically, he was saying that Secret wouldn't find a job paying enough to cover child-care expenses and that she would've been working just to go back to work with no financial or other benefits. The arguments flew back and forth between the lawyers at the behest of their clients, and so did the requests and denials for alimony, child support, and full custody of the children.

Secret was on her feet when she heard that David was asking for custody of her kids. "He doesn't care about them! He hasn't visited them since he left us! He left us with no money to eat! They barely know him aside from just seeing him and calling him Daddy! He doesn't know what they eat, their favorites toys or shows, or even how to put them to sleep at night!" Secret yelled out. She had had enough of David's bullshit. She had heard enough from her soon-to-be ex. There was no way she was going to sit and be quiet while David and his bitch tried to take her kids from her so they could go play house. No fucking way!

The judge ordered Secret to sit down and refrain from those types of outbursts. If Secret didn't know any better, she would've sworn that the judge had a thing for David. She looked at him with googly eyes a few times, and Secret caught her.

With six hours of back and forth and still no fully agreeable terms, the judge finally granted a temporary order of alimony and child support to Secret. At first, Secret felt a sense of relief when she heard she would be getting some financial help from David, but her relief was short-lived. When Secret heard the judge enter the amount of $1,200 a month, she started screaming again. What could she possibly do with that little bit of money when the house mortgage was over $2,000? How could she feed herself and the kids?

"He makes well over two hundred thousand dollars a year! I can't even pay the mortgage on the house with that! I can't feed my kids! He fucking emptied the bank account and took everything! That's how much of a man he is," Secret screeched, shooting daggers at David with her eyes.

The judge gave Secret one last warning about her lack of control and her loud screaming outbursts. Before she knew it the proceedings were put on hold. The hearing was adjourned for eight weeks. That meant two months of mortgage that Secret had no clue how she'd pay with the bullshit amount of money the judge had ordered David give her. David was smiling and shaking his attorney's hand like he'd just won a big lawsuit settlement. His girlfriend was smiling and holding on to him like she'd just won a grand prize.

Secret literally felt nauseous. David made Secret sick to her stomach now. Even if he ever wanted her again after this, Secret didn't think she could ever accept him back.

Before Andrea could hold her back, Secret stormed over to where David stood milling about and laughing with his attorney and his woman.

"David! You piece of shit. I can't fucking believe you! I knew you could be a low, selfish, self-serving bastard, but I never thought you'd do this to me and the kids!" Secret screamed. With that, she charged into him like a bull-dozer.

David turned toward her, wearing a look of shock that quickly dissipated and turned into disgust. Before he could react, Secret was up on him, and she slapped his face so hard his head snapped left to right. She didn't waste any time grabbing David's little eye candy. Secret wound her hand in the girl's hair so fast no one could do anything about it.

"Mrs. Johnson, I will have you arrested if you come near my client again!" David's lawyer growled, grabbing Secret by the arm to restrain her. Andrea wedged between David's attorney and Secret and tried in vain to get Secret to loosen her grasp on the screaming girlfriend. Secret wasn't deterred in the least. Secret's attorney got into the mix. He rushed over to the scene to break it up too.

"Mrs. Johnson, you can't afford this type of display. They will surely remove your children for this," her attorney warned. Those were the words that made Secret let go of her new nemesis.

"You are such a fucking man, David Johnson, a real man. You would take food out of the mouths of your children all for some high-class ho bitch! You will rot in hell for this shit, David. I will see to it. You will never live a good life doing this to us! Your life was committed to hell the day you betrayed me!" Secret screamed as her lawyer and Andrea dragged her out of the courtroom.

Chapter 8

Secret held the first alimony/child support check in her hand as she sat in front of the bank. She felt like a total idiot. What a fool she'd been. She had not opened an account for herself in years. In fact, it had been since she was dating David, to be exact. How could she be so stupid? She didn't even know exactly what she needed to open the account. She had literally let her husband run every aspect of her life like she was a child. He had convinced her early on to let him open a joint account, which he told her would be the easiest way for the both of them to "share" their money, although at the time all of the money going into the account came from her.

Secret and David had combined their separate accounts, his $20 with her $5,000 at the time. Secret had always been good at saving her own money since she was a child. She had worked at several different fast food restaurants throughout high school, and when the modeling started, money was rolling in faster than she could save it at the time. Instead of buying a bunch of bullshit with her money like her model friends did, Secret saved half of everything back then. That was how she was able to get an apartment and move out on her own. When she met David, she had money in the bank, and he barely had any.

Secret's hand shook fiercely, and she gnawed the skin off of her bottom lip as she sat with a measly $1,200 check in her hand when she had over $4,000 in bills associated with the house alone. Secret didn't know how the judge, a female, could've ever allowed something like that when clearly David was bringing home nearly $15,000 a month with his salary. The system was set up for women to fail and for men to get ahead.

After she opened a new checking account with the money David had sent, Secret drove out of the bank parking lot, but instead of heading to Andrea's to pick up the kids, she headed in the opposite direction. As she drove, Secret didn't know what it was that was urging her forward, but she drove until she was finally in front of David's new building. She had a need right then to see him. To see his bitch. Secret didn't know if it was a need to see him with the woman again or a need to confront him. She really didn't understand this overwhelming urge to be at the building when she knew damn well they had an order of protection against her. Secret couldn't help herself, and although her mind told her to go straight home, her heart told her no.

Secret attempted to get into the parking lot but realized she needed a swipe passkey. "That's all right. I'll wait right here," Secret whispered to herself. She had taken Andrea's Porsche truck and left her car with Andrea because it had the kids' car seats already in it. Secret tapped on the steering wheel as she waited. Not really sure what she was waiting for, Secret still refused to move. She waited and waited some more. Secret had to keep talking herself into being there.

Finally, Secret looked down at her watch and realized she had been waiting for over an hour. All she wanted was a glimpse of him, or maybe it was the woman whom Secret wanted to see again. Secret still couldn't be sure why she was there, yet she continued to wait. It was obsessive, she had to admit that to herself, but still, she waited and waited.

After another hour Secret sat up in her seat when she noticed the S550 swing out of the building's parking garage. Secret's heart jerked in her chest as she read the plate. "Lady Luck." Secret recognized the car and plates that had been parked at David's job.

That's the bitch right there! Secret screamed inside of her head. Secret put Andrea's truck in drive and slowly pulled out behind the high-end Benz. With her mouth as dry as the desert and her heart hammering against her sternum, Secret followed David's girlfriend.

"Fuck you, Lady Luck. Your ass ain't lucky, bitch," Secret said through gritted teeth as she followed the woman.

With every turn, every stop, and every block, Secret didn't lose sight of her. Secret didn't even notice that she had been biting her lip until the metallic taste of blood filled her mouth. The hurt she felt was palpable. Secret felt like David had taken her heart out and run over it with a tractor trailer. She was completely devastated, and no matter what she did, she couldn't pull out of it. Secret felt like she had nothing to live for anymore.

Finally, the woman who Secret blamed for her failed marriage pulled up to a storefront. Lucky Cakes, the sign above the store read. From the looks of it, it was an upscale cake and cupcake bakery. Secret had even passed there once or twice before while driving to Andrea's house.

Secret stopped her car far enough away not to be noticed, but where she could still see Lady Luck get out of her car. David's girlfriend sauntered up to the store's gates and fished around in her bag. After a few moments, she pulled out a set of keys. Secret watched carefully as the woman unlocked the big silver padlocks and pulled the front gate up to reveal a huge tinted and etched glass window. That was when Secret noticed the etching on the glass. It read, "Lucky and David's Love Cake." Secret squinted to see inside of the store. It was beautifully decorated with pastel and silver walls, and from what Secret could see there were rows of sample cakes and cupcakes all beautifully handmade and what looked to be expensive artwork hanging on the walls.

Secret felt sick again. She wanted to throw up. She was immediately jealous of the woman and angrier at David than before. David had made her give up her dreams of doing anything, but he was obviously supporting the business of another woman. Secret was struggling to make ends meet, and David had an executive's salary, and his girlfriend was a business owner who drove an S550 Benz and carried a different high-end designer purse every time Secret had seen her. Secret felt stupid and less than. She felt like the scum of the earth in comparison to David's new woman now. Secret reasoned that that was just what David must've thought of her in comparison to his new beautiful, successful woman. Secret didn't know what had come over her, but she had a need to see this woman again, to speak to her face-to-face, woman to woman. Their last meeting didn't count. Secret had been too violent to get her point across. She had made a fool of herself for sure. David's new girlfriend probably looked and thought of Secret as a dirty bum bitch at this point.

Suddenly, Secret was like a woman possessed again. This time, however, she willed herself to keep her hands to herself. Secret put the car in park and removed the key from the ignition. Some unknown force was moving her, and she was following its lead. Secret grabbed her purse and rushed up the block to the bakery. She tugged on the grand brass door handles and stepped inside. The door chimes made a tingling sound that reminded Secret of a fairy waving a magic wand.

"I'll be right there!" David's girlfriend sang out from somewhere in the back of the store. Secret wasn't able to see her, and she knew for sure the woman hadn't seen who it was yet. Secret's chest heaved, and she felt light-headed as she waited. Her nerves were standing on end, and her toes were balled into knots inside her shoes. She wanted to rehearse what to say to the woman, but nothing came to her blank, racing mind. Although Secret wanted to turn and run back out of the store, she was seemingly rooted to the floor. She needed to be there. She had to do this right now. Secret didn't realize how dazed she looked standing in the middle of the floor, her mouth partially open like someone who wasn't all there mentally.

"Can I help . . ." David's girlfriend started, but her words went tumbling back down her throat like oversized marbles when she saw Secret standing there.

The woman's face paled, and she began backing up with her hands out in front of her in surrender, quickly remembering the ass whooping Secret put on her the last two times they met. She went to scramble for her cell phone to call the police.

"I'm not going to do anything to you," Secret managed to say, and she meant it. She wasn't there for that today. The words and questions suddenly came rushing to her tongue. "What's your name?"

"I'm Lucky," the woman answered tentatively.

"I guess you know my name," Secret said.

Lucky shook her head in the affirmative.

"I guess you know a lot about me. That's what men do, right? They tell their mistress all sorts of things about their wives to paint their wives as the problem? Is that what David did?"

Lucky stood in silence like she didn't know how to ans-wer the question. Secret didn't really need her to answer though. She already knew the answer.

"Lucky, no matter what David tried to tell you, this was a total slap in my face," Secret said. She could feel a ball of grief forming in her throat. "I . . . I just want to know, how can you sleep at night with a clear conscience? David is my husband. He is a father. He was our everything. We are married, and we've been together for years, not months or weeks, years. As a woman, how would you feel if you were in my place? If I just came out of nowhere and snatched your entire life away like a thief in the night? Knowing your marriage was ending because of another woman, knowing your kids would be left without their father because of another woman?" Secret said pointedly.

Lucky was struck silent.

"I just want to know, how and why?" Secret's voice rose and fell like waves crashing against rocks. Lucky's eyes were as big as saucers, and she didn't say anything, but somewhere inside Secret could see sympathy, or maybe it was pity. She couldn't be sure.

"Don't you know breaking up something that God put together is a sin? Haven't you ever heard that what goes around comes around? Do you have any morals or scruples? I mean you've been to church, our church to be exact. Haven't you learned anything? Why couldn't you find a man of your own?" Secret said, her voice cracking in places as she fought mightily not to break down and cry. Her body shook all over.

Lucky shifted her weight from one foot to the other and sighed loudly. "Look, Secret. I'm sorry about every-thing that has happened to you, but I'm just as much a victim as you are. I didn't know Davie was married until the day you showed up at the office," the woman said almost apologetically. "So I was in the dark just like you were. But now I can't help who I love and who loves me. People do fall out of love. Maybe that's what happened. Maybe he just fell out of love with you."

"Davie? Really?" Secret repeated. "Did Davie tell you that it was my fucking blood, sweat, and tears that helped him get where he is while he went to school and did absolutely nothing? Did Davie tell you that I sacrificed my entire college career and sense of self just so he could be a success, only to have him turn around and pick up somebody like you who has no regard for the sanctity of marriage or our kids? No! I bet you he didn't tell you any of that while he was flaunting you at his big business dinners and at our fucking church, did he? So don't fucking talk to me about falling out of love when fucking loyalty should count for something," Secret growled, her voice rising ten octaves.

"I'm sorry about all of this, but he lied to us both. We met after his company did the marketing plans for my business. He never said he was married. I mean where were you when he was taking me on all of the trips, buying me all of the expensive gifts? I mean he would spend a week at a time with me. Why would I have believed that he was married? Didn't you ever question your own husband? I'm sorry, but I can't help who I fell in love with," Lucky said, making sure she kept a safe distance between herself and Secret. "He is with me now, and I am willing to be a part of the kids' lives if that makes you feel any better," she continued.

That was the wrong thing to say to Secret after questioning her common sense when it came to David. Secret felt like the woman had just spit in her face. Secret knew that Lucky was right. Secret had been so busy trying not to rock the boat that she let David tip the fucking boat over and cheat on her. The truth definitely hurt.

Secret started advancing toward the woman like a lion toward its prey. With her finger pointed toward her, Secret squinted her eyes into dashes and spoke through clenched teeth.

"You may have won the man with your hair extensions and your fake tits, but I'm fucking warning you, if you ever come around my kids for any reason, trust me, you will regret it. I would die before I let you and your Davie play house with my fucking kids," Secret said through gritted teeth, pointing her finger so close to Lucky's face she almost fell backward trying to avoid getting poked in the eye.

"Now you tell your Davie that Secret said that shit. Also, remember you reap what the fuck you sow, and I'll tell you, as soon as I gained ten pounds and got one little laugh line and my tits didn't sit up like two balloons, David's eyes were roving to bitches like you. Good fucking luck keeping him. I got the scars to show that nothing can keep that bastard happy. Nothing," Secret said, turning and storming out of the store. She could hear Lucky behind her, scrambling for her telephone.

Call your Davie and tell him. Tell him he will regret the day he left me, Secret thought as she headed back to Andrea's car. "Bitch better nail his dick to the wall or else she'll always be chasing that shit," Secret mumbled under her breath.

Chapter 9

Secret hadn't been sleeping at all. She was up all night, and only painkillers and sedatives could put her to sleep. Even then it would be for one or two hours. Secret kept replaying her interaction at the bakery with Lucky. Secret had started to believe that maybe it was all her fault for being such a passive wife. Secret had beaten herself up all the way to Andrea's house and all the way home. That evening, she had taken her sedatives, but they only put her to sleep for a few short spurts at a time, and she'd jump up in a cold sweat every couple of hours.

Secret kept obsessing about the situation: what she did wrong, what she could've done better, what she shouldn't have done, or what she should have done. The plastic surgery was bothering her the most. Not only had she botched her body, but she had lost her husband in the end anyway. She could never meet a man with her body in the condition it was. It was literally driving her crazy. To top it all off, she had to admit to herself that she missed David and the security of having him around. Even when he would travel for weeks at a time, Secret knew he would be back, so she never worried, and she still felt secure. Secret hadn't felt this lost and lonely since her childhood. Secret had always seen David as her savior from her past realities, and she also saw herself as just as much a savior to him from his past.

Secret tossed and turned thinking about how fast things had spiraled downhill in her marriage. Secret was also obsessing about her financial situation. The mortgage was due, and there were still four weeks until the next court date where she would find out if the judge was going to increase the alimony and child support payments.

Frustrated and restless, Secret threw back her bed covers and got out of bed. She looked in on her kids several times between her fitful bouts of sleep and wakefulness. She peeked at them again for the tenth time and watched their little chests rise and fall. It was like she was making sure they were still alive, still hers. She loved them so much, and they were the one thing she didn't regret now about her relationship with David. She loved him for giving her such beautiful children. The kids were all Secret had left, and they were the one thing Secret would fight to the death for.

After she'd checked in on the kids, Secret roamed the house aimlessly. She found herself standing naked in front of the tall mirror in her bedroom. She touched her botched stomach and ran her hands over her failed breast implants. Secret thought she looked like a real freak of nature. She collapsed to her knees and cried. The beauty standards in America made her sick. She had fallen right into the trap of trying to look perfect, instead of loving what God had given her.

"Pull yourself together, Secret. It's not the end of the world," Secret told herself. She got to her feet, wrapped herself in her bathrobe, and wandered into her kitchen. She made herself some tea and picked up her cell phone. She started off searching David's friends' social media pages, and one thing led her to another, and suddenly she was on Lucky's page.

Secret scrolled through the page, and there were mostly pictures of beautiful cakes and cupcake creations. But then Secret came upon pictures of Lucky and

David. There were some of them kissing. Some were of them on yachts sailing the Amalfi Coast in Italy. Secret's heart sped up with each picture. David hadn't taken her anywhere in years. She continued scrolling, and there it was: a picture of David on one knee, holding a ring box in front of Lucky, who had her hands over her mouth in surprise. The caption under the picture read, "When your best friend and lover asks you to be his best friend and lover for life."

Secret sucked in her breath and doubled over at the waist. It was like someone had kicked Secret in the chest, or maybe the feeling was more like she was having open-heart surgery while she was still awake. The pain in her heart was unbearable. Time seemed to stand still around Secret, and she was having trouble breathing properly. Her ears began to ring. She stared at the picture for what seemed like a lifetime.

"Engaged? We're not even fucking divorced yet and he gets engaged," Secret said through clenched teeth. She had been biting down into her jaw so hard blood filled her mouth and she didn't even realize it. Still dressed in her pajamas, Secret mindlessly raced out her front door and climbed into her car. She couldn't nor did she even think about her sleeping children being left alone.

Secret sped onto the highway not sure where exactly she was headed. She was driving with her hands at ten and two o'clock, and her back was erect like a zombie. A few times she had ignored traffic laws, and she had also cut a few people off. She had tunnel vision, which was dangerous for driving.

Before she knew it, she was in front of Lucky's bakery once again. The gate was pulled down, and the locks were put on. Secret wished the bakery were open and filled with people. She wanted to bust every window out of the place. Secret wanted that bitch Lucky to hurt. She wanted the world to know how much of a home-wrecking bitch Lucky was. Secret felt like if Lucky and David were in front of her, she could probably kill them both and think nothing of it.

Secret jumped out of her car. She scrambled around to the back of her car. Secret frantically dug around in the space behind the seats where she usually threw the kids' toys, emergency umbrellas, and stuff like that. Secret didn't know what she was looking for: a crowbar, a brick, anything. She had destruction on her mind.

Secret found a can of spray paint. Secret remembered how she and her husband had worked to revamp their deck furniture with the black spray paint after David bitched about buying a new set. With her heart pounding, she grabbed the can of spray paint and rushed over to the silver gates pulled down on the front of the bakery. She started spraying like crazy. Secret was, again, a woman possessed.

She sprayed the words "home-wrecker," "slut," "adulterer," and "bitch" all over the gate. With her chest heaving wildly, when she had finished the can of spray paint, Secret reached back into her car and grabbed a can of lighter fluid from her and David's last barbeque. She sprayed the gate with the fluid, retrieved the small flare lighter from her trunk, and lit the liquid afire.

"I hope both of you bastards burn in fucking hell," Secret growled. She jumped back into her car and sped off. Although it was the wee hours of the morning, Secret did notice a few people walking the streets. She wanted to get out of there before anyone took her license plate number or saw her face.

When she was about ten blocks away, she pulled over and put the car in park. With all of her windows up she started to scream at the top of her lungs and slam her fists against her steering wheel. She screamed and screamed until her head hurt.

Exhausted, Secret collapsed with her head lolling onto the steering wheel. She sobbed pitifully. Secret didn't know how long she'd been there, but before long she noticed winks of the sun coming through her windshield. Secret strangely looked out of the windshield at the sky. It was then that Secret realized that she was in her car and that something had definitely happened to her. It was the first time she had lost touch with reality. Looking around wildly and realizing she was in her pajamas, Secret lurched around to check the back seat of her car.

"My kids! Oh, my God! Where are my kids?" she shrieked, whirling her head around. She sped out of the spot she was in and headed back to her home. It was not until she burst through her front doors to find her babies screaming and crying that she realized she had left them all alone again.

It was the first but not the last time Secret would let the situation get the best of her. Secret realized that something inside of her was slowly coming apart, and she didn't know what else to do about it. Secret couldn't understand how her life had become so complicated so fast.

Chapter 10

"Secret! What were you thinking?" Andrea asked, pacing after Secret told her what she'd done.

Secret sat silently, wringing her hands in her lap with no explanation for what she'd done.

"You know they'll know it was you, right? This will reflect badly on your court case. Oh, my God, Secret," Andrea ranted, running her hands through her hair in exasperation.

They both almost jumped out of their skin when loud knocks reverberated through Secret's front door. Andrea looked at Secret with huge, round eyes. Secret nodded and lowered her head.

Andrea was the one who answered the door for the police. Andrea had told the police that Secret was out running errands right then and that when the incident allegedly occurred, Secret had been home the entire time with her children.

"These kids are babies. Y'all can't possibly be accusing my cousin of some early morning vandalism. Does that even sound right to you when she has babies? You just said the witness got a glimpse and said the person was alone. Look, I think this is all a ploy by her ex-husband to paint her in a bad light so he can win his divorce and get away without giving my cousin anything," Andrea told the police.

"I mean, come in, take a look at the kids," Andrea said. Andrea showed the police officers the kids for good measure. The cops observed the kids from the door. They seemed to kind of back off when they realized that the children were very young and Secret leaving them alone to drive from Long Island to Brooklyn to vandalize the salon might just be a far stretch. They had seen these types of tit-for-tat divorces in the past. Satisfied for the moment, the police officers gave Andrea their card and asked that Secret call them anyway when she returned home.

When they were gone, Andrea gave Secret the signal. Secret emerged from her bedroom closet where she had been cowering while her cousin covered for her ass. Secret was embarrassed but relieved at the same time that her behavior had not cost her much more than flushed cheeks.

"Secret, you have to stop. David is not coming back, and it's not that woman's fault. David is to blame. Please, get your shit together and fast," Andrea scolded her.

"I know. I'm sorry for putting you in this whole thing. Everything you do is appreciated. I'm okay now," Secret lied.

"I hope so. If you ever feel impulsive again, call me first," Andrea emphasized.

Secret just hung her head, again, embarrassed by her impulsive and crazy behavior.

"Are you sure you're going to be okay until I get back from work? Can I trust you with these kids, Secret?" Andrea asked seriously.

Secret smiled and hugged her cousin. She was putting on a good act. Secret just wanted to be alone. "I got it all out of my system. I'm sure. I swear. I'm all good now," Secret said.

Andrea looked at Secret with skepticism but love at the same time. "Okay, I'm trusting you," Andrea replied, finally relenting. "But no more wigging out spray paint-ing and setting fire to people's shit. My ass is not visiting

your ass in jail. You know I'm allergic to jail," she continued, waggling her finger at Secret and then chuckling
to lighten up the mood. Secret forced herself to laugh.
Inside she was crying and coming apart, but she put up a
front to put Andrea at ease. Andrea finally took Secret's
word and left her alone.

Secret gave DJ and Bella something to eat, more
Benadryl, and put them down for a nap. She decided that
she would just relax and watch some television to clear
her mind. She was going to try to go drug free from now
on. That was her plan until she checked her mailbox and
retrieved a notice that the mortgage company was about
to proceed with foreclosure on the house.

"How much can one person take? What the fuck am
I supposed to do?" she said to herself. With her hands
shaking, she picked up her phone and dialed David's
number without even thinking. She didn't know what
she would say to him, but she dialed the number anyway.
When it began to ring, she hung up. Secret repeated the
call at least ten more times. She never spoke to him. He
kept ignoring her. Eventually, he turned his phone off,
and it just continued to go straight to voicemail after
that. Secret continued to call until his voicemail prompt
said his mailbox was full. It was full of blank messages
because Secret had just kept dialing, listening to his voice,
letting the voicemail pick up, and listening until his
voicemail cut her off. Secret just wanted to hear his voice
over and over again. She did it until her phone battery
died and she was no longer able to make any more calls.
Secret was definitely not herself anymore. She was at the
edge and slipping.

At Andrea's urging, Secret spent almost an hour on the
phone with the mortgage company trying to negotiate a

deal that would work out for her. Secret didn't know the first thing about refinancing, loan modifications, or the like. When the house was purchased, it had been all David. All Secret had done was signed on the dotted line. She wasn't even sure she owned half of the house the way David had been sneaking behind her back, doing grimy shit.

After being transferred almost ten times, Secret was finally put in contact with a foreclosure specialist, only to be told that David was listed as the sole owner of the home and that Secret had no authority to negotiate on his behalf.

"Even though I'm his wife and I am living here with my children?" Secret had asked incredulously.

The foreclosure specialist had apologized to Secret but told her only David could save the house from foreclosure. Frustrated and angry, Secret broke yet another telephone by sending it sailing across the room. She paced around inside her house for almost an hour, feeling aimless and helpless. Secret continued to glance over at the ever-growing pile of household bills that littered her kitchen table. She hadn't paid the light, gas, telephone, or cable bills. She was getting doubled up bills for just about all of them.

Secret felt like the walls of life had completely closed in on her. Suddenly a flood of tears dropped from her eyes. "What happened, David? Why are you doing this to me? What did I ever do to deserve all of this but love you?" she sobbed.

Blinking rapidly, Secret started seeing flashes of Lucky's Instagram page playing in her mind again. Secret blinked and wiped her eyes roughly. The images were still there. Lucky and David kissing, Lucky by herself: it was all too much for Secret to handle. She pushed back from the table like a poisonous snake had just bitten her.

She rushed into the living room and grabbed all of the pictures of her and David, her, David and the kids, David by himself from the shelves. "Bitch!" Secret hissed as she began smashing the glass frames and snatching the pictures out of them.

"I hate you!" she boomed as she drove a jagged line across David's face in one picture. Secret ripped and shredded each picture until she was exhausted and her hands ached. Flopping down onto her couch breathing hard, Secret looked down at the mess in front of her. Her bottom lip quivered as the severity of her deed set in.

"Oh, no! What did I do! What did I do!" Secret screamed, putting her hands up against each side of her head, pulling at her hair roughly. Secret looked down at the tiny slivers of pictures that now resembled the pieces to a 1,000-piece puzzle. They were impossible to put back together, just like her marriage.

Secret sobbed one minute, and she was angry with herself the next minute for losing control. It had been happening more and more often now. Taking a deep breath, Secret roughly wiped her tears away.

"Pull your fucking self together! Stop this shit now!" Secret whispered harshly to herself. She scrambled out of the chair and to the kitchen. Peeling off a large garbage bag from the roll of bags, she raced back to the mess and frantically picked up the cut-up pictures and put them into the bag. Secret couldn't risk Andrea stopping by and seeing the complete mess she'd made. Secret knew that Andrea would think she was losing it again and the lectures would start all over again.

When everything was finally all cleaned up, Secret placed the bag down near the back door. Something told her to see if her children were okay. Secret checked in on her children. They were playing quietly in their playroom. Secret came back downstairs and tiptoed out of her back door into the backyard. She placed the bag with the pictures into David's large stainless-steel GrillMaster Grill. Secret squirted lighter fluid on the pile and dropped a match inside. It was definitely a *Waiting to Exhale* kind of moment. Secret felt sad that she no longer had her pictures, but for some reason, she also felt vindicated as well. She looked around nervously to make sure her neighbors weren't watching, while she burned away remnants of her past.

When she was satisfied with the pile of ashes before her, Secret went back into the house. She washed her hands and changed her smoke-scented clothes. Then she picked up her cell phone and called her attorney. Secret pleaded with him to ask the court for an emergency hearing. She explained to him that there was no way she could wait another three weeks to go to court with the situation the way it was. Secret even confessed to him that she could feel herself losing it, her mind, her home, her life as she knew it. She was losing it all, to be exact.

Chapter 11

Andrea held Secret's hand as they returned to court. Secret was elated that her attorney was able to push the hearing up.

"You okay?" Andrea asked, feeling the trembling in Secret's hands.

"I haven't been okay in months," Secret finally confessed.

Andrea could tell her cousin wasn't okay by the way Secret looked. Secret didn't bother to dress up like she did for the first court appearance. She was at the point where she didn't care any longer. She threw on a pair of jeans and a regular mom T-shirt from the Gap. Her hair was slicked back in a lumpy, uncombed, cakey ponytail, the result of her not really combing her hair out in weeks. She didn't bother to make up her face either. Secret knew she had bags the size of pillows under her eyes, but nothing mattered to her anymore. She only went from day to day for Bella and DJ, that was it. If not for them, Secret would have ended it a long time ago.

Secret leaned in and whispered to Andrea, "I want to see what way this motherfucker is going to fuck me over this time," Secret said.

Andrea was silent at first, but Secret's appearance and behavior were just killing her inside. It just wasn't right. In fact, Andrea thought her cousin looked and sounded like she was snapping.

"Girl, why are you dressed like you're going to the store, or even worse, like you are going to put the damn garbage out or something? I mean, you want to present yourself well, don't you? Do you want this nigga to think you're pining over him and falling apart?" Andrea asked seriously.

"What nobody seems to understand, Andrea, is that I don't give a shit about him, the judge, or my life right now. I couldn't give a fuck less what anybody thinks about me and whether I'm pining over him or falling the fuck apart. I mean it's the truth at this point. Whether I was dressed to the nines or naked, if shit is going to go in my favor it just is and vice versa," Secret replied, her tone cold and flat.

Inside the courtroom, Secret's lawyer gave her the same kind of reaction that Andrea had. He eyed her up and down as if to say, "What the fuck were you thinking?" Secret sat down next to him and folded her hands in front of her. She didn't say a word.

"I think all of the parties are here. We can begin," the judge said.

Secret shot the female judge an evil look. *This fucking bitch,* Secret thought as she noticed the judge smiling hard at David, who by the way, was dressed sharply as usual.

David's smug-ass lawyer stood up and adjusted his suit jacket. He looked just as smug as David. Secret figured that was why David had hired him.

"Your Honor, my client would like to make the divorce final today. We feel there is no need to prolong these proceedings at the expense of either party. We are prepared to present our requests today and trust that you will find in our favor or whatever is favorable to the court," the lawyer announced.

Secret finally looked over at David and his lawyer, and then she noticed a world-renowned plastic surgeon she'd consulted with sitting in the courtroom.

What the fuck? Why is he here? Secret screamed in her head. Her heart jerked in her chest, and her stomach cramped at the sight of him. She hadn't seen him in a long time. She couldn't imagine why he would be at their divorce proceedings. The doctor being there made Secret uneasy and overwhelmingly nervous.

"We are prepared to hear your client's request as well as Mrs. Johnson's requests," the judge replied.

David's lawyer smiled. "Your Honor, my client is asking for an immediate divorce from Mrs. Johnson. His request is not out of the blue. My client wants to end his marriage due to lies, theft, which he is prepared to prove today, due to cruel and unusual treatment, which he is prepared to prove today, and finally due to violence and erratic behavior by Mrs. Johnson throughout the course of the marriage, which he can also prove today," David's lawyer said loudly.

Secret's head whipped around so hard she felt her neck crack. She thought she'd fall out of the chair. Was David fucking serious? She leaned into her attorney and began whispering harshly in his ear. She was telling him that it was all bullshit. David was lying on her. Her attorney shushed her and promised that she would get her time to speak. Secret needed to shut David's lawyer up.

"Go ahead and present what your client has today," the judge told David's attorney.

Oh, my God! He can't continue talking, Secret said inside her head, a cold sweat breaking out all over her body.

"Your Honor, as to the lies and theft and secrecy during the marriage: as Mrs. Johnson had correctly argued during the last hearing, Mr. Johnson spent four years working hard studying for his degree at business school. After his graduation, he was the only source of income in the marriage. Mr. Johnson worked hard and put all of his income into the marriage. My client has physical proof that during that time, his wife, Mrs. Johnson, stole thousands of dollars to have secret plastic surgeries, which caused significant financial distress to my client. I have an expert who is in court today to give a statement about the surgeries. If you look at the screen, you will see I have also obtained pictures of Mrs. Johnson's last plastic surgeries, which left my client completed aghast and unable to be turned on sexually by his wife," David's lawyer announced proudly.

"You motherfucker!" Secret erupted when she saw her botched body on display. Lucky stared at the pictures. Andrea stared. Everyone was staring at Secret's horrible body.

Secret's ears were ringing, and the room began to spin. Her vision became blurry, and she felt like she would faint. She jumped up out of her seat and pushed away from the table. The chair she was sitting in went crashing to the floor, startling everyone in the room. Secret covered her face and bolted down the aisle and out of the courtroom. She raced into the courtroom hallway and spun around and around wildly like a lost child. Finally, she noticed a sign for the bathrooms and she sped toward the doors. Her chest was aching like she was having a heart attack.

Inside the bathroom, Secret splashed water on her face, but it didn't help. She stumbled into one of the stalls and threw up. Secret felt like dying. If she had a weapon, she would take her own life right now. She could not believe David had betrayed her like that. David was the one who had constantly called her an ugly, disgusting pig. He was the one who had pushed her to get the surgeries. Secret couldn't understand how David would've obtained those pictures. How did the judge even allow that? Secret couldn't believe this. Secret leaned up against the courthouse bathroom wall for support. It was all she could do to keep from fainting.

After a while, Andrea entered the bathroom. She was coming to the rescue as usual. But Secret didn't want to face her or anyone for that matter.

"There you are! Oh, baby, I'm so sorry," Andrea said, grabbing Secret and holding her. That made Secret feel even worse, and all of her tears came flooding back to the surface along with her sins.

"I don't know why he would do this. What have I ever done to him?" Secret cried.

"He is a bastard. I can't believe it either, but you have to go back in there with your head up high. Nothing he says can change the fact that he also committed adultery with that bitch and that is the real reason your marriage is ending," Andrea comforted her.

Secret knew she had to go back, but she damn sure wished she could just disappear.

When Secret walked back into the courtroom, all eyes were on her. She felt like the gazes were burning holes into her. She apologized to the judge for the interruption and took her seat next to her lawyer again.

David had a smirk on his face, which sent a flash of heat through Secret's chest. *Die, you motherfucker.*

The judge started the proceedings again. Secret was only half listening. She could no longer focus. David presented pictures of the damage that had been done at his girlfriend's bakery and told the judge that he had witnesses who said Secret had done it.

He produced surveillance video from his building showing that Secret had been outside and followed Lucky's car on numerous occasions. He produced a written statement from Lucky about the beat down Secret had put on her and about Secret showing up to her place of business, threatening her.

Secret took proverbial slap after slap. She just sat there and let David run her name into the ground. But then the gloves came off. He finally had Secret's attention.

"Your Honor, my client is also asking for full custody of his two children ages two and six years old. It is my client's belief that Mrs. Johnson is mentally unstable, as we have witnessed by some of the items of proof my client brought to the court's attention today, and that he would be the best parent to care for the children," David's lawyer said.

The words seemed to explode in Secret's ears and touched her someplace deep. "No! He cannot have my children! They are all I have, Judge. Please if you have any mercy in your heart, I'm begging you! He can keep all of his money! I will live in a shelter! But please don't take my kids from me! They're all I have left!" Secret screamed out.

Her lawyer grabbed her by the arm and forced her to sit down. He was watching Secret prove David and his attorney right about her mental state with her seemingly erratic behavior. Secret put her hands over her mouth in an attempt to squash her sobs. She could still be heard whimpering. Secret could not believe David was digging so deep to be so malicious. She knew he had no interest in caring for their children, but it was an attempt to make her suffer. Secret couldn't for the life of her understand his need to be so cruel to her.

The judge asked to hear from Secret's attorney, but his requests and arguments seemed like small pebbles compared to the huge boulders David's lawyer had thrown. But the attorney did argue for Secret to keep her children. She explained to the judge that David had had little or no real interaction with the kids. Secret tried to read the judge's face, but she was unable to tell what the judge was going to do. Secret started to silently pray for her children as the judge gathered up all of David's pictures, video, and written proof. She also took some documents regarding the foreclosure and household bills Secret was facing. Secret's insides felt like someone was putting them through a meat grinder.

"I will review the information in chambers, and I will return in one hour with my final decision in this matter," the judge said. Secret tried to plead with the judge with her eyes, but the judge had never looked at her, only at David.

With that, the judge dismissed them all for a lunch break. Secret had her head down on the table. She couldn't even move, much less eat. Andrea watched as David laughed with his attorney as they exited the court-room together.

Andrea chased after them. "David!" she huffed, catch-ing up to them. They turned to face her. "You both think you're smart, don't you? You think I couldn't figure out how you set my cousin up? You fucking purposely encouraged her to get those surgeries. You even paid for the consultations, you piece of shit. What did you do, David? Did you fucking pay these doctors to botch her? I believe you're just that fucking low! You did this. You fucking did it all!" Andrea spat.

They both looked like deer caught in headlights. "Yeah, I'm on to you. It will be a cold fucking day in hell before you get those kids, David. You don't even know anything about them, what they eat, when they sleep. All she ever did was love you. All she ever did was try to please you. Mark my words, you will get what is coming to you. Trust, revenge is a dish best served motherfucking cold," Andrea said through gritted teeth.

She turned swiftly and went back into the courtroom
to get Secret. Andrea didn't know how much more Secret
could take. She knew hands down that if the judge gave
David custody of the kids, Secret would lose it once and
for all.

Secret watched nervously as the judge sat down behind
her tall desk. Secret balled up her toes inside her shoes
and clenched her ass cheeks tightly. The judge shuffled a
few papers and then she started speaking. The first thing
she said was that she was granting the divorce decree. It
was final. Secret's marriage to David was officially over.
Hearing the words made Secret have an empty feeling inside her chest. She likened the feeling to a cross
between severe hunger and severe emotional deprivation.

Next, the judge granted Secret alimony in the amount
of $2,000 per month, but it was only until Secret found
gainful employment and could support herself. Secret listened intently and quickly noticed that the judge hadn't
said anything about child support like before. Secret
kept listening. Then the judge got to the topic Secret had
been dreading: her children and who would win physical
custody of them. Secret's heart was hammering painfully
against her sternum as the judge's lips moved.

"In the matter of the Johnson children, Bella and David
Jr., ages six and two years old, respectively: at this time,
I am granting temporary full custody to Mr. Johnson
until such time as Mrs. Johnson has completed a full
psychological evaluation. The matter of custody will be
added to the family court docket, and the children will
be assigned a guardian ad litum. Mrs. Johnson, you have
until Monday of next week to produce the children at
this courthouse. Mr. Johnson will take custody of the
children, you will complete the evaluation and whatever

other recommendations the psychiatrist makes, and after that, I'm sure a family court judge will return custody to you. That is, if you're deemed to be stable," the judge said.

Secret felt like someone had just shot her in the chest. There was no pain like that she'd ever experienced. She finally knew what a stab to the heart felt like. Her legs went numb. Her head spun. Everything around her started to move.

"No! Oh, God! No! Please don't do this to me! I can't take it! I have nothing else! Please don't take my kids away from me!" Secret let out a high-pitched, ear-shattering wail that could've stopped traffic in New York City. Her screams sent chills into everyone in the room, even the judge. It was the kind of scream an animal in the wild being slayed would emit.

Secret had no control of her body. She shook her head and flailed her arms wildly. She really resembled a crazy person. Secret's attorney tried to contain her, but Secret was inconsolable. Andrea raced over to her, but Secret just flailed her arms wildly and screamed some more.

"Andrea! Please tell them! I can't lose them! Please! Please, Judge, don't do this to me!" Secret screamed some more.

"Shh," Andrea comforted her. "I know. Oh, baby, I know." Andrea cried herself. There was nothing like a mother's love being shattered.

"Mrs. Johnson, I'm sure you will get the children back when you get yourself together," the judge said, standing up to leave. The judge wanted to get out of there as fast as she could. Secret's screams of anguish had even threatened to make the judge shed a few tears.

"Fuck you! Fuck all of you! You can't do this! David, you won't win! I will die first! I will kill you first!" Secret screeched as Andrea forced her down the center aisle of the room. Andrea didn't want her cousin to get arrested for making threats or cursing out the judge on top of everything that was already happening to her. It was a sad fucking day for everyone involved.

Andrea turned around one last time to see David smiling and shaking his attorney's hand. She shot him an evil look and returned her focus to her cousin, who was now a shell of a person.

Secret rocked back and forth in the car during the ride back to Andrea's house where her children were. Andrea didn't bother trying to speak to Secret on the way. She knew it was useless.

The mere thought of having them for only three more days made Secret just want to die. A million thoughts danced her in head, one of which was eliminating the threats: David and Lucky. What else could she do? What else did she have to lose?

When they arrived at Andrea's house, Secret was out of the car before Andrea could fully pull up. Secret banged on the door frantically as if somebody were chasing her. When the babysitter pulled back the door, Secret almost knocked her down, racing to find her kids. Both of the kids were just fine, sitting in front of the television.

"Oh, my God, my babies," Secret sang out. She grabbed both of them up, struggling with the weight of both of them. She squeezed them up against her so tightly they started to whine.

"Nobody is going to take you from me. I won't let anything happen to either of you," Secret whispered through tears. Secret didn't want to let them go. She held them like that for the next half hour although they squirmed and complained for her to let them go. Andrea had to force her to allow them to get down and go play.

Andrea had also begged Secret to spend the night here with the kids, but Secret wouldn't hear of it. She told Andrea she just wanted to be home alone to spend the next few days with the kids before she had to turn them over to David. Andrea was very worried about Secret, but there was nothing she could do to convince Secret to stay over for the night.

Andrea watched as her cousin, who now resembled a soulless zombie, loaded her two kids into her car and pulled out. Andrea said a silent prayer that Secret and the kids would be okay. She promised herself that she would go check on Secret first thing in the morning. She couldn't imagine that anything could happen in less than twenty-four hours.

Chapter 12

Secret scrolled through her cell phone screen after she'd Googled guns for sale. There were tons in her county. She looked at everything she needed to purchase one, and it was a lot. This wouldn't be a street transaction and untraceable.

Secret lost her nerve and closed the screen. Shaking her head, she scolded herself. She had to stop the shit. What was she thinking? What the hell would she do with a gun anyway?

Secret pinched the bridge of her nose, trying to relieve the banging tension headache she had been battling for a few days.

"I can't deal," she whispered. "There is just no way I can turn my kids over to David and his bitch. There is just no way. I can't do it." She spoke to herself in earnest. She would have to find another way.

Secret climbed the stairs in her house and looked in on her sleeping children. They were so innocent. They didn't deserve to be in the middle of her and David's battles. Secret still couldn't believe he would throw them into the mix by petitioning the court for full custody. It was all a ploy to avoid paying child support. Secret knew David's selfish ass better than he knew himself. Secret was still absolutely flabbergasted that David wanted the kids to live with him full time when he hadn't ever paid them any attention when he lived with them. David had never fed, changed, cuddled with, or even comforted either of the kids after they'd been born. He never took them to a doctor's appointment or took care of them when they were sick. David didn't know his own children's likes or dislikes. He didn't know how to comfort them when they were in distress, and more importantly, the kids didn't know him as well as they should at their ages. Secret knew that David saw the kids as a hindrance to their marriage. She also believed that he was secretly jealous of how much attention Secret paid them after they were born. Prior to their births, it was all about David, but after they came along, he had to share her time and attention with the kids. David didn't hide his feelings about it either. Secret remembered one night David held her down in the bed, having forceful sex with her while she fought to get up so she could go comfort Bella, who was a newborn at that time and screaming from the other bedroom. The memory made Secret shudder now. The thought of handing her kids over to David made Secret physically sick. She had thrown up three times that day alone. She only had one and a half more days with the kids and Secret didn't know what she'd do, but she did know giving them to her now officially ex-husband and his bitch was not an option.

It was the middle of the night and Secret banged on Andrea's door with urgency. Andrea swung the door open and looked at her cousin like she was crazy.

"Shit! Secret? What's going on? Are you okay? Did something happen?" Andrea asked, noticing how disheveled and frantic Secret appeared. It was very early in the morning, and it was not like Secret to be out with the kids this early. Andrea suddenly had a bad feeling about the situation.

"I have to go someplace real quick. Can you keep an eye on my kids until I get back?" Secret huffed, her hair wild and her eyes wide. "Just promise me you will not give my kids to anyone else. Please, Andrea? I'm begging. Please guard them with your life," Secret pleaded.

"I . . . I promise, but what's going on, Secret? You're in your pajamas. Are you all right?" Andrea replied, looking Secret up and down. Nothing about this visit could be good, Andrea was thinking. "How about you come inside and let's talk before you just run off? Let me help you think things through," Andrea urged.

"No. No." Secret threw her hands up. "I'm good. Please trust me. I just need to make a run, and I swear I'll be right back." Secret rushed her words out. She was moving as if she had to go to the bathroom or something. Like whatever she had to do was so urgent it couldn't wait at all.

Andrea had to think about the kids and their safety right now. "Bring them inside," Andrea relented. "I promise to keep them safe."

She wasn't going to ask Secret any more questions because it was clear she was having some sort of episode. Andrea wanted so badly to shake Secret by the shoulders and tell her to snap out of all this erratic behavior. It was just a divorce, which Andrea didn't think was the end of the world. Andrea realized that she had always been the stronger of them even as children growing up. Secret was always the nice one. She was quiet, and people often walked all over her and bullied her. People often referred to Andrea as the bitch who would fuck up anyone who messed with her cousin Secret.

Shaking all over, Secret handed her kids over to Andrea for safekeeping. She promised Andrea she'd be back real soon. Secret didn't want to miss her last minutes with the kids, but what she had to do was imperative. Secret had made up her mind what she needed to do.

She raced through the streets until she finally pulled up to a gun store. A feeling of sick nerves came over her, and little beads of sweat lined up at her hairline. There were so many guns to choose from. Secret swallowed hard. Secret whirled around a few times, contemplating just leaving. Then she thought about her kids again. She thought about Lucky tucking them in at night while Secret would be home, crying herself to sleep. She thought about David acting as if he were father of the year, bribing her kids with candy and shit she didn't want them to have. Once the thoughts came to mind, Secret decided she was doing the right thing and that she was in the right place. Soon, her life would be free of all of the complications, or so she hoped.

Secret tapped her foot impatiently as she sat outside of David's building. She had rented a car neither David nor Lucky would recognize. Secret told herself she was just there to talk to David, to reason with him about the leaving the kids with her. Secret practiced under her breath how she was going to ask him to drop his custody request. The more she thought about it, the more Secret remembered how ignorant David could be. Since negotiations might not work, Secret had her newly purchased Glock stashed between her thighs. Sweat drenched her back and underarms as she waited. Secret had played the scene over and over in her mind. She would scare the shit out of David and Lucky, and he would agree to leave the kids alone. She would force David to listen to her and leave her and the kids alone for good. Yes, those were her plans. He wouldn't have a choice, she reasoned.

Secret promised that whenever David and Lucky pulled up, whether separate or together, Secret planned on jumping out of the car and trying to talk to them. The longer she waited, the more irrational she felt. She went between being calm and being totally enraged about

David's betrayals. Secret replayed having her botched body on display for the world to see. David really wanted to hurt her.

Secret started nodding as she waited for Lucky and David. It had been hours, but she wouldn't give up. She pulled out her cell phone and scrolled through her address book. Secret retrieved the number of Lucky's bakery, which she had gotten from the store sign and saved the very first time she followed Lucky there.

"Yes, may I speak with Lucky please?" Secret said, disguising her voice to sound like she had some sort of accent. The store clerk told Secret that Lucky was out of the country and would be back tomorrow. Secret knew right away that she was with David. All of these trips out of the country and Secret was scrounging to pay bills. She was infuriated even more now. The information might as well have been a knife in Secret's chest. She really wanted them both dead now.

"That motherfucker couldn't even let the ink dry on the divorce papers. He expects me to turn my kids over in the morning so he can come back and play house with my fucking kids. He will see what I turn over to his ass," Secret growled as moved the rental car from in front of David's building and headed to Andrea's to get her kids.

"It's okay. You'll regret the day you fucked me over, David Johnson. You will regret it," Secret continued, speaking out loud to herself. It wasn't over just yet. She wasn't going to give up that easily. Her kids were all she had in the world, and David had already taken everything else, including her fucking soul.

Chapter 13

As usual, Secret hadn't slept a wink the entire night. Secret had the kids in the bed with her, real close to her. She had lain next to them, weeping on and off for hours. She would teeter between anger and sorrow and back again. Secret was suffering now with huge knots in her stomach on top of sleep deprivation. Secret kept picturing her kids screaming and crying when she handed them over to David and had to walk away from them at the courthouse. The thought alone threatened to make her hurl. She envisioned David forcefully putting them into their car seats while they writhed and kicked in protest, their little faces blood red and covered in tears. Secret would also see that bitch Lucky trying to console her crying babies like she was a doting stepmother. Secret just couldn't let that happen. She wouldn't let her babies suffer like that. It wasn't their fault that their father was a selfish, adulterous, cowardly asshole. She had contemplated going on the run with her kids, but she knew that they would put out an Amber Alert for the kids and she would be found and put into jail. That wouldn't help the kids either. Besides, Secret didn't have any money to be on the run with her babies.

With her heart hammering, Secret suddenly bolted upright in bed. A serious feeling of anxiety came over her. "Fuck him. He can't have them," Secret spoke to herself. She threw her legs over the side of the bed and stood up. Secret walked the length of her bedroom, the unbearable feeling of anxiety getting worse and worse. Her stomach

seized and released over and over again, causing Secret
to sweat. She had to prevent David from getting the kids.

"I can't let them go. I can't," Secret finally whispered.

She raced into her closet and retrieved the new gun
she had purchased. Secret examined the black steel,
and she felt powerful as she held it. Secret wasn't finished with the mission she had started. This time Secret
would end this ordeal once and for all. David had turned
her into this monster. Now she was going to show him
just what she could do, just how much of a monster she
really was. In Secret's mind, her life was over anyway.
Secret felt like she had suffered enough embarrassment
and humiliation. She also felt like she had nothing else to
live for. This was it. Secret was going all in now.

When Secret arrived at David's building, she didn't
wait outside and stalk David and Lucky like she normally
did. Not today. Secret wasn't living in the shadows today.
No, she planned on being seen and heard. Secret boldly
entered the lobby of the building and rang the door
buzzer. She'd gotten the exact address from the divorce
papers.

"Who is it?" Lucky sang through the intercom.

"FedEx," Secret said with a gruff voice, trying to sound
like a man.

"We're not expecting anything," Lucky said suspiciously.

Secret twisted her lips and silently mouthed the word
"bitch" at Lucky's comment. Just as she was trying to
come up with another method of getting into the building, someone came out of the door.

As soon as the door swung open, Secret rushed through
it. She smiled because now she was in. Secret reached
into her coat pocket and touched the weapon. She
wanted to make sure it was still there. She didn't need to
give herself a pep talk or build up her confidence. This

was it. All or nothing. David had fucked with the wrong person. He had driven her to all of this, so he had no one to thank but himself.

When the elevator stopped on the floor, Secret felt a flitter of excitement. She wasn't afraid at all. This was part of what she needed to do. When she exited the elevator on the floor, Secret crept up to the door. She listened for a few minutes, and she could hear that both David and Lucky were home.

"Bastard." Secret smiled wickedly. Secret pressed the small bell that sat at the side of the door and stepped aside so they couldn't see her through the peephole.

"David, I think this is the FedEx person who rang the downstairs buzzer," Secret heard Lucky call out. "No, I didn't order anything nor am I expecting anything, unless it's a package from your lawyer," Lucky said. Secret was listening the entire time.

"Maybe she brought the kids early," David said.

David snatched open the door, and when he did, Secret rushed him. He didn't even have time to react. Secret barreled into him like a battering ram, sending him stumbling backward.

"What the fu—" David started to scream, but his words were cut off. David's eyes grew as wide as dinner plates when the cold steel of Secret's Glock was pushed into his face.

"Now, motherfucker! It's time for my revenge for everything you ever did to me," Secret growled.

"Oh, my God!" Lucky belted out when she saw that Secret had a gun.

"Shut the fuck up and get over there," Secret growled, directing Lucky and David to sit down in front of their fireplace.

"What are you doing, Secret? Where are the kids?" David huffed. He had never felt his heart beat like that in his entire life.

"Don't ask about my kids! You don't love those kids, and you'll never have them!" Secret said through clenched teeth. She moved the gun around haphazardly, which caused David and Lucky to flinch.

Secret started laughing seeing their fear. She wanted them to feel just like she had felt over the past couple of months.

"What are you going to do to us?" Lucky cried as she gripped David's arm so tight her knuckles paled.

"You'll see," Secret said calmly. "David, you drove me to this. What I know now is that you never loved me. You never cared about me, oh, no. David only cared about himself. Why would you take everything from me? After all I've done for you. Why would you drag my name through the mud and flaunt your bitch at our church? And then, the biggest one yet, you tried to take my kids from me? Those kids are the only thing you have ever done that was good. They are all I have, you bastard!" Secret barked, waving the gun in their faces.

"Listen, Secret. There is no need for violence," David said, trying to stay calm with his hands up in defense. His voice was cracking, a sure sign that he was fucked up and nervous as hell. He was trying his best to calm Secret down, but little did he know that the more calmly he tried to speak, the angrier it made Secret. She took it as him being the same smug bastard he had been in court.

"Shut up! You piece of shit. You caused all of this! You're a selfish piece of shit, always was and always will be. Yes, you drove me over the edge after everything I did for you, for us. Look at me. Look at how I look compared to your little skinny bitch there. You made me feel so fucking bad about myself I sacrificed my entire body for you! My soul! I'll never be good for anyone else, ever! You turn around and leave me with no money to even feed my kids!" Secret barked. This time she placed the gun against Lucky's temple. Lucky started to cry uncontrollably. She was holding on to David's arm, and her body was trembling.

"Awww, look at your little beautiful bitch. She's scared, David. I guess she didn't know what she was getting into when she got with you, huh? Tell her, David. This is what you get when you steal someone's husband," Secret taunted, moving the gun from Lucky's temple to David's forehead.

"Shh," David instructed Lucky. "Let's just all remain calm. I can call someone to help us through this, Secret." Lucky muffled her cries, and they came out more like small whimpers.

"Shut the fuck up! You're not calling anyone!" Secret barked. She turned her attention to Lucky. "Did David ever tell you all of the things I did for him, Lucky? All of the nights I stayed up writing his research papers because he wasn't that fucking smart? All of the days I worked like a dog and handed all of my money over to him? How I gave up my modeling career because he was jealous of it? I bet he never told you any of that," Secret said to Lucky, placing the tip of the gun by her ear and moving it through her long, silky hair. Lucky peed on herself from fear.

"I knew he didn't tell you any of that shit! Why would he tell you that I gave him every bit of myself? My heart, my soul, my mind, my body, and now my kids!" Secret screamed, a large vein pulsing in her neck.

"Secret, where are the kids?" David asked, his voice taking on a frantic tone.

Secret tilted her head and started laughing. "Oh, now you want to know about your fucking kids? When you left them and barely visited them, you weren't worried about them. You weren't worried about them when you decided to fucking leave for this little stupid bitch you got here. Where's the kids? How fucking dare you! Shut the fuck up and don't ask about my kids!" Secret said through clenched teeth. The thought of the kids sent a wave of nausea through Secret's stomach. She had had enough. It was time for her to end this bullshit once and for all. Secret extended the gun in front of her and trained it on David and Lucky.

"Oh, God!" Lucky screeched, ducking her head and closing her eyes tight. David closed his eyes as well. His nose flared in and out rapidly.

"Say you're sorry, David. I want to hear you say that you're sorry for everything you've done to me," Secret said through tears.

"Say it, David! Say you're sorry to her so we can live," Lucky cried out.

"Stay out of this, bitch! You ended my marriage! You stole my husband! Soon you're going to be ex-wife status too, bitch!" Secret screamed, snot and tears covering her face now.

With that, Secret placed her pointer finger in the trigger guard and pulled back the trigger. The gun erupted in her hand. Secret jumped. She watched as Lucky's body flew back and slumped to the floor. Blood was running out of a hole in Lucky's head. It almost made Secret vomit, but she was too numb to react. She turned her attention to David. Lucky had just been a casualty of their war, but he was Secret's real intended target. He had been the one to leave her with nothing to live for.

"Secret! Don't do this!" David pleaded, his hands out in front of him. She looked at him wickedly and aimed her gun at him. Facing the barrel of the gun, David pissed his pants.

"I will always love—" David started, his mouth curled like he was about to say the word "you." Bang! He didn't have a chance to let what Secret considered a big lie leave his lips. His words were cut short after the shot rang out. David's body fell to the side and sprawled on the floor. Secret felt the powerful reverberation from the gunshots. She just stood there, staring. She wasn't going to let him tell her another lie. Secret blinked rapidly. She was paralyzed. It was over. It was all said and done.

Secret placed the gun to her and tried to pull the trigger, but she couldn't. Secret knew she should've run, but she couldn't move. She didn't know what had paralyzed her, but she was completely stuck.

It seemed like forever, but Secret finally heard the sirens in the distance. She was about to face the consequences of her decision. That meant someone had heard it all go down. Why else would the police be coming to the house? There were four gunshots in the end. Secret could still hear them. Two each. That's the punishment she had meted out. It was what they deserved.

Secret shook her head. She never expected it to come to this. All kinds of complications were what she'd gotten in the end. All she wanted was to be loved for who she was, now. She hadn't asked for much: loyalty, love, acceptance. It was too late. The sirens continued to close in on her.

Secret flinched thinking back on how the gun had exploded at the command of her fingertip. She'd dropped the gun at her feet and stood there shivering. No screaming, no hysterics, no immediate feeling of regret, nothing. Even when Secret saw all of the blood and watched the terror move across their faces, she didn't cringe and barely moved, much less screamed. She was numb. Numb from all of the physical and mental anguish she'd endured trying to please him. Numb from the way he'd treated her, his lies and secrets.

Secret's self-esteem and mental stability had taken several blows over the past year. Everything had gotten complicated. She wished she could turn back the hands of time. Do things differently. It was too late. Now here she stood, blood speckled on the front of her clothes, a burner lying at her feet, and two dead bodies in front of her.

"Police! Let me see your hands! Let me see your fucking hands!" the first arriving police officers screamed.

Secret lifted her hands slowly, but it was as if someone else had control over her body. She couldn't move her feet. Something had her rooted to the floor. Her mind was fuzzy, but she smiled at the sound of the police officer's voice. It was definitely not a smile of happiness. Instead, it was like she had begun to lose her mind. That's what he had wanted all along anyway. All of the cruelty and harsh treatment over her weight gain. Secret closed her eyes, and her nostrils flared again. Every time she thought about it all over again, that happened.

With about ten police weapons trained on her, Secret stood stock-still. One officer rushed over and kicked the weapon away from her. It skittered across the marble floors with a screechy noise that made Secret's ears move. Finally, she could feel something. The numbness had worn off. It was her blood rushing as her heart thumped wildly. Secret quickly realized life as she knew it was over.

She wanted to speak, but no words came out. She wanted the opportunity to explain herself. She wanted to tell the officers what had driven her to this. But she couldn't speak. It was only a matter of seconds before she was being manhandled and thrown roughly to the floor. Secret landed on her stomach with a thud, and the wind was knocked out of her. Several officers laid hands on her, and not with soft touches either. They were treating her like she'd just assassinated the president.

"Search her good for weapons!" one of the officers barked.

Secret struggled to breathe. She hoped they didn't beat her to death right there. She had thought about her kids, but those thoughts were too painful. She couldn't do that to herself now. She'd done enough damage.

"She's clean," a female officer called out.

Secret didn't have anything else. She had only purchased one gun: a .40-caliber Glock. It was in her despair that she'd made the purchase. She hadn't been in her right mind. Maybe she could blame it on the painkillers she'd gotten addicted to after the surgery. Just thinking about the surgery now infuriated Secret. *All of that pain! All of those complications! All for nothing!*

As she was being lifted up off the ground to be placed into the squad car, Secret looked over and stared into his eyes, the familiar eyes that she had fallen in love with years ago. His seemed to glare back at her, cold, glassy, and dead.

"You did this to us. You made me turn into a monster," Secret mumbled, staring into the dead, dilated pupils of the man who was once the love of her life, the father of her children, and most of all, her husband.

"This shit is like an episode of *Snapped,*" one officer spoke loudly, forcefully pulling Secret away.

"Looks like she really fucking snapped. This is one of the worst crimes of passion I've seen in a while," another officer commented.

They had no idea just how bad it was. Secret had been through the wringer.

"I wonder what led to all of this. What would drive someone to just murder in cold blood like this, with no remorse?" the other officer commented.

Secret was forced into the back seat of a squad car. She closed her eyes and let the tears drain from the sides as she thought about the officer's questions. What would drive someone to just murder in cold blood? What led to all of this? The words played over and over in Secret's mind, and just like that, she started replaying the events that had driven her to the edge . . . to murder.

Chapter 14

"Mommy!" Bella screamed out as she rushed toward Secret.

Secret bent down and grabbed both of her kids in bear hugs. "Oh, my God, I missed you both so much," Secret cried as she layered kisses on them. "Thank you for keeping your promise," Secret said, barely able to speak from being choked up by her own tears.

"I would never let you down, Secret," Andrea said. "I will be here for your forever. This time will fly by and you'll be home. I'm just glad they understood that he drove you to this," she said.

All Secret could do was sob and hold on to her kids. All she ever wanted was a life free of complications.